Born in the Ashes

by Elisabeth Kaye

PublishAmerica
Baltimore

© 2006 by Elisabeth Kaye.
All rights reserved. No part of this book may be reproduced, stored in a retrieval system or transmitted in any form or by any means without the prior written permission of the publishers, except by a reviewer who may quote brief passages in a review to be printed in a newspaper, magazine or journal.

First printing

At the specific preference of the author, PublishAmerica allowed this work to remain exactly as the author intended, verbatim, without editorial input.

ISBN: 1-4241-1927-8
PUBLISHED BY PUBLISHAMERICA, LLLP
www.publishamerica.com
Baltimore

With love to my husband, Thomas, whose support has never faltered. He has made me countless mugs of tea as I wrote this book!

Special thanks to my dear friend, Marsha McBee, whose expertise, affection and patience never fail me. Thanks, too, to Allyson House—my RVing buddy—who helped with computer problems while we were workamping together. Paul Aron has offered advice and encouragement for which I am grateful. My family has tolerated my mental absences and late nights at the computer with understanding, never once objecting to quick meals or a messy house. Thanks, Tom & Kaitie. Finally, thanks to my elder daughter, Aimée, for her merciless editing.

Emilia heard the footsteps in the hall and managed not to cringe in her bed only by using all the courage she could muster. It was her husband, of course, the man she detested, who pulled the door open and looked at her with eyes which she knew would be cold and calculating. She realized she was holding her breath, so she released it in what she hoped would pass for the light snore of someone who was fast asleep. She wanted to squeeze her eyelids tightly closed, but she forced them just barely open, knowing they would appear, from a distance, to be naturally closed in sleep.

Sometimes he left her alone if she was asleep. Sometimes, but not often. He wasn't a man who inconvenienced himself for others.

"Are you really sleeping, Emilia?" His voice was smooth, refined. "I can never tell." His low chuckle sounded as though he were closer. "Not that it matters…"

She did flinch when the covers were throw off of her, she couldn't prevent the automatic movement. His only response was cruel laughter as he joined her on the bed. Now she was gone, her mind, her soul, sent someone else as he completed his disgusting mission to degrade her and—he hoped—to make her pregnant with the one thing which he wanted but could not obtain by himself, a son and heir.

In only minutes, he was gone again. Emilia lay rigid until the door closed behind him and the sound of his departing footsteps could no longer be heard. Then she jumped from the bed and ran into the adjoining bath, retching even before she could lift the lid of the toilet.

"I can't do this," she whispered to herself after she had rinsed her mouth and rehung the towel. Years of training by the nuns made her neat, no matter how chaotic her life was. "I can't stand this much longer."

She turned on the shower and stood under water which was so hot that the impurity left on her skin by the man she hated finally seemed to have been rinsed away. When she had dried off, she pulled on tailored pajamas. Then she went back to the bed, pulling the linens from it and piling them outside the door, gagging at the smell of her husband's cologne which clung to the expensive sheets. Finally, she remade the bed.

She was shivering when she pulled the clean, fragrant sheets up to her chin. It wasn't cold, but shock. She knew it, knew the pattern by heart by now, but it was nearly an hour before she stopped.

She remembered her doctor telling her and her husband six months ago that pregnancy was more likely with infrequent sex. She didn't know if he was telling the truth or trying to protect her—it had not required much sensitivity for him to realize she was both terrified and repulsed by the man she had been forced to marry—but she was grateful.

Still, she acknowledged that what she had told herself earlier was true. She knew she wouldn't be able to tolerate her life much longer. Almost nightly, she dreamed of killing her husband. Her subconcious provided various involved means of doing away with him, stabbing, shooting, poisoning, even setting him adrift in an open boat near the Polar Ice Cap. She was rather awed by the creativity of her imagination.

But she knew she was very unlikely to be successful in eliminating him from her life. Before long, she might have to face the fact that the only way she could get away was to eliminate herself.

* * *

Emilia gazed out the window of the taxi, watching the early morning sun as it broke through the tall buildings beside the wide avenue. It disappeared behind the bulk of one glass and concrete edifice and then briefly reappeared before vanishing again. Within half an hour, it would have risen enough to clear all but the highest buildings, but it was already apparent that this was the beginning of what would be a beautiful, clear day. Not too hot yet, the air was just cooling toward fall.

"Jim's plane should be landing now." Emilia turned to see her cousin's bent head. Fiona was peering at the tiny gold watch at her wrist, an impractical bit of jewelry which was more elegant than useful. Her chin-length auburn bob obscured her face, but swung smoothly back into place as she looked up with a radiant smile, revealing her light olive, faintly freckled skin.

"I know," Emilia responded dryly. "I told you it wasn't necessary for us to come into town this early." She looked at her own more substantial watch, confirming the time herself with a quick glance. "It will take Jim at least another hour to get to his office."

"Well, we missed the bad traffic at least." Fiona's bubble was sailing high, and there was nothing Emilia could do to make it burst even if she had wanted to, which she didn't. If she occasionally felt envy for her cousin's happiness, she never felt jealousy. "We'll go ahead and check into the hotel and have a Danish and coffee, then I'll head downtown."

"And I'll go to my doctor's appointment." There was resignation in Emilia's voice. Fiona reached for Emilia's hand and squeezed it, but said nothing. She knew how hard Emilia had tried to avoid the tests her husband insisted she have to determine why she had failed, in nearly two years of marriage, to conceive the heir he wanted.

"If only we could get you away somewhere," Fiona mused as she had so many times before. Until midnight before the day of Emilia's wedding, her cousin had been proposing outrageous schemes to spirit her away. But Emilia's father had followed a longtime familial involvement in organized crime, and she had left his control only to exchange it for the control of a husband, her father's "boss," Antonio Scarpellini.

The FBI knew him as "The Torch." Several burned-out buildings owned by Antonio's opponents in the New York boroughs and across the river in New Jersey explained the handsome and debonair man's moniker.

The taxi stopped at the door of the boutique hotel where Fiona had spent her wedding night. She generously tipped the driver as he handed her luggage to the doorman, and both men's faces wore sincere smiles as they watched the ebullient girl run up the shallow steps. Her pink, softly swirling dress stopped just below her knees, and her heels accented her slim ankles.

Following at a more sedate pace, Emilia sighed. She weighed ten pounds more than her cousin. No matter how much she dieted, how carefully she watched what she ate, she could never quite match Fiona's slender shape. Fiona claimed to envy Emilia's curves, but Emilia would have been thrilled to trade bodies with the half-Irish pixie.

Fiona stood by the ornate entrance, waiting. Emilia forced a smile and increased the speed of her steps. Jim had been in Los Angeles and Seattle on business for nearly two weeks, and Fiona was nearly bursting with excitement about his return. It wasn't her cousin's fault that Emilia's life was a mess.

Fiona checked in for the night, discreetly pulling the cash from her purse. Paying in cash was one of the few things she did which showed their grandfather's influence. Poppo had not believed in banks, and his suspicion of them had been passed on to his children and grandchildren. Money held in cash was more difficult to trace—and tax.

Even Emilia's purse held several hundred dollars. Her husband gave her only a small allowance, but he had been generous with his funds last night, because he was uncertain what the doctor would charge for today's visit. Antonio hated bills arriving at his house nearly as much as he hated federal law enforcement.

"I put the reservation in my name," Fiona whispered, "Just like the time I lured Jim here to seduce him." Her soft laugh had a wicked edge. "Poor guy, he didn't have a chance." She smiled smugly over her shoulder, and Emilia grinned back. This was a side of her cousin which few ever saw. Because of her small size and cheerful attitude, people often failed to see the steely, determined Fiona. "Before we left here, we were engaged."

Tucking the old-fashioned room key into her purse, Fiona grasped Emilia's arm and led her into the oak-paneled breakfast room. She moved purposefully to a small table set into the curve of a deep bay window, breezily ignoring the gestures of the hostess who was obviously hoping to steer them to a less desirable area. The woman shrugged, recognizing she would lose any confrontation. A middle-aged, somber waitress promptly brought them menus and poured coffee into their upturned china cups.

Emilia had never been in this hotel. She looked approvingly at the real linen table cloths, the crisp napkins, and the delicate porcelain. Time had stood still here in the cozy, elegant hotel, and it was so like Fiona to select a place of such quiet opulence. She could only guess what this luxury cost.

"Danish?"

Emilia shook her head in response to Fiona's inquiry. "No, a quick Danish seems almost obscene in this place. This time with you is the only good thing about my day, so let's relax and have a real breakfast."

"That sounds great!" Fiona's response was immediate. "And it's my treat."

"Oh, no, let me pay, it was my idea."

"Forget it." Fiona's slim, tanned hand with its pink painted nails and large diamond engagement ring waved Emilia's suggestion away. She looked quickly around the room to see if they could be overheard and leaned across the table. "I have thousands of dollars on me, remember? I'm stopping at the travel agency to pay for our trip when I leave Jim's office. And then, of course, I need to do a little shopping before I meet him for dinner." She winked exaggeratedly at Fiona, giggling.

"Ah, yes, a second honeymoon only a year after the first," Emilia teased.

"No, a first year anniversary trip," Fiona corrected. "It's just a month late, because Jim had to take this trip to the west coast."

"Well, the weather will be better in September and the crowds will be smaller. I can't imagine how you could see any of Paris and Rome when you were there on your honeymoon last August."

"This time we plan to see more of the sights." Fiona's wicked little laugh sounded again. "On our honeymoon, we didn't see much except hotel rooms and the food service cart." She leaned forward as the waitress approached. "Did I tell you about that huge tub in Rome?"

Emilia slapped her cousin's hand with the menu. "Yes, it was more information than I needed. Someday I'm going to tell the world about the real you!"

"Threatening blackmail again?"

"Yes, it's going to cost you millions to protect your reputation."

"Oh, I was hoping you were going to *give* me a reputation." The waitress stopped at their table, obviously disapproving of their nonsensical banter.

"Cream cheese and strawberry stuffed French toast, please." Fiona ordered primly, adjusting the napkin on her lap with elaborate dignity. "And I would like a glass of pineapple juice." She nodded in Emilia's direction.

"I'll have the same, except I'd like grape juice." Emilia matched her cousin's schoolgirl manners. They giggled together as the waitress walked away, her back as stiff with reproof as her straight, thin mouth had been.

"Why don't you come with us?" The question surprised both of them. "We could find you a place to hide in Europe, and you know I could send you money."

"You're back to saving me from my dreary life?"

"Well, I feel so guilty sometimes." For the first time that morning, Fiona's face was serious, and her voice grew quiet. "Even though we were apart when we were small, it's as though we were connected somehow. Remember when Mama died, and Daddy and I moved back to New York? When we met, it was like we were sisters, finding each other at last."

Emilia nodded. The two of them looked so much alike, they were accustomed to people assuming they were sisters, or even twins. Her own eyes were a darker shade of brown, and her brunette locks had no hint of the red in Fiona's rich auburn, but those were the only differences other than her own slightly more rounded shape.

"Remember when you took that history test for me?" Fiona asked.

"And Papa spanked *you* because *I* opened his humidor and ruined his expensive Cuban cigars?"

"Well, he didn't have his glasses on…"

"Not that he looked at me very closely anyway." Emilia sobered. "Enrico is the only child who counts; I was just something he could barter away, trying to gain a better position."

"Sh-h-h." Fiona looked at the couple nearest to them, but they were smiling into one another's eyes as the very chic middle-aged woman reached across the tiny glass-top table to butter the balding man's toast.

"You don't know what it's like." Emilia lowered her voice to a whisper. "Aunt Francesca ran away with your dad when he was just a young Irish gardener, and they lived in New Jersey. You weren't raised like I was, in an Italian 'Family.'" Emilia's voice and look stressed the "family," in a way with which Fiona was familiar.

Once again, Fiona's eyes scanned the room. "I still don't really know much. Even you and I have never discussed it. I never actually lived with my Italian relatives. I grew up more Irish. When Mama died in the accident and Daddy was so badly injured he had to sell our nursery business..." She glanced down briefly at her plate, blinking away the quick tears which even now came at the mention of that awful time in her life. "You know that was the first time I met all of you. And the only good thing about that was you."

"And Poppo."

Fiona looked up with a smile. "Yes, of course, it was wonderful to finally get to know Poppo. I guess he could be truly awful at times—after all, Mama ran away because he wouldn't let her even talk to Dad. Even though he was in the Mafia all his life, you and I would never have known it. He was the best grandpa; he was crazy about you and me."

"You especially." Emilia had been aware that their grandfather favored her cousin, but she had understood why. "You were Poppo's chance to make up for the way he treated your mother, I think."

"Probably." Fiona absently stirred another sugar into her coffee, and Emilia wondered if she would be able to drink the syrupy result. "In any case, Daddy and I never had to deal with the negatives you've had."

"Are you sure? You seemed to have so much money, I thought Uncle Sean went to work for Poppo."

Fiona's face registered horrified shock. "Of course not!" Her tone was indignant. "Daddy would never do anything illegal! He sold our land to developers who were building a shopping center and country estates. He made lots and lots of money."

"But he bought the land with money Aunt Francesca stole from Poppo when she ran away." Emilia regretted the words as soon as they left her mouth, though she didn't doubt they were true. Poppo did not lie; he might have been the head of one of New York's more notorious—if smallest—crime families, but he had had his own integrity. He had hated liars.

"Stole is the wrong word." She quickly corrected herself as she saw the conflicting emotions—anger, confusion, doubt—chase one another across Fiona's face. "Aunt Francesca had the same situation with Poppo as I do with Papa, I'm sure. No freedom or money, just unpaid work and then marriage to a man she wouldn't have loved." Emilia smiled gently at her cousin. "I'm glad she escaped. And I'm sure she earned every cent she took with her."

The shadow lifted from Fiona's pretty face. "Yes, she never said anything to me, but I suppose she would have if she hadn't died when I was seven. Daddy told me a little later. I think he was very brave to take her away."

"I do, too. I think he was even braver to come back here with you. Particularly since my father threatened his life the night before they eloped."

Fiona looked quizzical. "I never thought of that. It never occurred to me that he might have been in danger from your father—certainly not from Poppo."

"I think he might have been in a lot of danger had he not already been so badly injured in the accident." Emilia's voice was grim. "The fact that he had you—and Poppo loved his granddaughters more than anything—helped. I don't think Poppo would have let my father hurt Uncle Sean." She sat back as the waitress set her plate in front of her, the plump strawberries peeking out from the French toast, rich cream cheese stained a tantalizing pink oozing around them.

"But Papa hated him." Her brown eyes were bleak when she looked at Fiona.

"Never think he didn't hate Uncle Sean, and the hate just grew because he couldn't do anything about it." Emilia touched her cousin's hand. "He hates Jim, too." She ignored Fiona's shocked gasp. "The night Uncle Sean had his heart attack, when I called from the hospital to say he'd died, he said he was glad he was burning in hell with your mother. And he told me the night of your engagement party that you were lowering yourself as your mother had, marrying shanty Irish." Emilia went on quickly, "You know I don't feel that way. I love Jim, and you two are wonderful together, but you can never trust my father. I want you to realize that."

Fiona had known Emilia's life was very different from her own, but they rarely had the privacy to talk. She now saw for the first time how much Emilia had suffered, how much she had held back from her, the depth of her fear and sadness. While her life had not been perfect, Fiona had lived surrounded by the love of her parents and then her husband. Her uncle's cruel comments about her parents and husband did not touch her; she had no fondness for the man.

"And Poppo?" She took a forkful of the delicious food, trying to not show how much her beloved grandfather's opinion meant to her.

Emilia smiled at a remembrance. "Once Papa was raving about your father, saying he wished he had died with your mother, and Poppo roared at him." She laughed softly. "'The man has guts,'" she quoted in a quieter rendition of their grandfather's rumbling growl. "'He's Irish trash, but he's gutsy Irish trash, and he's my granddaughter's father.' Papa backed off then!"

Fiona laughed too, in relief, and helped herself to another bite. "Poppo wasn't all bad."

"Never to us," Emilia said. "But Papa…" she shrugged.

"We'll get you away, someday," Fiona whispered.

Emilia shook her head. "I can't imagine how."

But the key to her freedom was already in the lock, and it had begun to turn.

* * *

The rest of the cousins' conversation was lighter. They discussed their memories of Fiona's intimate wedding, skirting any talk about Emilia's. They talked about the trip Fiona and Jim were to leave on the following evening. It would be a leisurely tour of Great Britain, with an emphasis on Ireland. Jim wanted to get to know County Kerry, from which his grandparents had emigrated, and Fiona wanted to see County Galway, her father's ancestral home.

Someday, they planned to have a family. "Two boys and two girls!" Fiona said, never doubting it would happen the way she wanted it to.

Fiona had paid the bill after another quick skirmish with Emilia, and she looked at her watch for the umpteenth time. Emilia was not offended and understood that, while Fiona was enjoying the rare chance to spend time alone with her, she was still more excited at the prospect of seeing her husband soon. Again, Emilia envied her, as she could never have produced any feelings of expectancy, no matter how long her husband had been away.

"This watch is impossible! A single diamond on a blank miniscule face is not readable! What time is it, Emilia?"

When Emilia told her, she rose, her cheeks pinking with excitement. "Oh, Jim will be at the office by now. I have to go!" She rounded the little table, and hugged her cousin. "I'll call you tomorrow before we leave," she promised breathlessly, "and we'll bring you back a wonderful piece of Waterford crystal…or something equally impressive," she giggled and her hands flew about in the air, diamonds sparkling on her fingers.

She grabbed one of the handbags on the chair between them and rushed away, turning at the door to give Emilia a final wave and smile. Her face was lit with joy at what the day held for her, then she was gone, only a silhouette in the taxi which drove past Emilia's window. She turned to watch it, a bright dab of yellow against the New York skyline dominated by the twin towers.

Emilia lingered a while longer over her coffee. She ignored the waitress's glances, feeling a small triumph that she was not allowing herself to be intimidated as she so often was. Lingering here allowed her to dwell in the happiness of the time spent with her cousin before she had to consider the rest of her day. She tried not to think about the bleak contrast between her cousin's joyful anticipation of her vacation with a beloved husband and her own misgivings over an unpleasant doctor's visit.

Someone's cell phone jarred the dignified hush of the room and an, "Oh, dear God!" was heard before a couple near the arching doorway rushed out, their napkins floating to the marble floor. They apparently had not yet paid, as the waitress ran out behind them.

Without the waitress to annoy, it was no longer fun to sit at the table alone. She guiltily added money to the tip Fiona had contributed, and then made her way to the powder room, having to weave her way through a crowd which had gathered in the lobby. She wondered where they had all come from and where they were going. They were noisy, chattering excitedly, but she was not sufficiently interested to attempt to make out any words.

She took her time in the ladies' lounge, absently reaching into the small inner compartment for her lipstick and stroking it on before combing her fingers through her long, dark hair. She had wanted to cut her hair for years, but her father had forbidden her to when she was a teenager, and now her husband insisted that she keep it long. Sometimes she nearly forgot that she had ever wanted it done differently.

The face she saw in the mirror was so like Fiona's, it even startled her at times. She wondered what had become of the auburn wig she had worn to take that long-ago history test. No matter, it would take more than a wig to transform her life into one as happy and free as her cousin's. Having been married since she was eighteen, Emilia took constant companionship for granted. For her entire life, she had spent most of her time accompanied by a family member, then after her marriage by either her husband or a member of their housekeeping staff. There had never been a time when she lived alone, when she spent the day in her pajamas, never having to consider what someone else would think.

Fiona had lived with her father, of course, but then had gone off to college, made her own friends, found someone with whom she chose to spend time. Emilia wondered what it would be like to share a home with someone she actually wanted in the same room and whose companionship she sought. Lately this prospect had seemed more and more desirable, and compared to the happiness she saw between Fiona and Jim, only empty years stretched ahead of her.

She was afraid the doctor would discover the real reason she was childless. Would the tests show she was taking birth control pills? Fiona sneaked them to her, and she had them carefully hidden in her room. She was determined to win on this one point; she would not provide her husband with an heir if there was any way she could avoid a pregnancy.

Emilia leaned closer to the mirror. There was something not quite right with the way she looked. Her lipstick was paler than usual, only a glimmer of soft rose. She owned only a single lipstick, a warm peach. She frowned and opened the handbag again. Even as she undid the clasp, she realized what had happened. The handbag was the same neutral gray as hers, almost the exact size and shape, but it did not belong to her.

Fiona had taken the wrong purse. Emilia looked at the sizable stack of bills in the bottom of the bag and sighed. Now she would have to go downtown to Jim's office to exchange handbags with her cousin. It was fortunate her appointment wasn't until 11. She should have plenty of time. She suddenly shivered, icy cold as though a draft had blown around her. "Someone walked over my grave." She whispered to herself the words Poppo had said when anyone mentioned a sudden chill or sense of foreboding. She really *was* upset about that doctor's appointment, she supposed. Traffic was always unpredictable, so she decided she had better start for Jim's office. Antonio would be furious if she returned home with a lame excuse for missing the tests he himself had arranged. Life was very unpleasant when Antonio was not happy. Emilia sighed and slowly walked out of the plush powder room. A few people were still milling about in the lobby, and several people ran past and out the door ahead of her. She exited onto the street and heard screaming. Some people were running and others were standing, as though shocked into immobility, gazing downtown. Sirens sounded, almost drowning out the screams. A fire truck raced past, followed by an ambulance, and then another fire truck. Emilia's eyes followed the emergency vehicles into the distance, and then she saw what she had missed while she was musing in the hotel. Hordes of people stood in the streets, some silent, some crying, some pointing toward the horizon where clouds of smoke billowed from both World Trade Center buildings. The constant activity of the city seemed to have stopped while everyone watched what was happening at the two towers. A man next to Emilia collected himself sufficiently to mutter something about an airplane crash, but Emilia didn't understand how smoke could be coming from both buildings. So much smoke was pouring into the sky that the sun would soon be obscured. Jim's office was in one of the towers, but Emilia couldn't recall which. Surely the people lower down would be able to safely exit the building. Obviously the damage was horrific, and God knew what was happening in the damaged areas of the towers, but the greater part of each building still seemed sound from this distance.

 Where was Fiona? Emilia knew there had been plenty of time for Fiona to reach her husband's office before the disaster occurred. She sank to the steps and watched the mayhem of the next minutes. People around her were full of speculation; she heard that an airplane had hit each building, but that seemed a ridiculous impossibility. The streets were full of people now, no one was working or going about their business. Everyone's attention was focused on the smoke that continued to pour into the air and the neverending stream of police cars, ambulances, and firetrucks that tore past at full speed. The air was filled with the harsh shriek of the sirens when Emilia felt a low rumbling fill her body. She looked around but couldn't gauge the reactions of others in the crowd. The rumbling grew, and as she looked back toward the scene of catastrophe, one of the towers slowly began to sink toward the earth. Surrounded by an increasing cloud of dust and debris, it gently vanished from view. Emilia watched, stricken. She knew Fiona and Jim's chances of survival were diminishing by the second, but there was no way for her to reach them now. The smoke and dust veiling the bereft space where once a mighty tower had stood was billowing up the avenues of the city, reaching for what looked like miles. Emilia sat with her elbows on her knees and her head in her hands until the second tower gracefully followed the first. Now the smoke and dust had reached her, far away as she was, and she felt the stinging in her eyes and choking in her throat.

She took the key from Fiona's purse and went into the hotel, passing groups of spectators who either wailed their fear or stood stoically silent. Numbly, she found the room where her cousin had planned to welcome her husband home, from which they had planned to leave the next day for their trip. She knew with awful certainty that they would not be coming to the hotel; the tickets at the travel agency would go unclaimed.

Emilia sat on the bed, placing Fiona's purse lovingly beside her. She supposed she could turn on the television, but she didn't feel ready to see the bombardment of images she knew would be on every station. Through the solid walls of the old building she could still hear the wail of the sirens, but the curtains were drawn, and she left them that way. Her thoughts were haphazard, turning from the shock of what she had just witnessed to many memories of time spent with her cousin, especially Fiona's happiness she had envied just a short while ago. Emilia opened the drawer of the desk, pulled out scissors, and walked woodenly into the bathroom. She wouldn't let herself dwell on the thought which had flitted through her mind, unbidden but logical. Even as she refused to think about why she was doing this, her mind was beginning to develop a plan, think of problems and resolutions. She didn't want it to be possible, but she knew it was. If she did have a chance, this would be her only one. It would not help Fiona to not grasp it; indeed, Fiona would demand that she do so.

She began to cut her hair, slowly and methodically, until it was the exact length of her cousin's. The drone of the sirens went on and on. Finished with her hair and unable to tackle anything else yet, she curled up on the bed and began to sob, tears of both grief and release.

THE BEGINNING

Maria Domenici married Gianni Bellini on August 9, 1980, only three days after they met. That she did not know him or know how she felt toward him was insignificant. Her father had chosen him, with a minimum of input from her mother, and the marriage was arranged, the wedding plans made, before she even knew what was happening. She saw him for the first time at a pre-wedding party.

Gianni eventually would nearly double his weight, but he was then a very slim man of medium height, with a full head of black wavy hair. His neatly-trimmed mustache gave him a dapper look. Indeed, he was a cultured man who enjoyed opera and art. He was also a man who could strangle the life out of someone who opposed him, then straighten his tie and go on to dinner at an elegant restaurant.

Maria was convent-educated and unworldly, but she immediately sensed the lightly-leashed killer animal within the sophisticated man. She was instantly afraid of him, but she knew any pleas she might make to her parents would go unheeded. She would have to be careful with this stranger; she had no choice but to make a life out of the little she would receive from him. It was really no more, no less, than she had been taught by her parents and the nuns to expect.

Life turned out to not be as bad as she feared. Maria became pregnant on their honeymoon in Florida, in spite of her bridegroom spending most of his time with his friends and business associates. He was even gone overnight on several occasions, much to her relief. He offered no explanations for his absences, and she asked for none, grateful for the time she had alone.

She did a lot of shopping and lounging on the beaches. It was the most freedom she had enjoyed in her life. When they returned to New York, her parents' efforts to rein her in were rebuffed by her husband's amused contempt. He enjoyed being the king in his particular castle, and he frankly didn't care if his bride's new lifestyle shocked his in-laws. He found her pretty and occasionally amusing, he appreciated the fact that she did not intrude into his personal or business life, other than to rarely preside regally over a dinner party, and he really didn't care if she spent the day in the city, unescorted by a male member of her family.

Maria breezed through the pregnancy, active and energetic until Emilia was born on the first day of June, less than ten months after her marriage. The delivery was quick and uneventful, giving the disappointed father, who had expected a son, the false impression that this one wrinkle in his perfect life would soon be eliminated. He fully expected his wife to present him with a son within the following year.

Maria, too, was unhappy that her baby, though healthy and perfect, was female. With the exception of her husband's unwanted attentions, she rather enjoyed her new life. She had hoped he would spend all his time with his women friends once she produced a male heir.

Maria became pregnant again within months. She miscarried shortly thereafter. Again, she was pregnant almost immediately. But this time she was almost continuously ill. By the time her much-anticipated son was born, after seventeen hours of labor, it was obvious something was very wrong. He died the following day, during emergency open heart surgery.

Enrico's birth, only a week prior to Emilia's third birthday, was greeted as a miracle. He immediately eclipsed her in importance.

A third son was stillborn, a little more than a year later. Then there were two more miscarriages in quick succession, followed by an emergency hysterectomy.

Emilia only vaguely remembered Enrico's birth, but there was one occasion in her childhood which she remembered very well—her sixth birthday, the only birthday when she actually had a party. Her father gave her a wonderful dollhouse, complete with tiny ornate furnishings which mimicked antiques and miniscule painted reproductions of the Old Masters. Even a small Rolls-Royce sat in the circle driveway which was lined with eight-inch tall manmade "trees." The whole thing sat upon a heavy walnut base.

The birthday card was also signed "Mamma," but Emilia gave the credit for the lavish gift to her father. Her mother had had little to do with her before Enrico's birth; now she left her upbringing totally to her nanny. Even though Gianni rarely spoke to her, the little girl told herself her father was busy, that he really loved her much more than the squalling baby boy who so captivated her mother. She constantly waited for him to notice her, glowing with happiness on the occasions when he did.

Gianni was a charmer, and he did sometimes turn his charm in the direction of his daughter. She was a pretty girl, and he thought she might someday be of use to him. He was a member of a small crime syndicate, but he longed to be more important. A lovely daughter who adored her father enough to not question his choice for her husband might make a profitable alliance sometime in the future.

An Italian family which refused to pay for protection of their very exclusive restaurant was convinced by the violent death of their younger son that it was in their best interest to return to their homeland. They left so quickly they were able to take only a few of their possessions with them, so Gianni helped himself to the young daughter's expensive dollhouse. It would impress his own daughter, he was sure, and there was something about it which also appealed to him.

Emilia treasured the dollhouse, even after she could no longer convince herself that her father loved her more than he did his son.

She loved it even after she accepted that in her father's eyes, compared to Enrico, she was nothing.

* * *

With the exception of four years of dancing lessons, and her complete ineptitude with a sewing machine which made her nanny give up the attempt to teach her any domestic skills, Emilia's childhood was exactly like her mother's. She was also sent away to convent school at nine. The housekeeper was the only one to wave goodbye, because the nanny had left the previous week to go to work at another home.

Emilia's introduction to her future husband was during the Christmas vacation of her last year at school. Her parents were to leave for Florida the next day, taking Enrico with them, so she would be left alone in the big house for the final week between school terms. Antonio came to dinner the last night her parents were home.

His reason for being there was soon obvious. Emilia tried to ignore the situation, but she felt a sense of foreboding which would only increase during the last months she was in school. Twice, he sent her flowers, huge, ostentatious bouquets which were more suitable for topping a casket than wooing a young girl. She sent notes of polite thanks and increasingly dreaded returning home.

He was there for dinner the day after she moved back. She heard the housekeeper and maid talking in the pantry the next morning as she sat in the big kitchen alone, sipping a mug of coffee and eating buttered toast. Antonio was not only part of her father's syndicate, she discovered by listening carefully, he was the head of it. Of course, his organization wasn't as large and powerful as some others, but he was known to rule with an iron hand. Those who opposed him would be burned out. He had done it multiple times. Anna, the maid, whispered loudly—the only way she could whisper, as Emilia knew from years of experience—that her own uncle had lost his produce business to fire when he refused Antonio's "protection." Emilia was troubled, though not surprised, by what she heard. Though sheltered all her life, she could hardly grow up in her father's house without realizing how he made his living and paid for his family's extravagant lifestyle.

Antonio was just a couple of years short of 40, and he was extremely good-looking, Emilia had to admit. He was of only average height, but he was muscular, and wore his expensively tailored suits and stiffly starched shirts, complete with monogrammed cufflinks, with style. His hair was immaculately cut and brushed, his nails manicured and buffed, his ties (he was never without a tie) of the most expensive silk. He wore a massive solid gold Rolex on his left wrist and a large diamond ring on his right pinky finger. He had season tickets to the opera, he danced with effortless grace, and he had read every book in his impressive library. He was the picture of a renaissance man. But it was only a picture, which he himself had painted with skillful strokes.

He made Emilia's skin crawl. The civilized veneer was thick, but she could smell a rat when she was near one. Her mother's glance of sympathy at dinner her second night at home made her blood run cold. Mamma feeling sorry for her meant that Antonio was definitely *not* going to be a good husband, and it was clear that that was to be his future role in her life.

Gianni seemed either unaware or disinterested in Emilia's feelings or his wife's worries. He barreled along, making plans, giving orders about the soon-to-be-announced engagement and the autumn wedding. Antonio looked smug, his eyes glimmering with reptilian satisfaction.

As the fifth of November, 1999 approached, Emilia became more and more numb. Even her cousin, Fiona, couldn't cheer her up. Fiona's half-baked plans to rescue her from her certain fate began to annoy her.

"I can't just run away, Fiona," she said with undisguised exasperation as they both studied her strained expression in the cheval mirror. She was trying on her wedding gown and veil for a final time following the dressmaker's alterations. She turned to check the way the veil flowed from the pearl and rhinestone-encrusted tiara which held it to the crown of her hair. She had hastily piled it up to mock the elaborate coiffure she would wear on her wedding day.

The dress had been chosen by her mother, who did not typically show interest in such things where Emilia was concerned, but it was beautiful on her. The Queen Anne neckline emphasized her slim, graceful neck; the tightly-fitted waist and flowing silk organza skirt made her appear very slim. If she were marrying someone else, almost anyone else, she would have been excited, but she felt only dread and despair. She knew, whatever Fiona said, there was no way to avoid it.

"Fiona," she continued as though it had not been several minutes since she last spoke, "I can't run away like your mother did. Aunt Francesca had someone to take her away. I don't. And even if I could get away, if they didn't find me and drag me back, I don't know where I could go, or how I would live when I got there. I have no money, no training, no way to make a living. I know you would let me live with you, but Papa would never allow that. And you know it can be dangerous to oppose Papa."

Fiona sank to the floor and propped her chin on her hands. Her elbows rested on her drawn-up knees. She was ever the optimist, always sure she could make what she wanted to happen to just *happen*. But now she had to admit defeat.

"I just keep thinking there should be a way." But even her voice was feeble.

"There isn't." Emilia's face in the mirror looked strained, almost old, not the least bit pretty at that moment. "My world is controlled by men, and they are men who do not love me. I am serving a purpose for them."

Fiona's sigh was the only indication that she agreed. She stood up behind Emilia, resting her chin lightly on her cousin's lace-covered shoulder. Her smile in the mirror was a little shaky, but she managed to smile nonetheless.

"Whatever happens, you'll always have me," she promised softly. "I'll always be there for you, Emilia."

Emilia smiled back, her face again pretty. "I know," she whispered, "and that helps more than you can possibly realize."

* * *

The wedding was lavish, almost to the point of bad taste. Antonio was delighted with the extravagant amount on the money tree, as well as the expensive gifts they received. He gallantly danced with his new bride, his bow to her making the guests clap in appreciation.

Emilia was not surprised that his hands were cold, almost clammy. She giggled a little as he escorted her onto the dance floor. She had decided during the wedding ceremony, when her irreverent thoughts were darting from subject to subject rather than concentrating on the words she was saying by rote, that she was marrying a snake. She and Fiona had called him a rat, but didn't snakes devour rats? Antonio would dispatch a rat with ease. She looked for Fiona in the crowd which watched her husband twirl her around the dance floor. She wanted to tell Fiona what she was thinking, but she was whirling too fast to make out the only friendly face in the hundreds which surrounded her.

She had sipped enough wine that she felt almost detached from the events. She smiled on cue, she danced with her father, she danced with a few men whom she knew and many more who were strangers. She ate cake and posed for pictures. It was all done in a state of numbness.

More quickly than she expected, she was in her room, looking at the orderly arrangement of the antique furniture in her dollhouse as

Mamma and Fiona tugged at her wedding garments, and helped her into her lilac cashmere suit. Neither commented on her silent acquiescence as they turned her this way and that, unfastening one thing and fastening another.

"Fiona," she said suddenly when they stood away from her to admire their work, "he's a snake, not a rat. He would swallow a rat whole then very properly wipe his mouth with a linen napkin and take a sip of champagne." She giggled irreverently before becoming suddenly sober again.

Her last view of her cousin before she resolutely walked from the room was of Fiona's face crumbling into tears. She was remotely aware of her mother's gasp of surprise, but she was afraid to allow Fiona's show of emotion to evoke any response from her. Controlling her own tears, she avoided Maria's hand which reached for her.

By the time Antonio had handled her into her mink coat, his wedding gift to her over her objections that the almost sixty-degree weather did not warrant a coat of any kind, her mother and Fiona had regained control of themselves. Fiona joined the young girls trying to catch the orchid bouquet (Emilia hated orchids), when it was thrown from the second step by the bride.

She could have caught it, but something made her pull back in distaste as the enormous bunch of blooms approached her. She saw Emilia's eyes as she turned around to watch the would-be brides strain for the bouquet she had been happy to discard. She looked relieved when she saw Fiona would not be the one to catch her flowers. They were somehow tainted by the groom who had purchased them...as he had his bride.

* * *

The honeymoon in Miami was not a success. Emilia, thanks to the birth control pills which she took surreptitiously and religiously, did not become pregnant. She quickly learned that her violent husband enjoyed her reactions when he hurt or frightened her. She discovered the way to diffuse his ardor, or at least decrease his excitement, was to show no reaction whatsoever. She confided later to Fiona that the most difficult thing about sleeping with her husband was managing not to throw up on him.

While in Florida, Antonio spent even more time with his business contacts than Gianni had when he was there on his own honeymoon. Antonio knew many people in many illegal businesses. He was much more powerful than his father-in-law had ever been.

He wanted his new bride to shop in the best stores, flaunting his wealth and success. He enjoyed seeing other men admiring what belonged only to him, when Emilia sunbathed on the beach in bathing suits which would have shocked her parents.

Though he was pleased with her as a showpiece, she quickly became personally less and less attractive to him because he could elicit no emotion from her. She had screamed at his brutality on their wedding night, which had delighted him, but she had indicated no feelings toward him since then. Even when he furiously struck at her, and his ring cut a deep slice in her right hand as she threw it up to protect her face, she stayed controlled. The cut required eight closely-sewn stitches to hold it in place.

He at first tried to conquer her, make her show her fear, but he became bored with the game and decided she wasn't worth his efforts. She would make a good decoration and admirable hostess, but he could find more pleasure elsewhere.

By the time they left Miami to return to New York, he was anxious to again see his old girlfriend. Unfortunately, he still wanted a legitimate son, so he did not completely neglect Emilia, but her life was somewhat more bearable.

As their second anniversary approached, Antonio became more anxious about Emilia's lack of fertility. He was forty now, and he was beginning to think he had chosen the wrong wife. Did he not give her everything she needed, luxuries which few women could afford? She owed him an heir; it was her sole duty.

If the doctor's tests indicated she would never conceive, he would have to do something about the situation. He could not divorce as he was, after all, a good Catholic. But he was determined to find a way to have a son.

AFTERMATH

It was afternoon of the following day before Emilia realized she had not eaten in over 24 hours. She had called the hotline and the hospitals, checking for Jim's name on any roster—living, injured, or dead—but there was no information as yet. She remembered the time Fiona took her to his office, shortly after their engagement, but she still wasn't sure what floor it was on. It seemed that she should be able to remember at least if it was on the upper floors or nearer to the ground, but she just couldn't pull that information from her memory.

Emilia couldn't process all the data coming at her from each television channel as she flipped through them. But she feared it would be days, perhaps weeks, before reliable information regarding the thousands of people involved was available.

But still she called, trying to find out if Jim were alive. She didn't ask about Fiona. She knew she would find her if she found Jim. If the worst had happened, she did not want anyone to remember that someone had been asking about Fiona; who could it be, except herself?

In any case, she had already decided Emilia, whose handbag was certainly in one of the towers when it collapsed, had died. Fiona herself, or Emilia posing as Fiona, would live, waiting here for her husband until she was sure he had not survived. Her family, such as it was, knew she had met Fiona that morning. Whether or not any identification was possible, they would assume she had still been with Fiona, and that they had died together, when Emilia never returned. Certainly no one would bother looking for Fiona.

Emilia had been surprised that she fit into many of Fiona's clothes. She dressed in a casual outfit and pulled on a hat. She would dye her hair later, if she needed to complete her disguise. Now she wanted to be as anonymous as possible.

She paid for two more nights at the hotel. The clerk was inefficient, finally apologizing for her ineptness.

"This isn't my job," she said, consulting scribbled notes. "I've never worked behind the desk before, but the day clerk's husband was in one of the towers and the night clerk's dad was one of the firefighters killed." She added figures on a piece of scrap paper.

"We only have about half of our staff working." She seemed sad rather than annoyed. "I don't think there's a person in New York who didn't lose a family member or friend. You probably know." She handed the cobbled-together bill across the smoothly-polished marble.

After only a glance, Emilia paid the amount in cash, nodded grimly at the distracted woman, and whispered her thanks. Then she went out into the street, vaguely looking for a place to eat.

The city was eerily familiar and normal in some respects, drastically changed in others. Businesses were open, but the customers all seemed to be in shock. People were silent or spoke only in hushed tones. Emergency vehicles were everywhere. The smoke had mostly cleared from this part of town, hanging only very high up in the air, but not far away Emilia could still see the pall that remained, unmoving, over the empty place where yesterday two gleaming towers had dominated a city.

Emilia entered a deli and looked at the selections. She was normally a decisive person, but she seemed almost unable to choose what she wanted to eat. She finally bought several slices of provolone cheese, a loaf of fresh bread, and a jar of sun-dried tomatoes. Then, as she was paying the cashier, she grabbed some candy bars. Her body suddenly craved the sugar.

* * *

The next day she was sitting on the bed and gazing with unseeing eyes at the view from her window, when words and phrases pierced the fog which shock and incessant repetitive news had wrapped around her brain.

"Fewer than a half dozen of Frasier-Stroboski's one hundred and twenty-eight employees seem to have survived the tragedy. These workers were attending a training session across town while the others were in their offices on the seventy-ninth floor." The newscaster's voice was slightly hoarse, maybe from the smoke, or strain, or the fact that she had been talking almost non-stop for most of the previous two days. "None of the other employees has been reported alive or injured."

She held the microphone in front of a blonde, middle-aged woman who probably normally looked very attractive, but who now appeared to have been sleepless for untold hours, her makeup smeared around her eyes. "They're all gone," she said, and fresh tears followed the tracks of the others down her haggard face. A man and a woman behind her were sobbing, their heads bowed. "We haven't been able to find anyone anywhere."

Obviously moved, the commentator murmured a few words of comfort before returning the program to the somewhat insulated and controlled atmosphere of the station. The newscaster, looking almost strange in his crisp white shirt and suit jacket, smoothly commented that some evidence had been found from Frasier-Stroboski. Papers had floated to earth a couple of blocks away, and a leather chair had landed on a roof not far from the gaping hole which had swallowed the rest of the business.

Emilia's loss was confirmed, and with that confirmation came firm resolution. She pulled on Fiona's hat and went to the store in the next block. She purchased only a single item, a bottle of hair dye in a dark auburn shade.

The next day, she paid dearly for a taxi to drive her all the way to Connecticut. Then she boarded a bus for Maine.

* * *

The bus was uncrowded. Fiona, for that was the way she had decided she must refer to herself, didn't know if that was normal. She had never been on a public bus of any sort. She was almost amused, reflecting that her husband and father would be shocked to know she was riding one.

No husband or father, she reminded herself. Fiona had neither, and she must not forget to think of herself in terms of Fiona's life rather than her own.

The seat next to her was empty, for which she was grateful. Across from her, a very young mother held a fussing baby. As Fiona watched, she expertly popped a bottle into the infant's mouth, and the silence was immediate. She glanced up, saw Fiona's smile, and tentatively smiled back.

The bus stopped in the glare of fluorescent lights outside a small building in a nameless town. Three of the few people on the bus disembarked, and it was again on its way. Other than Fiona and the young mother with her baby, only four others remained. An elderly couple leaned against one another in the front row of seats, and a teenage couple was rarely visible in the back row.

"How old is your baby?" Fiona spoke softly. She could have had one this age or older by now, she thought.

"Three months." The girl smiled proudly. "Her name is Rae Ellen," she added. "My husband's name is Raymond, and he wanted her named after him. I told him we'd probably have a boy next, but he said she's his firstborn, and he wanted her named 'Rae.'" It was apparent she had been pleased by his request. "You know, lots of men want a boy first, but Raymond was mighty happy with Rae from the first moment he saw her."

"Where is your husband?"

"He's a firefighter," she responded proudly, with more pride, Fiona was sure, than she had felt a few days ago. "He's helping in New York, so I decided to take Rae for a visit with my parents."

Fiona was just about to offer to hold the baby for a while so the girl could rest, when the bus again stopped. The girl struggled to her feet with her sleeping burden, smiled a good-bye, and walked to the front, the diaper bag catching on each row of seats as she passed, causing her to have to jerk her arm slightly forward with every third step. A couple waited to greet her. The woman reached to take the baby while the man kissed the girl's check before grabbing a nondescript suitcase from the compartment below.

As the bus pulled away from the curb, Fiona watched them wistfully. The girl seemed very young and not very well off, but she was obviously happy, in love with her husband, elated with her baby, and cared for by decent parents. She would so gladly have traded places.

* * *

Fiona had chosen her destination not completely randomly. Maine was far from New York not only geographically, but also culturally. Fiona wanted someplace where she could give up the fashionable, expensive clothing her previous life demanded and vanish into a simpler crowd. She had no reason to believe anyone would look for her, but if they did, they surely would not look in a small town in New England. She had never been here before and had no ties here. While looking out the bus window she quickly selected a place called Seafair. From the bus it looked large enough for her to remain somewhat anonymous. (She would soon realize this original impression was wrong. The fact that the village stretched so far along the coast made it appear larger than its actual size.) The place appeared to have a charming downtown district where she could hopefully find work, and she could smell the ocean, a crisp scent that always pleased her, before she stepped down to the street. The village of Seafair was not pretentious enough to call itself a city, or even a town. It was, and had been for nearly two hundred years, a village with a church defining each of its three inland corners, a prosperous main street which fronted the cliffs overlooking the ocean, and a tiny marina at its north end just past the Congregational church. It was picturesque as a village overlooking the waves of the Atlantic should be, full of Victorian and Cape Cod-style homes surrounded by ancient trees and grassy parks, but it was too small to hold as many tourists as would have liked to stay there. At any one time, the inns and bed and breakfasts could accommodate no more than eighty or so. The nearest campground was nearly fifty miles away, and there were no chain motels, hotels, restaurants, or stores.

Many towns claimed to have maintained the charm of previous eras, but Seafair was one of the few which actually did. There was even one family living at the edge of town which used oil lamps and water from a cistern. The village council had insisted they join onto the sewer system, although their once well-used "outhouse" still stood, supposedly as a decorative item, in their yard.

Seafair had in its history produced a famous general, an opera singer (although some were embarrassed because James Frankenberger was a tenor rather than a baritone), and was now the home of a United States senator.

Senator Keith Shane was a moderate, a conciliator in Congress. He was known for his ability to get things done for his people without caving in to special interest groups. He was considered incorruptible, and the citizens pointed proudly to their small public school where he had been educated before going away to Annapolis. He had retired at 42 from the Navy and immediately and successfully run for office. After a term as a representative, he had easily won election to the senate.

Senator Shane and his wife, Libby, owned a house north of the village, overlooking the water. It was a lovely house, although it was not overly large and anything but ostentatious. A four-over-four clapboard Cape Cod, downstairs it had a living room in front of a small office to the right of the open hallway. A dining room adjoined a cozy kitchen on the left. The curving stairway hid a powder room beneath as it led up to two bedrooms on each side of the upper hall. The master bedroom was much larger than the other one on the right side, which had once been a nursery and was now Libby's private office-sewing-craft-reading room. A large bath—the most opulent room in the house, Libby acknowledged, with its huge pedestal tub and skylight—separated the two rooms of the master suite. On the other side of the upper floor were two bedrooms of equal size, with their own small bath between.

There were two cottages on the grounds. The senator's parents had moved to the larger one when their son came home from the Navy, giving the old house over to their daughter-in-law and her long-stifled urge to remodel. She was tired of living in houses which were not her own, and she relished having a home with which she could do anything she wanted. They watched with consternation which became amusement, as she tore into her project, removing wallpaper which predated her husband's birth, tearing up carpet to restore wide plank oak floors, scraping coats of paint from woodwork. They ultimately agreed the outcome was well worth her efforts.

Libby, untiring, next went to work on their cottage. They quickly decided to move into the smaller cottage while she whipped through the dated décor which they had failed to even notice. They appreciated her efforts when they moved back in, less than six months later. As they requested, Libby kept their antiques, even though they were more well-worn than elegant, but the chintz fabrics, warm woods, and tiled surfaces added life to what had been rather drab and plain. Their two bedrooms and baths, living room and country kitchen were just what they wanted, even if they had not known it.

Libby was elbow deep in the last cottage, which had three tiny rooms—living room, kitchen, and bedroom with a little bath—when Keith won his first senate election. The news people photographed her in paint-spattered overalls, brush in hand on a ladder, with a scarf tied around her short salt and pepper hair.

She didn't mind that people throughout the state saw her with no makeup ("Well, I *was* wearing mascara," she later admitted. "I *always* wear mascara."), and Keith's constituents loved that she didn't care. When she danced with the president at the White House, otherwise beautifully groomed and dressed, the fact that her hands were stained from refinishing a cabinet the previous weekend only added to the lore about the senator's wife. She was one of his best assets.

Keith and Libby Shane lived much of the year in an old brick townhouse which had been converted into a duplex just outside Washington in Arlington, Virginia. Keith's parents, Thomas and Margaret, shared the other half of the duplex. While they enjoyed cultural events offered in the nation's capital, they all considered Seafair home. Even Ethan Shane, who lived in Boston where he was an attorney with the Department of Justice, spent as much time in Seafair as he could. He had never shared his grandfather's and father's love of sailing, didn't like to even swim in the water, but he loved to be near the sea, to be able to look at it, nonetheless.

It was not, perhaps, surprising that the newly-born Fiona was instantly drawn to the village when she first saw it. The sun was just beginning to set as the bus crested the hill and then began the descent onto Main Street. For the first time that she could remember, she felt at peace.

Fiona stepped slowly from the bus when it finally stopped. There was an inn with a wide porch running around the entire first floor, across the street and two houses down. She retreived her suitcase from the storage compartment, walked the short distance to the house, opened the gate, and trod the brick path to the painted steps, studying the Victorian fretwork which she had only seen before in photos.

A very plump, rosy-faced woman answered the ring of the shell-shaped brass bell and welcomed her. She led her upstairs to see the room which overlooked the ocean. "It's the best room," she boasted. "You'll be happy with it."

Fiona doubted she'd ever be happy, but she did like the old-fashioned room with its walnut canopy bed, quilted coverlet, and china basin and bowl on a marble-topped washstand. A big bathroom was through an open door, the pedestal sink wide and the claw foot tub roomy. She smiled and placed the suitcase by the bed.

"There are a couple of restaurants on down the street," the woman, who introduced herself as Mrs. Haddington, said gently. She seemed to somehow sense Fiona's sadness and smiled at her. "Breakfast is at eight. We'll fatten you up a bit," she laughed.

"Mrs. Haddington, I've never had anyone say I need to fatten up."

The woman laughed, a rollicking sound which made Fiona blink. "Why, you're a tiny little thing," she said. "If the wind picks up when you're walking along the cliffs, you might be blown into the sea."

Fiona couldn't help but smile back.

* * *

After she unpacked, she walked a couple of short blocks to a rustic café where she actually enjoyed her cola and lobster roll. It felt strange to dine alone, but it tasted better than anything she had bought at the high-priced New York deli. On the way back to the inn, she stopped in a little shop and browsed for a while among the souvenirs and fishing gear. She handed a couple of quarters to the leather-faced man behind the counter, nodded at his gruff thanks, and took a newspaper.

There was no one in sight when she entered the inn. She stepped out of her shoes just inside her room, turned on the floor lamp by the single armchair, and read through the paper, page by page. There were of course articles regarding the recent tragedy, speculations of who the guilty parties were, how long it would take to sift through the rubble, and accolade after accolade for those who died. It was a relief to be far away from it all, in a place where she could look out her window at the last glow of daylight on the ocean and almost pretend it hadn't happened.

The last page was made up of classified ads. There was a fishing boat for sale, a refrigerator, a washer and dryer set, and several items listed under the heading "Antiques" which sounded as though they should be more accurately listed under "Used Furniture." She looked at the "Help Wanted" ads. The last one caught her attention. She read it twice, then carefully tore it out, turning the paper around to keep from ripping through it.

"Wanted: House-sitter who will also do cleaning when residents are at home. Cottage and meals plus small salary. Apply in person at Cliff House."

She had no idea where Cliff House was located, but she planned to find out tomorrow.

* * *

Fiona was on time for breakfast, just barely. She had slept soundly in the wide bed with its feather ticking and goose down pillows. The slight chill in the air had made the warmth of the room welcome. She could faintly hear the waves crashing below the cliffs, a melodic rhythm which lulled her into a fatigued sleep.

In the darkness, she had dreamed of her room at her parents' home. She had taken a few cherished items with her when she married, but her father had not allowed her to move her treasured dollhouse. In her dream the dollhouse was with her, displayed in a room in a cottage by the sea. She was sitting in a chintz chair, looking at the dollhouse as it slowly revolved on its base, smiling at how beautiful it was, when her father burst through the door.

"How dare you steal that from me!" Her father ran toward the dollhouse, lifting it up so she could see under it. Something was shining there, dully catching the light of the candles which glowed in her dream room.

"No, Papa!" She called out in her sleep, waking herself even as she reached to snatch the dollhouse back. She was so tired, the dream was soon a fuzzy memory and she was awake for only a few minutes before she again fell asleep. This time, she did not dream.

When the smell of coffee awakened her, it was a quarter till eight. She brushed her teeth, threw on jeans and a light sweatshirt, swiped a brush through her hair, then decided she could take a minute to apply a sweep of blush across her cheeks and mascara to her lashes.

By the time she arrived at the table, her stomach was growling. She could smell the bacon and biscuits; even the strawberry preserves gave off a sweet and homey scent.

The only other guests, a couple from Charlotte, North Carolina, were at the door, bidding their hostess good-bye. They had a long drive ahead of them today, Fiona heard them comment. Then Mrs. Haddington returned to the table, sitting down at the head so that Fiona was at her right.

"Did you rest well?" She helped herself to another biscuit, although her plate showed evidence that she had already eaten. "Looks like you're hungry this morning." She smiled with satisfaction at the scrambled eggs, bacon, and biscuit on Fiona's plate. Butter oozed from the biscuit, and strawberries were at the side, ready to be added.

"I am." Fiona couldn't remember when she had felt so relaxed and comfortable with her surroundings. "I had a strange dream last night," she added thoughtfully. "It even woke me up, but it wasn't really scary—just odd."

"You were tired," the older woman said, solemnly nodding her head so that the lowest of her several chins moved from side to side. "Your mind was likely dealing with a lot."

Fiona looked at her sharply to see if she showed any sign of suspicion, but Mrs. Haddington was busily fitting two thick slices of bacon onto yet another biscuit. She closed the biscuit, then paused before again opening it so she could layer strawberry preserves on top of the bacon. Then she took a bite and smiled.

"Nothing like breakfast, it's my favorite meal." She carefully set the remainder of the creatively made sandwich back on her plate and poured more coffee. "Now what are your plans for today, dear?"

Fiona swallowed her bite of cheesy scrambled eggs. If she didn't find somewhere else to live, she thought, she would soon be the size of her hostess!

"Where is Cliff House?" she finally asked.

"You thinking of applying for Mrs. Shane's job?" Mrs. Haddington quickly put two and two together. "Have you decided to stay in the village?" She poured more cream into her already pale coffee. "That would be good. You'd like it here, I'd wager."

"I do like it here." Fiona leaned forward earnestly, grateful that Mrs. Haddington wasn't prying. "It's so pretty and peaceful."

"Well, the Shane family is a good one. They live at the north end of town, close to the marina. There's a stone wall on either side of the drive. You'll see it. You can't do better than to work for the senator and his missus, even though they're not really wealthy. You won't be gettin' rich!" She laughed and took a generous swallow of coffee. It was so diluted with cream, it could not be overly hot, Fiona thought vaguely.

"Mind, they're rich enough, rich compared to the rest of us around here, but they're not likely to put on airs and such. And they've traveled, been everywhere nearly. They won't have trouble understanding you with your funny accent." She smiled gently to temper the criticism. "Where are you from anyway? We get people from all over, but no one's been talking the way you do."

The New York accent was influenced by the melting pot of students with whom she had associated at convent school, she supposed. Plus, the Italian often spoken at home probably colored her speech patterns. "I guess it's a combination of the people I've been around and the places I've been," she vaguely answered. Then she asked for more juice, hoping food would replace any other subject in Mrs. Haddington's mind.

As she returned from the kitchen with the cold tumbler of juice, Mrs. Haddington paused to pull the gingham curtain aside so she could look out at the sea. "The wind's picking up a little," she said. "If you're heading up to Cliff House, you'd better not tarry too long. And be sure to take one of the umbrellas in the hall with you."

"I'll straighten up a little before I go and change to something a little less informal," Fiona replied.

Mrs. Haddington laughed. "You're dressed up enough for Mrs. Shane! Now old Mrs. Shane may be particular, but the young one will like you just fine the way you are. She only dresses up when she has to, when she and the senator are in Washington." She patted Fiona's arm. "Get along, girl. All I have to do all day is what needs doing in this old house, and that will be done in two shakes of a lamb's tail."

Fiona showered quickly and did add a little makeup, brush her teeth again, and change to a nice blouse with a leather jacket over it. She looked at herself in the mirror. She *was* Fiona. With the reddened hair, and Fiona's clothes, even though they were somewhat snug, she looked more like her cousin than herself.

"Emilia is dead." She whispered to herself, as if saying the words out loud would make them true. "Emilia is dead, and Fiona is alive." She looked out the window at the sea for a minute. Just looking at it made her feel stronger, more alive.

She was where she was supposed to be. She could feel it. She descended the stairs slowly. There was no hurry. She knew where she was going, and she felt it was where she was going to stay.

She remembered to take an umbrella only because, on her way out, she passed the rack where they were propped. The sky, she noticed, was clearer than it had been earlier. It looked as though the sun might try to come out from behind the enormous clouds which still hid most of its light.

She took her time walking through town, checking out the shops although she didn't actually go inside any. She passed the café where she had eaten the previous evening, and then a larger restaurant in the next block. Two more blocks, and there was a diner, complete with stools at a long Formica counter.

There were two dress shops, a drugstore, a fairly large grocery toward the end of Main Street, a library in a Victorian house which looked as though it might be better suited to be a teahouse or bed and breakfast. There were small shops for the tourists, with wares from antiques to crafts, imported china and crystal, souvenirs and lighthouses in every form imaginable. It would be fun to shop here, she decided.

The marina came in sight, and then she saw the rock pillars which made no effort to actually guard the road which led to Cliff House. The house itself sat uphill, surrounded by trees and wild gardens. A cottage was set behind it on either side, one smaller than the other. What wonderful views they must each have! Fiona couldn't wait to enter the house and see the cliffs and water from its welcoming windows.

She had been walking slowly until then, but now she picked up her pace. She was anxious to reach those stone sentinels, anxious to walk through the lush trees and flowers to the scarlet door which seemed to urge her to come in.

When she finally went through the picket gate, then reached the door, no one answered her knock. She continued around the house on the slate path. She looked around her at the profusion of flowers. She couldn't imagine what the garden must be like in the spring and summer if it was so fragrant and colorful now. It was unlike any garden she had ever seen before, thick and wild, with no discernable pattern.

"Hello! I hope you haven't been trying to find me for too long!" The voice was friendly, although the accent was odd. The speaker's English was perfect, but it was spoken as though it was not her first language. The woman pulled off a wide straw hat to reveal short, thick hair which was just long enough to touch her ears. The black was generously sprinkled with silver which glowed in the emerging sun.

"I'm Libby Shane," the woman said as she approached, pulling garden gloves off her surprisingly small hands and extending the right one. She was of average height, but her build was slight. When she removed her sunglasses, Fiona saw that she had very prominent cheekbones and unusual dark eyes, very round but sloping upward at the outside edges.

"I'm Fiona Patrick." She grasped the proffered hand, surprised to find it soft. "I've come about the ad." She had said the name with hardly a second thought. She really was beginning to feel as though she were a different person.

"Oh yes, finally someone who made the trek to Cliff House." Libby Shane replaced her sunglasses. "I've had three people call. That's the way it is in a village; they know us, so they don't bother to do as I asked. They just dial our number, and I have to traipse into the house and answer the phone. I think it's much more pleasant to chat outside, don't you?" Before Fiona could reply, she began to talk again. "I don't see any reason to go inside when we don't have to. Not when the weather is still so nice. Besides, I tend to track in dirt, and sometimes other messy things, too." She started walking briskly across the terrace, so Fiona followed.

"The larger cottage, the one behind us, is where my husband's parents live." Libby gestured over her shoulder. "The smaller one is for the house-sitter." A few more steps across the yard—here behind the house there actually was grass, although the wildflowers were nearly as plentiful as they were on the front lawn—and they were at the tiny cottage.

"It's very small." It was clear she was describing, not apologizing, as Libby threw open the door as though she were revealing a prize. Fiona stepped into the living area. It was nearly as bright as the outside, the front bow window let in so much light.

The room was all in blue and white, the fabric of the chairs and sofa striped, while the window seat was covered in a blue plaid canvas. The table between the chairs was painted white, as were the cabinets, table and two chairs in the kitchen at the back of the cottage. The floor was slate, but a large rug covered most of the area. Shells of various varieties were woven into its pattern.

There were real shells inside the glass tops of the tables and an enormous and breathtakingly beautiful shell mirror dominated the room. The beach motif could have been tacky, but Libby's deft sense of style had produced a warm, welcoming home. The more Fiona looked, the more shells she saw. They were even used as pulls on all the drawers, including the cabinet which hid the TV.

The single painting in the living area was of sand dunes and undulating sea grass with a lighthouse dimly visible in the distance. The dampness of the fog which obscured the lighthouse could almost be felt, the painting was so realistic.

The bedroom was to the left of the front door, and it also had a bow window. But here the window seat was covered in a pattern of cabbage roses, with pillows of coordinating fabric in stripes, plaids, and smaller florals. The blue was carried over to this room, but it was secondary to creamy yellow and rose.

The bed was a pencil post without a canopy. A thick comforter, in a duvet made of a patchwork of the fabrics on the window seat and pillows, covered the high mattress. There was a tall, narrow dresser and an equally narrow closet beside the door to the bath.

The bathroom had a claw foot tub, a pedestal sink and a reproduction "water closet" toilet. Here again were a beautiful shell mirror and white painted shelves filled with coral and large specimen shells.

All the curtains were of white lace, although white hurricane shutters rested outside against the weathered pale yellow clapboards. When the winter winds blew, the lace would be too wispy to offer any protection.

Fiona doubted that the entire cottage was more than 500 square feet. But it was charming, and she instantly loved it.

"It's wonderful!" Her eyes were shining when she finally remembered Libby. She didn't know that Libby had been watching her face as they toured, seeing the reactions as Fiona discovered every facet of Libby's creativity.

"Let's go sit on the terrace and chat awhile." Libby led the way back to the main house just as briskly as she had traveled away from it to the cottage.

As they stepped back up onto the low terrace, an older woman approached from the opposite end. She was quite tall, very lean, and dressed in natural-colored linen slacks and a matching shirt. Her curly hair was short and gleaming white.

"Mother, this is Fiona Patrick. Fiona, my mother-in-law, Margaret Shane." Libby's tanned face crinkled with humor. "Don't ever call her Maggie," she whispered loudly. "She can get quite ferocious!"

"Posh!" Margaret scowled at her daughter-in-law, but Fiona could see the two shared a close relationship. "I simply prefer my own name. Maggies have long hair which they toss about, getting it into food and other people's faces. And they wear tight jeans and tee shirts with logos on them."

Libby laughed. "Maybe I should change my name," she said, gesturing to her own snug jeans which carried a common label name. Her tee shirt boldly proclaimed that Virginia was for lovers.

"Hm-m-m," Margaret said reflectively. "No, everyone would get the two of us confused. Besides, it would take years for your hair to get long enough."

Libby stood up. "I'm going to get us something to drink. I never can win against you. But that's because I haven't had as many years to practice being snippy." She disappeared into the house before her mother-in-law could respond.

Margaret sat back in her chair, shrugging. "That's the only way she can get the last word," she said smugly. "She has to run away."

Fiona decided she liked both of the women very much. She couldn't imagine any of her own family teasing one another like this.

She cupped her chin in her hand, her elbow on the patio table, and listened to Margaret Shane as she pointed out the marina in the distance, her own cottage, and this and that in the garden.

Libby returned with glasses of ice and cans of several soft drinks. She set the laden tray between the two who were seated and sank into her own chair. "Pick what you want, Fiona," she said as she choose a drink, popped the top, and poured it over the ice. She wiped her finger down the side, removing the condensation.

"So where are you from?" she asked abruptly. "What brought you here to Seafair? Do you plan to stay here? What jobs have you had in the past? How old are you?"

Fiona did not hesitate. "New York, a bus, yes, I've never worked, 20." Her words were rapid fire.

"You've never worked?" That was the one thing which seemed to surprise her.

"Dictatorial, old-fashioned, difficult, over-bearing father."

"So you're running away?"

"No," now Fiona spoke slowly. "I'm running *to*."

Margaret was nodding, and Libby nodded, too. "I understand. You're determined to live your own life."

"More than that, I'm determined to live a peaceful life." Fiona had not really known her goal until she said the words.

There was no response. The three sat, sipping their drinks in silence for a few minutes.

"I don't think it's going to rain after all," Margaret remarked to no response.

"Can you clean?" Libby asked.

"I don't know how to do much, but I can clean." Fiona replied honestly.

"I could clean, cook, sew, do almost anything when I was married, but I rarely get to do anything, particularly when we are in Washington," Libby said pensively.

"Your mother taught you all that?" Fiona couldn't imagine a mother who would sit at a sewing machine, tutoring her child in the domestic arts.

"No, I learned everything in the orphanage in Korea. I was taken there when I was a few days old, by my American father after my Korean mother died. The women who ran it needed help, so we learned to do things as we grew up." She looked across the field of flowers, as though she were remembering the sometimes hard years of her childhood.

"Even though we had to be a tad creative to feed everyone, it wasn't usually bad," she said quietly. "Miss Louise, a spinster nurse who came two years before I arrived and stayed many years after

I left, took particular interest in me. I felt well cared for. Then, when I was 16, she talked her sister and brother-in-law into sending for me, and I came to America."

She popped open another can and poured the contents onto the melting ice. "I worked and went to college in Rhode Island. Then the second year I was here, a Navy officer came to visit a friend of his in the apartment below mine, and I met him on the stairs." She glanced at Margaret. Fiona wondered if this was an oft-told tale when she saw Libby begin to smile.

"He was so-o-o pretty in his dress whites," she finished, exaggeratedly rolling her eyes. "I just fell head over heels in love." Margaret made a noise which sounded suspiciously like a snort, and Libby laughed. "Within two months we were married, and Ethan was born exactly a year from the day we met."

"Isn't that romantic?" Margaret dramatically drew out the syllables of the last word, but Fiona thought she was trying to disguise her own emotional reaction to her son and daughter-in-law's love story. "It's amazing people as impulsive and silly as those two found one another."

Libby just laughed more loudly until Margaret's stern expression gave way to a glimpse of humor. "Well," she growled, "at least they produced a wonderful, quite sensible child."

"Who, unlike his father and grandfather, both Navy men, hates to sail," Libby said.

"As I said, quite sensible," Margaret responded.

Fiona finished the last of her drink and stood up. "Well, I certainly have enjoyed meeting you both," she began.

"Italian, that's it, isn't it?" Libby interrupted.

"What?"

"I could hear a little of a New York accent, but there was something else, too. Your dictatorial father is Italian, isn't he? That's why your accent is different."

She watched Fiona's expression close as she thought for a moment before answering. "Yes, my family is Italian, but I was taught in convent schools. I imagine that is why I don't have the usual New York accent."

Libby nodded. She was sorry she had made the girl uncomfortable, although she couldn't imagine why her question had caused Fiona to withdraw so quickly and completely.

"We'll talk about the job and give you a call, if you are still interested." It was what she had intended to say, but now she spoke too quickly, trying to change the subject. "Are you staying in the village?"

Fiona glanced once more at the tiny, perfect cottage where it sat in the distance, a few wind-bent trees shading it protectively. "Yes, I love it here." Her voice was very soft. She told them where she was staying, smiled shyly, and found her own way back down the slate path. The umbrella still leaned where she had left it.

"I like her." Margaret spoke firmly. "I don't know if we should trust her, but I do."

"Me, too." Once again, Libby swirled the liquid in her glass. "There's something wrong, but I don't think it's the girl. There's something that's happened to her." She looked into her mother-in-law's eyes. "Maybe we'll find out."

"And maybe not," Margaret said reflectively. "But she somehow seems to belong."

"That's it, Mother." Libby was pleased by Margaret's apt choice of words. "There's just something about her that fits."

* * *

The next day Fiona told herself, even as she descended the stairs and headed toward the yummy scents which had wafted up to her room to tempt her, that she would not eat as much as she had the day before. But her plate was filled with biscuits, eggs, and bacon within minutes. She did, however, deny herself any of the thick cream for her wake-up coffee. Coffee wasn't really necessary when the aroma of bacon was available, she thought as she helped herself to another slice. What did Mrs. Haddington do to make food so delicious?

"I've brought you some orange juice, dear." Mrs. Haddington glanced approvingly at Fiona's ample servings as she entered from the kitchen. "I didn't get to ask you about your visit to Cliff House yesterday, by the way. How did that go?" She sat heavily on the captain's chair at the head of the table.

Mrs. Haddington was just reaching for a biscuit when the knocker struck firmly against the front door. She pushed herself up as the knocker slammed against the door again, more loudly than before.

"I can only get there so quickly," she grumbled beneath her breath as she moved around the table. She pulled the door open abruptly—breakfast was her favorite meal, and she hated for it to be interrupted—but her tone of voice changed as soon as she recognized her visitor.

"Why, Mrs. Shane," Mrs. Haddington's voice was nervously friendly, the way one speaks to someone respected but also feared. "Come in! Join us for some breakfast."

Fiona turned to see which Mrs. Shane was entering the dining room, but she could tell by the voice before the new guest came into view.

"A cup of tea would be very nice, Winnifred." The elder Mrs. Shane's voice was dry. "I couldn't eat another bite of breakfast, however. I had toast only a couple of hours ago."

It was clear Mrs. Haddington could not think of an appropriate response. Fiona knew she wanted to exclaim that toast hardly qualified as breakfast, but she wasn't about to do that to the formidable and very thin village *grande dame*. "Yes, I'll put the kettle on," she murmured as she disappeared into the kitchen.

"Good morning, Miss Patrick." Margaret pulled a chair out, shook a napkin free of its folds and wiped it across the table to remove the few tiny crumbs which had been left by the previous occupant before settling across from Fiona. "I brought your umbrella back."

"Oh, thank you. I didn't even realize I'd left it."

"Well, I wanted to talk to you anyway. Libby is working on the yard, the house, whatever, to keep her mind off the awful tragedy in New York. That's her way to deal with trouble. And with Keith insisting he must stay in Washington, show the people he is ready to put himself in harm's way for them, she is doubly unhappy. The two of them don't do well apart." She laughed her dry, rather grating laugh. "Now Tom and I, we have to get away from one another every once in a while. Poor man can't stand me for long!" She absently fidgeted with her wide, flat platinum wedding band.

"Is Mr. Shane in Washington with the senator?"

"Oh, no, he's somewhere out on the ocean, sailing with three of his old Navy buddies. They go off for several weeks every year. I imagine they'll just sail off and never come back some day." Her tone was flippant, but she did look concerned. "They're all too old to be wandering about, but they love it." She shrugged. "One should go doing what makes one happy, I suppose."

"But won't they have heard about what's happened? Aren't they coming back home?"

"They won't hear the news until they come into shore. Sometimes they don't do that for a week or more. We'll hear from him when they do." She shrugged again. "He's always been a rover, anxious to travel, have adventures, see as much as he could of the world. When we were in the Navy, I loved living different places. And I like to travel still. But I enjoy having our little home. And I detest sailing."

Margaret gazed out the window for a moment, and then turned back to smile at Fiona. "Well, enough of that! The old man is 77 now, old enough to do what he wants. What I need to know is if you are planning to take the job? Libby really likes you, and she wants you to move into the cottage today if you're ready."

"Yes!" Fiona answered as Mrs. Haddington set a cup of tea and a Brown Betty teapot in front of the older woman. Margaret thanked her hostess, and sipped the steaming brew.

"You even make wonderful tea, Winnifred," Margaret commented. Mrs. Haddington beamed at the unexpected compliment, and they spent the next half hour chatting pleasantly. Then Margaret Shane left, promising to return that afternoon in her car to pick up Fiona and her baggage.

* * *

Fiona danced across the floor of the cottage, humming a wordless tune. It was the first place she had ever had of her own. Her mother had decorated her room at home in a suffocating style of heavy Mediterranean furniture and ponderous velvets and brocades. Antonio had hired a decorator to "do" their house, and he had not allowed his wife to move a single thing in the ornate, stiff décor. But now she was in a place which looked just as she wanted it to, warm and bright and cozy, and this place was to be her own, a place where she could settle in and spend time alone, doing whatever she wanted.

She had barely enough room in the closet for her meager clothing and three pairs of shoes. The remainder—underwear and nightgowns—filled the little dresser. With her makeup and other toiletries stored away in the bathroom, she let herself simply explore the cottage, touching this and that, looking into kitchen cabinets to discover pretty pastel dishes and blue glass tumblers as well as basic baking and cooking items.

The sun had set when Libby arrived, carrying a flashlight to guide her across the lawn. "Don't forget to leave the outside carriage light on at night," she said when Fiona opened the solid oak door in response to her light rap. "If you come to the house, or someone comes to visit you, it's impossible to see the way."

"I'm sorry." Fiona closed the door as Libby switched off the flashlight and walked into the room. "I was having so much fun exploring, I didn't realize it had gotten so dark." She had turned on two lamps in the room earlier, but more to enjoy the glow than because she needed the light to see. Now she moved to switch one on in the kitchen.

"Are you settled in?" Libby sank onto one of the chairs.

"Yes, everything fit in exactly. Would you like some tea or coffee?"

"Well, I guess we could move to the kitchen table and get to know one another." Libby vacated the overstuffed chair in favor of one of the white-painted wrought iron kitchen seats. She propped her chin against her clasped hands, elbows on the glass table top.

"Oh, the hours I spent making this table!" She looked through the glass to the arrangement of shells against the wood base. "It was such fun."

"You're so creative," Fiona said. "Does your mother-in-law like to work with you?"

"Heavens no! Margaret has no patience whatsoever. She's a walker; she walks miles every day, rain or shine. When she's not walking, she's reading. And sometimes she just visits with me when I'm gardening or working on a project." She leaned to pat Fiona's arm. "She scares people to death—she scared me to death when I first met her—but she's wonderfully funny and loyal. I adore her."

"But she scared you at first?"

"Oh, yes! She was gruff and abrupt, and I had taken her only child away. I thought she hated me. But after Ethan was born, I had to have emergency surgery and was very ill. For days, she sat beside my bed, reading to me, taking care of me. She said she didn't trust the nurses, or even Keith, to do what needed to be done. I've loved her ever since."

"I'll remember that story if she starts to scare me. But compared to the men in my family, she seems almost harmless. I liked her right away."

"She likes you, too. But don't think she's harmless. If anyone tried to harm someone she loves, she would turn deadly." Libby's voice was firm. "If you are her friend, you have a friend for life."

"I'll remember that, too. I like loyalty. There isn't much of it in the world." If Libby noticed the slight bitterness in Fiona's voice, she did not mention it.

They talked of other subjects then, Libby saying she would soon go to Washington, D.C. if her husband did not make a trip home. She also said she wished her father-in-law would return from sailing. "He's getting too old, his friends are too old, to go off for weeks out on the ocean." She shook her head. "I can't imagine why Mother doesn't try to stop him."

"Maybe she does."

"No, if she said she was worried and didn't want him to go, I'm sure he would stay. They fuss and fume, but they are devoted to one another."

"I think she doesn't want him to stay at home when he wants so badly to go," Fiona said. "She talked about it this morning. But she doesn't like to sail."

"Her father and brother were lost at sea," Libby said quietly. "They were fishermen, and they died when she was just fourteen. The family lived in this house, but it was just an old farmhouse with outbuildings then. Her mother remarried a couple of years later, and Margaret married Tom as soon as she finished school, but she never got over being frightened of the sea."

"It must have been awful for her, being married to a Navy man, but she somehow survived thirty years of it. Then she finally was able to come home to Seafair. She was so happy when Dad retired."

"If only he wouldn't take off sailing."

"Maybe this will be the last trip. Keith tried to talk him out of this one, but he was adamant. I hope..." her voice trailed off.

"Mrs. Shane said your son doesn't like to sail?"

"No, I think Mother got her points in early. Ethan is very like her anyway: pragmatic, serious, wry, loyal, and frighteningly intelligent. He even looks like Mother. And he can be as formidable as she is."

Libby glanced at her watch. "I'm sorry I stayed so late," she said as she pushed her chair back. "I know you must be tired. We'll get together tomorrow for lunch and I'll show you around the big house."

She smiled gently. "Don't worry, it's not all that large. And we'll help out when we're home. It will be your domain when you're here alone. It shouldn't be that difficult to keep up then."

She opened the door after flipping the switch which turned on the carriage light on the path which led to the terrace. "We mostly want you here to watch over things, not work yourself to death."

She took the flashlight from the table and went outside. "Lunch in our kitchen at noon. Relax and do whatever you want until then." She pulled the door to behind her.

* * *

Fiona was surprised at how late she slept. She woke to sunlight shining through the beautiful bow window. She had forgotten to close the lace curtains last night. The tragedy in New York seemed lifetimes away. She had not turned on a television since she arrived in Seafair.

In the kitchen, she made a cup of tea and some toast, thinking how appalled Mrs. Haddington would be at her meager breakfast. Well, a few weeks with Mrs. Haddington, and she would need a new wardrobe! It was time to get back to sensible eating.

She wiled away the morning, then put on her makeup and a pair of navy chinos and a linen shirt before crossing the lawn to meet the two Mrs. Shanes at the back door of the big house.

The kitchen, which was three or four times the size of hers, smelled delicious. While Margaret stayed to watch the simmering clam chowder, Libby gave her a tour. All the rooms were comfortable, but the house was not the least bit imposing. Fiona could recognize Libby's warmth in every room.

After a big bowl of Margaret's famous chowder, Fiona followed the other women to the terrace. They sat as they had when she first visited, drinking cool drinks and talking, only now Fiona's nervousness was gone. It was as if she had never been Emilia and never lived Emilia's unhappy life.

"You'll need to get to know some of the young people in town," Libby was saying. "You shouldn't be very busy here, so you can go to the village and meet Brenda at the co-op shop. She's about your age."

"What's the co-op shop?"

"The tourists love it. Nearly everyone around here gets together and sells something or other there. We all contribute to Brenda's salary, and the village council gives us the building rent free," Libby explained. "We even have a little catalogue which Mr. and Mrs. Wilkinson at the newspaper print. We send copies to people all over the country twice a year. I think our last printing was for three hundred catalogues. That's not too bad for a little village business."

"What's for sale?"

"Enough of a variety that most of us do our gift shopping there. I found Christmas presents for all of my husband's staff the last couple of years. Two years ago, I filled baskets which Mr. Jennings made with Mrs. Zelinka's preserves and the Hemmings' honey. I lined the baskets with Miss Mattie's embroidered linen towels— they had lovely tatted borders—and hung one of Lulu's gorgeous ornaments on the handles. Last year, the men each received one of Sam Water's ships in bottles—they're all numbered works of art and I had to grab them fast before the tourists did—and I chose Nettie Blankenship's tiny handmade porcelain ladies for the women. Nettie makes the outfits by hand, and they are incredibly elaborate. She uses real hair to fashion the fancy coiffures. They are just fabulous!"

"I thought you liked them," Margaret said dryly. "You have half a dozen yourself."

"Were they in the corner cabinet?" Fiona asked. "I saw them. They are beautiful. I really loved the lady who looked liked Madame Pompadour."

"Yes. I'm afraid I'm really not responsible when I go into the shop. I should send Mother in with my things, so I'm not tempted."

"What do you sell there?" Fiona couldn't imagine anyone paying for something she made. She didn't have a creative bone in her body.

"Shell mirrors and furniture, wreaths made of shells, dried flowers, beaded fruit, Christmas ornaments and pinecones, dried bouquets, this and that." Libby spread her hands wide. "I paint and decorate plain picture frames, I cut out felt or paper figures for cards and pictures. Whatever is fun." She laughed. "I don't make a living, but you'd be surprised at the prices some things bring.

"Nettie and Sam are getting quite well-known, and I'm planning to give Patty's blown glass and Carol's pottery as Christmas presents this year. Bob's carved animals and Noah's Arks are fabulous children's gifts which I buy when someone has a new baby, but lots of adults collect them for themselves. It seems someone finds another way to be creative each year. We may have to expand into a second building soon."

"*I* do the books for the business," Margaret added. Her angular face, Fiona decided, was actually quite handsome. She doubted she had ever been pretty, but she must have been very striking. "I'm not artsy, but I'm good with figures. The shop is important. It helps a lot of people make ends meet."

"Well, I'm going to go down there this afternoon," Fiona said. "I can't wait to see everything."

"It takes a while," Margaret said in her dry voice. "You'd better be on your way. Libby and I will clear up here."

"We're going to indulge and have pizza tonight, Fiona," Libby said as she stacked glasses onto the tray on the table. "Come on over."

"Would you like to come to my cottage?" Margaret held the kitchen door open for her daughter-in-law. "Fiona hasn't seen it yet, and pizza is the kind of cooking I like to do."

"That sounds like me," Fiona said. "Carryout food is the only thing I prepare for dinner. But I'm really going to have to learn to cook."

"We'll teach you," Margaret threw over her shoulder. "See you at six." The door slammed shut.

Fiona was humming as she wove her way through the flowers which all but obscured the path to the front gate. Yesterday had been wonderful, and she had enjoyed her morning. She felt a pang of guilt as her cousin and Jim came to mind, but it was quickly replaced by a wave of peace, as though the real Fiona was reassuring her, letting her know they were together and happy, and that she wanted her to be happy, too.

She looked out toward the sea. A large sailboat was coming in to the harbor. It seemed to glimmer in the sun. She thought she might like sailing. Perhaps she would go out on a boat sometime and sail across those foaming waves. She felt ready to take on new challenges and experiences, and live life more fully than she ever had been able to before.

Fiona took her time walking to the village. The day was sunny, even if there was a hint of the quickly approaching autumn weather in the air. There were several boats tied up at the marina, but she imagined it was much less busy than it would be in the summer. Would she be here when the weather was hot, and the tourists filled the village next summer?

She quickly found the co-op. It might have been a bank at one time, she thought. Its door angled onto the street with metal steps leading up to the entrance. A ramp had been added to one side so it was wheelchair accessible. It was the largest of the shops in town, one of those she had dismissed as an ordinary souvenir store. As she pushed the heavy, old-fashioned door open, she immediately saw how wrong she had been.

Artwork of various kinds covered every surface of the wall, cabinets were overflowing with fragile handmade items, shelves held food items, and racks displayed quilts and other fabric handiwork.

"Hi, may I help you?" A very tall blonde approached her. She had a beautiful smile and china blue eyes.

"Are you Brenda? Margaret and Libby Shane told me I should come see all the wonderful things in your store. I'm Fiona."

"I'm Brenda, but it's not my store, I just work here. I do sell some things, but most of the items are made by other people. They're amazingly talented."

A quilt caught Fiona's eye, and she pulled the rack out so she could see it better. The price was high, but not as high as it would have been in the city. Watching her, Brenda remarked that the co-op members had decided when the shop was opened that they would charge prices based on the worth of their talent and products, hoping there was a market for quality items. They were happy with the results.

"Nearly half of our sales this year have been through our catalogues. We have four high school students who work a couple of evenings a week, packing items for mailing. If this Christmas season is like last year, we'll sell more between Thanksgiving and

Christmas than we did during the entire tourist season."

"Does it pay to stay open all year?" The town seemed very quiet with little traffic right now.

"Part of my pay is the apartment upstairs. When it's not busy, I just pop into the store when the bell on the door chimes. The cases with the really expensive items are kept locked." Brenda reached into a pocket and pulled out some keys, then unlocked a huge old cabinet with deep, wide shelves. She handed a scrimshaw brooch to Fiona. It was incredibly detailed, the bone cut to show a scene of a sailboat with a lighthouse in the background.

"Teddy Bruin makes those. A lady bought half a dozen last week, on a rainy day when I thought no one would be here. Last December, a woman called from Massachusetts to say she wanted to come up here to buy her Christmas gifts, but the only day she had free from her law practice and social engagements was a Sunday evening. I opened up, and was I happy I did! She bought almost $4,000 worth of merchandise, including three quilts. And two more shoppers came when they saw the lights on. They each spent a ridiculous amount of money."

"What if you want to go out of town? Don't you ever get a day off?"

Brenda didn't seem surprised by Fiona's interrogation. "Oh, someone comes in. Even Mrs. Shane has worked here."

"Libby or Margaret?"

Brenda laughed. "Libby...Margaret would scare customers away! But I don't often leave town, so I usually just ask someone to stay for an hour or two while I get groceries or go sailing. The teenagers in town help out in the busy season."

Fiona returned the brooch and moved around the store as they continued their conversation, and Fiona explained to Brenda that she had just moved into the Shanes' small cottage and would be working at Cliff House. She admired the wreaths on the walls which she was sure were Libby's handiwork and the paintings of the ocean, the village, and even some city scenes. One looked remarkably like the one in her living room.

Brenda saw where she was looking. "Ethan Shane does those. He's a wonderful painter, although I have always preferred his watercolors. No one would guess those were done by an attorney, would they?"

Fiona wondered if Brenda was personally interested in Libby Shane's son, but the chime of the bell warned of another customer before she could think of a way to tactfully ask.

"Adam!" Brenda's eyes lit up as the big man turned from latching the door. His hair was nearly as golden as hers, but his eyes were hazel.

"Hi honey, been busy?"

"No, travelers are few and far between right now. Maybe it will pick up again next month if nothing else happens." She gave a little shudder.

"I hope it's over, but I'm not sure I think it is." Adam's open expression had vanished from his face, and his eyes were now sad. "I'll never forget that mess."

"Adam is a policeman and volunteer fireman," Brenda explained to Fiona, and apologized for not introducing them.

Fiona offered her hand, and Adam's huge one swallowed hers in a firm, but gentle handshake. "Did you go to New York to help?"

"Yes, and it was a nightmare. I couldn't stay, because Rick Lyle's wife got sick and had to go to Boston, so they needed me back here. I got to admit, I was glad to come home." He looked at the toes of his highly-polished boots, shaking his head.

Brenda gave him a quick hug. "Are you going to be off tonight?"

"Yep." His head came up, and he smiled at her, holding her to his side with one arm. He glanced at his wrist on her shoulder. "Time I was gettin' back, sugar. I'll see you later." He dropped a quick kiss on her upturned nose and released her. He moved with the grace some large people possess, his steps almost silent, and turned to wave as he closed the door behind him.

"Isn't he wonderful?" Brenda laughed at her own girlish gushing. "I've been in love with Adam since kindergarten, and he finally noticed me in high school. We got engaged on my birthday last month." She held out her hand, displaying a pretty diamond, the size not small but certainly less substantial than the one Fiona owned. Fiona thought to herself that this diamond ring, though not large, actually stood for something.

"I'm going to be staying at the Shanes' this winter, house-sitting," Fiona heard herself say. "Maybe you could come visit me, have lunch or a pizza when Adam is on duty?"

"That sounds great," Brenda replied. "You're always welcome to visit me here. I might even get you to help out in the shop."

"That would be fun. I'd like to learn about all these beautiful things." Fiona picked up a glass bottle in which an ornate ship sailed against a painted background of a harbor. "I've never seen anything like this before. I don't even know what scramshaw is."

"Scrimshaw," Brenda corrected. "Sailors used to carve scenes in ivory during their long voyages. Now ivory is difficult to find, but Teddy uses bone. Most artists carve on fake bone, but Teddy insists on the real thing."

She held up a basket, its shape odd to Fiona's untrained eye. "These baskets take hours to make, some take days. And people want that quality and are willing to pay for it."

"We'll try to make sure I learn enough to be able to help you out a little." Fiona thought a few hours volunteering in the shop would be fun. Besides, she might be able to get a little better price on the items she decided to purchase if she worked here.

"I'm glad I got to meet you, Brenda. Please come see me." She turned to leave, happy she had taken the first steps toward making a new friend. A stranger came through the door as she exited,

Brenda's "good-bye" to Fiona followed by her greeting to the customer.

Fiona retraced her steps back to the Shane estate. She had planned to visit Mrs. Haddington, but she decided she didn't have enough time if she was going to be back in time to freshen up and go to Margaret's for pizza. Tomorrow, or the next day, she would see Mrs. Haddington. There was plenty of time. She planned to stay in Seafair for a while.

* * *

"Are you out of your minds?" Ethan Shane's voice bellowed across the phone so loudly that his grandmother could clearly hear his words even though it was his mother who held the receiver. Margaret briefly left the room, returning with a cordless phone to listen to the rest of her grandson's tirade.

"...doesn't have references, hasn't given you her social security number, has no work experience, appears out of nowhere..."

"Ethan." Margaret's interruption made him pause.

"Ethan, I like the girl, your mother likes the girl, and I suggest you come up here and meet her yourself before you make any rash judgments about her."

There was the sound of an indrawn breath as Ethan considered her words. "I can't imagine how I could take time to come up there with what is going on right now," he finally responded. "Actually the reason I called was to tell you I've been transferred to New York. My stuff is being packed and loaded for the move next week. A bureaucracy can move quickly when it really wants to."

"How on earth can you find a place to live on such short notice?" Libby asked.

"I'll stay in one of those residence hotels until I have time to apartment shop. It's not as though I need that much space. We military brats learn not to acquire much that's extraneous," he answered. His voice had returned to its usual quiet tone. "But Mom, Gran…"

"We'll leave things as they are until you have time to see for yourself," Margaret said when Libby looked at her helplessly. "We think you will be pleasantly surprised, dear."

Ethan sighed heavily. "I have several days to move. I'll take a couple of them to run up there rather than unpacking my things in New York. I'll just live out of a suitcase for a while."

"That would be lovely," Margaret said happily. "We're anxious to see you."

"I'll be there tomorrow." Ethan could sometimes win against his mother, but never against his grandmother. They were too similar, and she had more experience with power struggles than he. "But I'll only be able to stay one night."

"Be careful, darling," Libby said. They said their good-byes and hung up.

"He'll see why we hired her," Libby said.

"Certainly," Margaret replied. "It isn't as though we are country girls with no experience with people. Working with criminals has made the boy overly suspicious."

She rummaged in a drawer and pulled out a menu. "Now what kind of pizza shall we indulge in tonight?"

"The works!" Libby immediately said.

"Good idea." Margaret dialed the number to order.

* * *

The pizza delivery truck was driving between the stone pillars as Fiona walked from her cottage to Margaret's. She could see the two older women through the open curtains of Margaret's living room window.

She studied the room as Margaret paid the pimply-faced boy. The colors here were creams, browns, greens, and blues. Here and there, Libby had added a touch of coral to warm the subtle palette. The furniture was antique, the fabrics chintz. It was twice the size of her little cottage, with a second bedroom and bath upstairs, and its rooms were a more generous size, she found. Libby gave her a quick tour while Margaret served pizza onto each plate on the dining table located between the country kitchen and the living room.

The conversation was relaxed and easy. Fiona told them of her meeting with Brenda and Adam, how much she liked the co-op store, her enthusiasm making her eyes glow. The two women smiled at one another, their shared glance saying they were glad the young girl seemed to have moved from under the cloud that had hung over her when she first arrived.

Libby mentioned that her son was planning to visit the next day, but could only stay the night.

"Oh, I saw some of his paintings!" Fiona exclaimed. "He's a wonderful artist!"

"Yes, I think he would have painted for a living, had he thought he could earn enough," Libby said. "But he's a very good prosecutor."

"Not many people can support themselves, let alone a family, as an artist," Margaret remarked dryly. "Of course Ethan isn't married yet, but he's nearly thirty, so we hope someone soon is willing to face that awesome challenge."

Fiona remembered Libby had said Ethan was a pragmatist like his grandmother, but she thought there had to be another side to someone who could produce such beauty.

They were all startled by loud knocking at the door. Fiona jumped, nearly upsetting a can of Coke.

"Home is the sailor, home from the sea!" a male voice yelled. "Open up, woman, and give me a kiss!"

Margaret's stern face transformed as she recognized her

husband's voice. She covered the distance to the door quickly, throwing it open and embracing the man who stood grinning at her.

He was only slightly taller than his wife, but more rotund. His hair was the exact white as hers, but his expression was as affable as hers was often forbidding. "Did you miss me, sweetheart?" He gave her another kiss then walked toward Libby. With his arm still around Margaret, he bent to kiss his daughter-in-law then turned to smile at Fiona.

"And who is this lovely young thing?" Fiona thought his gift of blarney exceeded her uncle's.

When the introductions were made, Fiona decided it was time to excuse herself and leave the Shanes alone. Tom Shane was eyeing the leftover pizza, which was stone cold.

"I'll warm the pizza for you, Dad, then I'll leave you two alone," Libby said. "I'm sure Mother wants to tell you how worried she's been about you."

"Of course I've been worried," Margaret said. "The ocean's too unpredictable for old men to go out on for weeks on end."

Her husband patted her bony knee, his leathery face crinkling into a grin. "You're right as usual, sweetie." (Sweetie? Fiona couldn't imagine anyone calling Margaret by that endearment.) "We decided from now on we will just go out for the day. We found out we're too elderly to handle emergencies."

"What happened?" Margaret demanded, alarmed. "What emergency?"

"Not really an emergency...I'll tell you later." The old man smiled at Fiona. "She's crazy about me," he whispered loudly. "Just crazy."

"You're the one who's crazy," his wife replied tartly. But she leaned toward him, resting her hand on his thickly muscled arm.

Libby set the plate of steaming pizza in front of Tom Shane, poured him a cup of coffee, and then kissed her in-laws' wrinkled cheeks. Fiona stood and followed her to the door.

"It was nice to meet you, Mr. Shane," Fiona said. "Thank you for the dinner, Mrs. Shane."

"'Night, darlings," Libby called before shutting the door behind them.

They walked a few yards together before exchanging their own good nights. Fiona was surprised and pleased when Libby hugged her. She had had little affection in her life.

She tried to stay awake for a while, reliving the events of the day, but she was asleep within minutes, snug in the warmth of her little cottage.

* * *

Ethan Shane arrived just before lunch the next day. Fiona had helped Libby make chef salads, and they quickly prepared another when he called to say he was about to reach Seafair.

Margaret and Libby went outside to meet him, so he was still smiling when he entered the house. He did look remarkably like his grandmother, Fiona saw. His face wasn't handsome, but he was attractive in a rugged way. His eyes were hazel in his tanned face. His brown hair was thick and inclined to dip across his forehead. He was rather thin and quite tall.

He studied her for a full minute, then seemed to at last notice her hand which she had offered and took it in a firm handshake. She thought he had decided he liked what he saw when he finally spoke, his voice warmer than Margaret's had been when they first met. "Hallo, nice to meet you. Ma and Gran have been singing your praises."

Fiona's glance at the two women recognized the relief on their faces. So they had been afraid Ethan would disapprove of her. They had not mentioned talking to him about her. She murmured some vague greeting and went back to the kitchen to bring the pot of coffee out to the dining table. Tom Shane came through the back door and followed her into the more formal room, grabbing his grandson into a rough hug.

"You need to come home more often, kid," he said.

"I shouldn't be taking the time to come now," Ethan replied. "Much as I would love to stay here, I have to make a living, and right now work is keeping me very busy."

"Yes, your gran told me about your move." The elder man sat down and took a sip of the hot coffee. "What do you think about living in New York?"

Ethan too pulled out a chair, seating himself at the opposite end of the table so that he faced his grandfather. He shrugged. "I guess I like Boston better as far as a city to live in, and it's closer to Seafair of course, but New York will give me a lot more experience. If I'm going to be a prosecutor, I might as well learn as much as I can and go as far as I can."

"But you'd rather be sitting outside with an easel, painting the harbor."

"Well, I'm not ever likely to be able to do that." Ethan added dressing to his salad. "Right now, for the foreseeable future, I won't have any time to paint." He moved his fork through the salad, mixing the dressing in. "But I'm a lot more fortunate than some people."

They all nodded, and Libby changed the subject, mentioning the increasing business at the co-op. The conversation became lighter then, the voices flowing around Fiona. She enjoyed listening to the family's chatter.

When the meal was finished, Fiona volunteered to clean up so the others could spend the little time they had together. The kitchen was spotless, everything tucked away where it belonged, when she quietly let herself out the back door. She called Brenda and arranged to meet her at the café for dinner, leaving a message to that effect on Libby's answering machine when she saw the four walking out toward the marina. She didn't want to intrude on their family time.

Besides, she had wanted to talk to Brenda again. She ordered the delicious lobster roll she had liked so much the first night she was in Seafair, and Brenda had a cheeseburger. They returned to Brenda's apartment, a huge loft which was as sparsely furnished as the shop below was cluttered, and talked until so late—Brenda mostly talking while Fiona listened—that Brenda insisted on driving her back to Cliff House. She dropped her off at the gate.

A light was on in the kitchen of the big house, and someone had turned on the carriage light so Fiona could find her way to her cottage. The elder Shanes' cottage was totally dark.

"Are you all right?" The deep voice from the terrace startled her, and she jumped.

"I'm sorry," Ethan Shane said. "I thought you could see me. Mom was a little concerned when you were still gone at bedtime."

"Oh, I didn't call, because I didn't want to intrude on the little bit of time you have together. I'm sorry I worried Libby."

"She went on to bed, so I don't think she imagined you'd been kidnapped or anything." His tone was wry. "I told her I was going to stay up for a while, that I'd keep an eye out for you."

For some reason, she wanted to join him on the terrace, chat with him for a few minutes. There was something so sure and solid about him, so grown up, although she knew he wasn't quite thirty. She wanted to get to know him better.

But she was married. Fiona or not, she was married. She hadn't given it any thought until now, but she would have to avoid men, this man in particular, because she found him very attractive. Antonio was much more handsome, but Ethan was real.

"Thank you for waiting up." She spoke quietly. "And thank you for turning on the carriage light. It was very nice to meet you."

He knew she was attracted to him, she could tell by his voice when he answered her. He sounded amused by her polite schoolgirl speech. "Why, you're mighty welcome, ma'am," he drawled. His voice was an excellent immitation of a southern gentleman's.

He was wishing he didn't have to leave in the morning. He understood why his grandparents and mother liked this girl so well. He did, too. He hoped he would be able to spend some time with her, that she would stay at Cliff House long enough.

He sighed and watched the light come on in her bedroom. Then he went inside and up the stairs to his own room, but it was much later before he slept.

Ethan left before noon. Fiona had spent the morning in her cottage. He suspected she was avoiding him, and he couldn't decide if that annoyed or relieved him. He'd have to think about that on the long trip to his new home.

Only minutes after his car disappeared from sight on the road to the village, Brenda called to tell Libby two of his paintings had sold. They, too, were going to New York City.

TRANSITION

Libby Shane was whirling about her kitchen when Fiona entered from the terrace the next morning. Her knock at the back door received a muffled response which she assumed to be permission to enter. The louvered doors which hid the washer/dryer combo were open, and laundry was piled over much of the open floor.

"Oh, Fiona," Libby glanced over her shoulder. "I'm glad to see you. Have you had breakfast?"

"My usual toast and tea," Fiona replied. "Have you eaten? Or did you just wake up and decide to open a laundry?"

"I ate a bagel." Libby picked up a handful of clothes and threw them into the washer, then opened the door of the dryer to check on the load in it. "I woke up early this morning and decided to go to Washington. I miss Keith."

The door of the dryer banged closed. "I just need to get all this laundry done first."

"I can do the laundry," Fiona said, wanting to be helpful. "I'm supposed to be working here for you, remember? So far, I feel more like a guest than an employee."

"Well, your main job is just to be here." Libby looked frazzled. "You're not a lady's maid. I want to get all my clothes washed before I leave."

"I have lots of time," Fiona insisted. "I can do some laundry for you at my cottage." The stacking washer and dryer there were much smaller than Libby's own super capacity ones, but they were adequate for Fiona's needs.

"That would be wonderful," Libby conceded. She grabbed a laundry basket and stuffed her washable lingerie in with a couple of delicate blouses. "If you'll just do a load of these on easy care, that would help so much."

"Do what you need to take with you, Libby," Fiona said as she picked up the small basket and retraced her steps to the door. "I'll do the sheets and towels, what ever stays here, and remake the beds. I'm here to help you, and you need to get going if you're driving all the way to Washington."

"Fiona, I don't know what I did without you." Libby's thanks followed her.

By the time Fiona returned with Libby's laundry, the lingerie neatly folded and the blouses hung, Libby was back in the kitchen, dressed in jeans and a sweatshirt, ready to travel. Two suitcases, each with a matching tote, were by the back door.

Margaret was also there, accompanied by three suitcases and a single tote. She was, as always, calm and pulled together. Although Libby had suggested only that morning that they join Keith in Washington, Margaret had been ready to travel in barely more than an hour.

"What do you need me to do, Margaret?" Fiona asked. "Do you have laundry that needs to be washed, the bed changed, or dishes to wash?"

"No thank you, dear, it's all done," she said crisply. "I threw the sheets and towels in the washer as soon as Libby said she wanted to leave today, and Tom remade the bed and put things away while I packed for us. Just keep an eye on things and dust and vacuum every once in a while." That was Margaret, efficient and organized.

"I hate to leave so much for you to do." Libby looked around at the laundry which remained on the floor and the small amount of dishes in the sink. "My bed isn't made, and neither is Ethan's..."

"I'll have it done in a jiffy," Fiona reassured her. "It's my *job*, Libby," she again reminded her.

Tom Shane walked in, grabbed a couple of suitcases, and was out again. Libby, Margaret and Fiona carried the remaining luggage to the car. Tom packed it in the back, instructed by his wife on the proper arrangement.

"Now you have copies of all the keys?" he asked Fiona, and she nodded. "You have the electrician's phone number, the plumber's number, you know how to operate the emergency generator, where to get fuel?" Fiona's head was bobbing in response to each query.

"Very well, I think we're ready to go. Keith's no doubt weary of a peaceful life in Washington and yearning to have the havoc of his wife and mother." He ignored Margaret's withering look, surprised Fiona with a quick kiss on her cheek, and got behind the wheel. After a flurry of hugs, Margaret got into the other front seat, and Libby climbed into the back. They were off down the road, sounding the horn as they drove through the twin columns.

"Whew!" Fiona shook her head in amusement. She wondered if she would ever get over the amazement she felt with this family. They could not have been more different than her own.

She went into the kitchen and started to work. By noon, the laundry was done, the beds remade, the kitchen spotless. She locked the house, checked the elder Shane's locks, and returned to her cottage for a lazy afternoon.

She knew she would soon miss Libby and Margaret, but it was a new experience for her to be on her own and able to do whatever she wanted. She had the keys to the Jeep which they had left in the garage, but she decided she wouldn't use it until the weather turned too cold to walk to the village. She might even go up the coast a little one day. She felt as though she were surrounded by nothing but space, a welcome space that she could fill by doing whatever she wished. She was excited at the prospect of days alone in her little cottage by the sea.

The following afternoon, Fiona visited Mrs. Haddington. The woman was happy to see her. She enjoyed having guests in her bed and breakfast, and the slow seasons were long for her. The two sat over tea and chocolate chip cookies while Fiona listened to the latest gossip about people she mostly didn't know.

Her ears perked up, however, when Mrs. Haddington began to talk about Ethan Shane. "That boy was always an artist," she said. "My sister, Millie, taught at the school here until she retired a few years back. When Keith Shane retired from the Navy, and Ethan started to school—I think he came here when he was 15 or 16—she had him in her art class. My, how she raved about his paintings!"

"It seems strange that he became a lawyer." Actually, Fiona had more trouble imagining the man at an easel than in court, but it was something to say that would hopefully elicit more information from Mrs. Haddington.

"His grandmother always wanted him to go to law school, old Tom Shane's father was a lawyer. And Margaret had always wanted to study law, but she married Tom Shane when she was barely out of high school. They say Ethan's a lot like Margaret—I guess that's true from what I know about him—but he also must have some of Libby in him. There's an artist there somewhere for certain."

Fiona stirred a little cream into her tea. She'd walked all the way to the village, surely a little cream wouldn't hurt her. She was thinking about the conflicted man who worked long hours as an attorney for the Justice Department when he was more suited to be at home in his village, painting the local scenery. Somehow, she was sure that was what he wanted to do. He had seemed so content when he was at Cliff House.

She wondered when he would again find the time to come to Seafair. She hoped it would be soon. Then she mentally chided herself for admitting she wanted to see him again.

By the time she left the village, the sky was losing some of its light. She glanced into the co-op, but Brenda was busy with a customer, so she walked on.

At her cottage, she studied the painting on the wall of the living room. The detail, the sunlight on the waves, the shading of the sea grass and the multi-hued colors of the water made the canvas nearly translucent. Even her untrained eye recognized that Ethan Shane was indeed a gifted painter.

* * *

The next morning, Fiona dusted and vacuumed the big house. She paid more attention to the rooms than she had before. There were custom made frames, all decorated by Libby, holding family photos. A shell wreath hung in Libby's bath, opposite a shell mirror.

Over the fireplace in the living room, an enormous seascape by Ethan held pride of place. Two additional paintings were in the room, smaller ones which depicted scenes in what she guessed to be Europe.

There was at least one of Ethan's paintings in each room. The subjects were varied, but his detail and subtle colors were unmistakable. She particularly liked the one which hung over his bed. It was of a beach community, dressed up in lights for the holidays, the glimmer of the colors reflecting in the water and on the white blaze of beach.

How did he see things so clearly, with such detail, and transfer his vision so precisely? She wanted to talk to him about his painting.

She wanted just to talk to him.

* * *

That evening, she was munching popcorn, a late supplement to her insubstantial dinner of salad, when the telephone rang. It was Libby.

"Is everything all right?" Libby always sounded in a hurry. "Are you frightened out there by yourself?"

"Everything is fine, I'm fine, and I'm not the least bit frightened,"

Fiona replied. "But I'm glad you called. How was your trip to Washington? How are things there?"

Libby's sigh traveled clearly across the miles. "Oh, the Pentagon looks awful, people are so dreadfully upset, there's so much going on…"

"But you are glad to be with your husband." Fiona smiled to herself because she knew Libby must feel at ease now.

"Oh, yes! And he said he'd been hoping I'd come down. It's such a wearisome long drive, but we all took turns at the wheel. I'm so glad we're here."

"Any idea when you'll be back?"

"I hope we can come in October. I love to see the fall foliage, but the way things are, I'm not asking Keith to make plans. We hope at least to get away for a couple of days and go south into Virginia."

"*I* hope you can come home," Fiona said. "But I know the entire country is topsy-turvy right now. It must be very different there."

"Oh, yes…"

After a moment's silence, Libby asked if she had heard from Ethan. She seemed surprised when Fiona said she hadn't.

"Brenda left a message here, asking him to contact her. She said she didn't have his new number in New York yet, and didn't think you did either."

"I don't."

"Well, write it down, please. I don't know that you'll need it, but who knows what will happen next?" She rattled off the number at the residence hotel, and Fiona scribbled it on the same sheet of paper by the phone on which the Washington, D.C. numbers were methodically listed.

"Here's his office number, too, but don't call that except in an emergency." Fiona dutifully penned the additional number, noting "emergency only!" beside it.

"Call us once in a while," Libby said. "Don't worry about using the phone."

"I will," Fiona promised. "I hope it isn't too long before you can come back."

"Me too, dear! I'm tired of wearing high heels already!" Fiona was laughing as Libby hung up, but she became solemn, thinking that the cities that had suffered directly from terrorist attacks must be so different from the peacefulness she appreciated in her little town in Maine. She had tried to avoid the scenes on the news, still ever-present, of the wreckage in New York because it reminded her painfully of the loss of her cousin, and it moved her beyond words to see that loss reflected in the faces of so many helpless people. It had been her home for a long time, and she couldn't help but still be affected. While she had stayed in the hotel in the first days after the attack, she had suffered from gruesome nightmares in which she visualized Fiona and Jim's deaths over and over, but the dreams had abated and were now, thankfully, infrequent. Even in the worst dreams, she knew she couldn't begin to imagine what thousands had suffered.

Within minutes, the phone rang again. It was Brenda, wondering why it had been so long (actually three days) since Fiona had visited her. Her cheery voice immediately pulled Fiona out of her reverie.

"I'm going to work in Margaret's cottage tomorrow morning. I'll probably come down to the co-op in the afternoon. Do you want to go out for dinner?"

"Sounds great! Adam's working the evening shift this next week."

"Well, I know I'm a poor substitute for that hunk of man," Fiona laughed, "but I'll fill in tomorrow as best I can."

She sat smiling for several minutes after she hung the phone up the second time. With the exception of her cousin, she had never had friends whom she called up on the phone, or went out with for dinner. Now she had Libby, Margaret, and Brenda. And sweet Mrs. Haddington, she reminded herself.

* * *

She was about to finish the dusting in Margaret's cottage the next day when the phone rang. "'Lo," she said, stretching to reach around the vacuum which she had yet to return to its closet.

"I was about to give up," Margaret's voice barked through the phone. "I called the big house, your cottage, and this is the second time I dialed there."

"I just finished vacuuming half an hour ago, and I'm almost through with the dusting. I guess you called when the vacuum was on." She moved the object under discussion and sat on a chair at the kitchen table. "How are you, Margaret?"

"Fine, I suppose," she replied. "Would rather be in Seafair, of course."

"Come back," Fiona urged her. "I miss you."

"Well, that's not something I'm used to hearing."

Fiona laughed. "You know it's true. And Brenda says there's bookkeeping to do at the co-op."

"Ah, now I know why I'm wanted." But she sounded pleased nonetheless. "I don't want to come back until Libby does. She needs someone around to take her mind off all the tragedy. Libby feels things deeply. She doesn't cope well, you know."

Fiona thought Libby was somewhat intense, even flighty, on the surface, but there was a core of steel beneath, tempered by her difficult and lonely childhood and her experiences as a military wife. She also knew Margaret liked to feel necessary in her daughter-in-law's life.

"Yes, I'm sure it helps her to have you there, someone else to suffer through high heels and pantyhose." Fiona could not completely stifle her laugh, and she heard Margaret finally snicker, too.

"Mr. Shane hasn't taken off sailing, has he?" She wondered what had happened on the elderly man's trip with his friends to make them decide to stay closer to shore in the future. She still hadn't heard.

"No, he swears he's never doing that again. Did I tell you why?"

"No."

"Jerry Wilstine fell overboard, and Lyle Huntstreeter nearly drowned when he jumped into the water with a lifejacket to help him. By the time they got the two of them back on board, one of the men was having chest pains—fortunately relieved by his nitro—and another could barely breathe because of strained chest muscles. They all realized they need to reduce the scope of their adventures." Margaret paused only a moment before continuing. "Honestly, it's a wonder they all survived!"

"I think you've been brave all these years to not try to stop your husband and son from sailing when you are so afraid of the sea." As soon as the words were out, Fiona felt she'd made a mistake. "Afraid" was not a word Margaret would appreciate being applied to her.

Fiona was right. "I am *not* afraid of the sea. I merely realize how dangerous it can be, how unpredictable."

"Yes, that's what I meant." Fiona quickly changed the subject. "I've been looking at your grandson's paintings. He really is a fantastic artist."

"He is a wonderful painter," Margaret agreed. "But one does not make a living painting. And Ethan is also a gifted attorney. He is as brilliant as Tom's father was."

Before Fiona could agree, there was rustling at Margaret's end, and she said she had to go. She was due at a luncheon given by the wife of some official whose name meant nothing to Fiona.

"Well, keep in touch, dear. We'll come to Seafair when we can." And she was gone.

* * *

Brenda was checking the locks on the cabinets when Fiona arrived at the co-op. "I want to be ready to go when it's closing time," she explained.

But a woman pulled up in a glossy black Lincoln with Connecticut plates at five minutes before Brenda and Fiona were to leave. She took her time perusing the merchandise, oohing and ahhing at the quality and variety. Fiona occupied herself by studying the three remaining canvases of Ethan's which were still in the store. The prices were steep, but she thought the quality justified them.

The woman had chosen several items, and she left them on the counter by the cash register, crossing the room to see what so fascinated Fiona. Hearing her footsteps, Fiona moved aside.

"That's exquisite!" The woman's high society tones revealed her wealth as much as her car and enormous diamond rings. "That would be a perfect wedding gift for my niece next month. I'll take it." She hadn't even looked at the discreet price tag.

Another painting was to the right of the large one, but this one was very small. She grabbed it off the wall. "This one will be perfect in my alcove. It won't take much space at all; I can simply move my Chagall over a little…"

Ethan's painting on a wall beside a Chagall? A Chagall being moved so Ethan's work could be hung? She could hardly wait to tell him.

They finally locked the door behind them a little after six. The Lincoln's taillights were still visible in the distance.

"Whew, she was something! She didn't even look at a price tag," Fiona said as they crossed the street toward the café.

"That happens all the time," Brenda said. "Some of the people who come in here are very, very wealthy. And quite a few come back again and again, or they come because one of their friends told them about the shop. They like being able to buy something which is unavailable in any other store."

"You're down to only a single Ethan Shane now."

"I know. I called Libby in Washington and got his number, but he hasn't answered the messages I left for him in New York. I know he's busy, but I need paintings before the Christmas shoppers begin to arrive. He paints very quickly, but he needs to do several."

"Maybe he'll come up with his parents in October."

"Maybe." But Brenda didn't sound too hopeful. "All law enforcement people are so busy right now."

"He's working on the case with the hijackers?"

"I don't think so. Adam said he was taking over the Mafia cases so the New York guys could concentrate on the hijackers. That's why they brought him there from Boston."

Mafia. Ethan Shane was working on Mafia cases. Life was ironic. Fiona shivered, though she asked herself what the chances were that Ethan would cross paths with anyone she knew. There were many Mafia families, and it wasn't likely Ethan was concerned with hers. Papa was small potatoes. But Antonio wasn't, she thought; Antonio was increasingly important. If "The Torch" did anything while Ethan was in New York, what might happen?

She wouldn't worry about it, she decided, and determined to enjoy her evening with her friend.

"Cafe or restaurant?" Brenda asked as they walked away from the shop. "Shall we eat in style tonight?"

Fiona didn't hesitate. "Let do! We can take our time and have a nice chat without having to stop and open a case for a shopper."

They strolled to a restaurant in the next block. It was situated so that the ocean was visible from the windows, giving an impression that they were suspended over the water. The windows were cool to the touch, the darkening of the sky replacing the warmth of the sun.

Brenda knew everyone at the tables they passed on the way to a booth. And Fiona was surprised at the number of faces which were familiar to her. She smiled at the greetings she received, answering with shy smiles and quiet 'hellos.'

"Have you lived in Seafair all your life?" she asked Brenda as the waitress approached their table.

"Except when I went to college." Brenda glanced away. The waitress set tumblers of water and menus in front of them and rattled off the short list of specials. The clam chowder with scallops sounded good to Fiona, but she dutifully opened her menu in case there might be something else she preferred to try. Brenda chatted with the waitress for a minute, asking about her small son, then took a sip of water before opening her own menu.

"The scallops here are great, not rubbery as they so often are. Grant, the owner, told me they get them from a supplier who packs them wet, not dry, and that makes all the difference."

"I was just thinking about the scallops," Fiona replied. "And I think I might treat myself to the special with the clam chowder. I'm becoming addicted to clam chowder since I moved here."

"Did you eat a lot of seafood growing up?" Brenda lowered her menu. "I had seafood nearly every day of my life until I went to college, but I never get tired of it."

"Where did you go to college?" Fiona asked.

Brenda looked away and didn't answer for a minute. Then, "Pennsylvania," was all she said, before the waitress returned, carrying a tray with mugs and small teapots of steaming hot water. She set a china bowl filled with an assortment of teas in front of them and then placed a pitcher of cream near Brenda.

"Marie knows my weakness for cream," Brenda smiled up at the woman.

"There are worse weaknesses," Marie smiled. Then she turned slightly so she faced Fiona. "You must be the new house-sitter at Cliff House?"

"Oh, I'm sorry, I should have introduced you." Brenda hurriedly interrupted. "Marie, this is Fiona Patrick. Fiona, Marie Collingwood. She was a year ahead of me in school."

"Back when it seemed desirable to be older," Marie said with mild chagrin. "Now I'd like to be able to say *I'm* the younger one."

Brenda laughed. "Well, Fiona's only 20, so she's a lot younger than I am, if that makes you feel any better."

"Twenty! I can barely remember being 20." Marie was smiling.

"Oh, yeah, that was all of seven years ago for you," Brenda teased.

"Hey, Marie, how about a coffee refill?" The man at the table a few feet away was grinning in their direction and holding a mug aloft. Marie quickly swung around in his direction, then refilled a couple of more empty cups before returning to take their order.

"I didn't get to go to college," Fiona returned to their former subject. "I wanted to, but…" She realized she had been about to say she'd gotten married at eighteen, and swallowed the words. "It just didn't work out." She finished lamely.

"I wish I hadn't." Brenda's face and tone of voice were grim.

"What? Why not?" Fiona was as surprised by her friend's manner as she was by her words.

"My life was wonderful here in Seafair, I had an idyllic childhood which did nothing to prepare me for what I found at college." Brenda poured cream into the mug in front of her and absently stirred it into her tea.

"Look, Fiona, there is something about me only Adam knows." She looked into her friend's eyes. "I'm not sure if I should tell you or not."

"You can trust me, Brenda." Fiona's voice was earnest. "But please don't feel you have to tell me anything which you'd rather not."

Marie arrived with their salads, but said nothing. A small group of people had entered the restaurant, apparently tourists, and she rushed off to show them to a table.

"I've known nearly everyone in Seafair all my life, but no one knows what happened to me while I was away for those four years." Brenda added dressing to her salad and took a couple of bites before she resumed.

"My third year of school, I met this terrifically good-looking guy by the name of Lenny Good." She laughed mirthlessly. "Even after all these years, I can't get over how incongruous that name is!"

She didn't say anything more, seemingly absorbed in her salad until she had eaten half of it. Something told Fiona not to ask any questions, however, so she picked at her own plate. Then Brenda pushed the remains of her salad away and looked into Fiona's questioning face.

"Lenny had a lot of money. I asked him what he did, where he worked, but he always just answered that he was in business for himself. And I thought I was in love, so I didn't want to upset him. I actually *trusted* him. He bought me jewelry and clothes and took me to fancy restaurants. Then one weekend, only a couple of months after we met, he convinced me to elope with him. We flew to Las Vegas and were married and back in time for my Monday classes."

Brenda looked away, swallowing hard. "I wasn't long after I moved into his apartment that I realized something was wrong. Lenny took all his phone calls in another room, he left at all hours of the night, and he became furious when I started asking questions.

"One night, Lenny got a call, and I could tell he was frightened. I asked him what was wrong as he pulled on his clothes, but he told me to shut up. When I grabbed his arm as he was leaving the room, he swung around and hit me. He had to hear me fall against the dresser and onto the floor, but he didn't even glance back."

Brenda smiled wanly as Marie returned and removed their salad plates. She didn't speak again until their meals were in front of them. "I never saw Lenny again. The police showed up at the door less than an hour after he left. My eye had swollen shut by then and my lip was still bleeding. They took me to the hospital, and there I found out that Lenny had been killed in a drug deal that went bad."

Brenda opened her roll and buttered it, but Fiona realized that her friend was unaware of her actions. Smoothing the butter with exaggerated precision, Brenda seemed to have forgotten that she wasn't alone.

"And that's also when I found out I was pregnant." The words were doubly shocking, because Fiona had thought her friend's story was finished.

"At first, the police thought I might be involved in Lenny's drug business, because they couldn't believe I was naive enough to not be suspicious. But the lawyer the state appointed to me was able to convince them of my innocence. Or at least there wasn't enough evidence for them to charge me."

Brenda began to eat her meal, and after several minutes of waiting for the rest of her friend's story, Fiona also ate. Some portion of her mind realized the chowder was excellent. And the scallops were, indeed, the best she had ever had. She was just thinking that it was impossible to know what was in anyone's past, impossible to totally understand another person, when Brenda methodically patted her lips with her napkin before sitting back. Her eyes were distant when she regarded Fiona across the table.

"The lawyer found me a place I could stay, a home for unwed mothers. I had the baby, never saw it, refused to even hear if it was a boy or a girl, then I left the next day and came home to Seafair."

"I'm so sorry," Fiona whispered.

"I was a fool and then I was a coward," Brenda said the words in a rush. "I finally went to a doctor, one who was able to help me deal with the things that happened to me, with what I'd done. But I'll always suffer about giving up my child, even though I know I did the right thing. I would do it again, but that doesn't make the hurt go away."

"Oh, Brenda, and I thought your life was so perfect."

"It is now, and I can't believe Adam and I are back together after

I broke up with him when I met Lenny. He knows everything that happened, but he understands. But being perfect now doesn't mean it always will be, I know that. And I know I can't change the past. I'll always carry guilt and loss in my heart. But I *am* finally strong enough to carry it and not collapse from the load."

"You've had enough sadness for a lifetime," Fiona reached to touch her friend's hand. "I hope the troubles you and Adam encounter will only be small ones." Her voice was intense with the emotion she felt.

"Whatever they are, we'll face them together. That much I'm sure of."

"Would you like some dessert?" Marie was back at their table.

"Some pie, Fiona?" Brenda's smile was more natural now. "To celebrate our friendship?"

"Perfect!" Fiona responded. She was honored that Brenda trusted her. Why couldn't she bring herself to reveal her own past to her friend? She told herself it was because knowing about her could put Brenda in danger, but was that true? Or was she just unable to trust anyone, be close to anyone?

That night she dreamed of her dollhouse. Again, she and her father argued over it, and again Papa took it away from her.

What did it mean?

* * *

The days passed more quickly than Fiona would have thought they could. She still rarely watched the news, because it brought back the tragedy which had made it possible for her to come here. She supposed she would always feel some guilt, although she knew her cousin would have wanted her to take advantage of the situation. Hadn't she insisted she would someday find a way for her to get away? Well, inadvertently, she had.

Inspired by the items in the co-op shop, Fiona decided she would learn to do something creative. She wanted to make Christmas presents for the Shanes. Mrs. Haddington offered to teach her to knit, and she gave it her best effort, but the rhythm of "knit-purl" made no sense to her. She was hopeless at keeping track of where she was in a pattern.

She thought she might be able to make wreaths, but her single effort was somehow out of balance when she finished it. Besides, Brenda gently reminded her, Libby made wreaths of all kinds. It was unlikely that a wreath was what Libby or anyone in her family would want for Christmas.

"I guess I'm better at shopping than creating," Fiona told her friend. Brenda was discreetly silent, but it was clear she agreed with her.

"We'll find just the things for them," Brenda assured her. "New items are coming in almost daily." Indeed they were. Fiona spent a couple of afternoons each week helping Brenda display the new merchandise, and the Christmas catalogues had been completed and mailed. Before long, orders would be coming in.

* * *

Libby called the first week in October to say it was unlikely they would make it to Seafair before Thanksgiving. She was lonesome for home, she said, but she didn't want to come without her husband.

When Fiona talked to Margaret a couple of days later, Margaret said she and Tom planned to drive part of the Blue Ridge Parkway and see the trees. They were anxious to get out of Washington for a day. Margaret assured her they would be in Seafair for Thanksgiving.

So Fiona was resigned to spending another several weeks alone. But she hadn't heard from everyone in the family, and Ethan Shane did manage to get away from work for a couple of days.

* * *

The vacuum was roaring loudly as she whipped through the upstairs rooms of the big house. Fiona hadn't put on any makeup that morning, because she was going to clean before getting ready to meet Brenda and Adam in the village for dinner. She had joined them several times now, and she really liked Brenda's fiance.

She was leaning over to reach the wand beneath Ethan's bed when she heard someone say, "Hello!" She jumped with a squeal, turning around even as she landed back on her feet.

Ethan was laughing. "I'm sorry, Fiona. I really didn't mean to frighten you."

"Well, you did." She knew she looked awful, and that did not improve her mood. She resisted an urge to put her hand up to her messy hair.

"I did try to call, but I guess you were vacuuming. At least you didn't answer the phone."

She didn't spend that much time running the vacuum, but it seemed everyone tried to call when she did. She wrapped the cord and steered the offending machine into the hall closet where it lived.

"I'll get out of your way," she said. "I was just needing to dust, and then I would have been finished, but I can do that later."

He was puzzled by her unfriendly attitude. He hadn't noticed her lack of makeup or the old clothes she wore. He had hoped she would be glad to see him. "I'll be here just a couple of days," he said. "I've been working 70 to 80-hour weeks, and I finally told my boss I was leaving for a while. I have weeks of unused leave."

She was walking toward the stairs. "Let me know if you need anything."

"I thought we might have dinner in town tonight." He spoke quickly, before she could get away.

She stopped and turned around. It wasn't his fault that she looked like a charwoman. When she spoke, her tone was softer. "I'm supposed to meet Brenda and Adam for dinner. I was trying to finish the cleaning so I could take a bath and get ready to go." She shoved an errant strand of dirty hair back from her face.

He finally realized she was self-conscious about her appearance, but he thought she looked cute, if very young, with her scrubbed face.

"Would you mind if I joined you?" He was sure he had felt her attraction to him when he was there before. If he was honest, he would admit the main reason he had told his boss he wanted to use some of his leave was so he could come here and see her. Now he was wondering if he had been wrong. Maybe she really had no interest in him at all. He mentally scolded himself for wasting time and effort worrying about what she thought about him.

"I'm sure that would be fine." She disappeared from view.

* * *

She was perfumed and prettied when he knocked at her cottage door. He had waited for a while in the house, uncertain whether she expected him to pick her up. She had hesitated herself, not wanting to go to the big house to get him, so she was relieved when she saw him strolling across the lawn.

She smiled when she opened the door. "I'm sorry I was cranky this afternoon. You frightened me. And I certainly wasn't at my best."

"Well, you are now," he said gallantly. He looked her over, noting the soft gauzy pantsuit in a becoming peach color. She wore dangling amber earrings and a long chain with a matching amber pendant. There were no rings on her fingers, although a toe ring peeked out from her low-heeled sandal. She smelled vaguely of vanilla.

"I usually walk to the village," she said.

He nodded. "Sounds good to me. I did a lot of walking in Boston, and I do quite a lot in New York. Sometimes it's the fastest way to get around."

Fiona glanced at the mantel clock. She didn't want to say anything which would tie her to New York. "We're early," she said. "There's plenty of time."

Ethan took the key from her and locked the door. By the time they rounded the big house, they were chatting companionably.

Brenda and Adam were happy to see their old school friend. Brenda showed him the empty wall space in the shop before they left for the restaurant. "I need paintings, Ethan, and I need them now!"

"Unfortunately, the government thinks it has first dibs on my life," he replied. "I don't have time to get a good night's sleep or go to the theatre, let alone paint."

"Please paint something while you're here," Brenda suggested later at dinner. "Your work is getting known." At his skeptical expression, she leaned earnestly across the table toward him. "I mean it, Ethan. People are asking to see your paintings when they come in. I want to have something for the Christmas crowd."

"I'll drag him down to the sea tomorrow with a picnic lunch and make him paint," Fiona offered.

"It's a deal," Ethan said quickly, ridiculously pleased at her suggestion. "You fix a lunch, and we'll go to the cliff edge at the crack of dawn, and I'll paint all day."

That decided, they excused themselves early and returned to Cliff House. Ethan unlocked Fiona's door, thanked her for the evening, and left.

She had enjoyed herself, more than she could ever remember. She relived the evening, thinking she might have trouble going to sleep, but she dropped off quickly and awoke at dawn the next morning, excited at the prospect of the day with Ethan.

She dressed in layers. It might get very warm in the afternoon as it had the last two days. She packed sandwiches, fruit and drinks in a cooler. It was all ready when Ethan arrived, carrying his easel, paints and canvases.

"Ready to go?" He looked younger, more rested than he had the previous day. "I'm glad we don't have far to walk with this load."

"Ready!" Fiona responded as she threw a blanket over her arm.

They were in his favorite spot within a few minutes. He quickly set up the easel and prepared to paint as she spread the blanket behind him so she could watch. The view of the rising sun was breathtaking, the sea in one direction, the marina in another, the village below, and the treed mountains off in the distance behind them. The light grew quickly, changing the colors of the sky and clouds distinctly so that Fiona wondered how Ethan could capture it all.

Ethan painted rapidly, with sure strokes of the brush, and spoke to her only rarely. It was as though the painting had been repressed in him and was trying to get out onto the canvas. He added detail, leaning to examine a section which was not quite the way he wanted it to be. It was nearly four hours later when he stood back. "I'll finish it up this afternoon," he said. "What's in the cooler?" He joined her on the blanket and accepted the sandwich she offered. "Crab salad, um-m-m," he murmured approvingly. She handed him an opened Coke, and he nodded his thanks before taking a thirsty swig.

"I almost can forget to eat or sleep when I'm painting," he said. He squeezed some paint from a tube, then held it up to show her. "Azure," he explained. "I must use a gallon a year, painting the sky and the sea."

"You love it, don't you?"

"Yes." He turned to look at the rolling sea. "I can paint some things from memory or photographs, but this I have to see. It changes…the colors, the shapes, the light. I can't remember it well enough to paint it."

"The one in my cottage living room is so pretty. It looks like the ocean when it's deserted, the wind blowing through the sea grass. It's a simple painting, but it says a lot. At least it does to me. I can just look at it and feel the calm."

"Exactly!" He was glad she understood the painting. "I painted that one a couple of years ago, on an Easter weekend before all the tourists arrived. The beach hadn't been walked on for weeks, and the wind was chilly. The sun was just starting to come up."

"I love the one in your room, the Christmas lights at the beach."

"That one is more fun than soothing."

"One of the many moods of life. You show so many moods in your paintings."

"Well, thank you, Fiona. I guess that's the purpose, to paint not just the scene, but the *mood* of the scene."

"You do it well," she said simply.

He leapt to his feet. "I want to show you something before I get back to work." He pulled her up beside him, smiling down at her for several moments. Then he kept her hand in his as he strode across the cliff.

The land suddenly dipped abruptly and arched sharply inward. A few more yards, and they were on the beach. The tide was out, and the beach seemed to stretch forever, wide and clean with shells scattered about it.

"The cliff gives away just here for a narrow space so you can get to the beach without climbing the stairs you see everywhere else along the coast of the village," Ethan pointed out. "The rocks out there," he pointed a few hundred yards away where boulders marked the edge of a little bay, "guard the opening where the sea comes in." He walked her around to where there was a deep cave. "When the tide comes in along the rest of the beach, those rocks hold it back for a while here. But when it gets over the rocks, it fills the cave within minutes. Dad almost got caught in here when he was a boy."

She was pleased that he continued to hold her hand as he led her into the darkness. Further back, faint light showed that the cave curved to the left. Before she could ask the source of the light, Ethan showed her. He pulled her sharply to the right behind what appeared to be solid rock but was actually a cleft in the wall. Rough gouges in the wall formed uneven steps which led up to the opening from which the light could now clearly be seen. Pushing her up the natural ladder, Ethan followed her through the opening. They were again above the water, on top of the cliff. Standing just a few feet away from the opening, it was invisible. Fiona doubted she would ever have found it on her own.

"When Dad got caught in the cave, he happened to see the light in there, and he found the way out. As far as I know, he and I are the only ones who know about it. Now you share our secret."

"Thank you for showing me." They were walking back toward where the easel stood waiting, but she turned to try to see the opening again. There was no sign of it. "If your father hadn't seen that little bit of light and found his way…"

"He would probably have drowned," he finished her sentence. "Yeah, the tide is strong when it's concentrated in a small area like that."

As soon as he was back at the easel, he seemed to forget her, absorbed once again in the painting. When he stood back this time, he was finished and obviously pleased with his work. "I'll try to do one of the village tomorrow, then I have to head back the next morning," he said. He plopped down, opened the cooler, then took a big bite of the apple he found there.

"I appreciate your patience. It must have been boring, sitting all day while I painted."

"No, I enjoyed watching you. I had no idea someone could paint so quickly."

"I don't know that everyone does. I just start painting and it seems to get finished in no time. I don't do portraits often, though.

When I do, they take quite a few days. It's easier for me to show the mood of the sea than of a woman." He smiled at her. "I guess I know more about one than I do the other."

"I don't know that they're all that different," she responded with a grin. She gathered up the blanket and almost empty cooler, and they headed slowly back toward Cliff House.

"Let's give Adam and Brenda a call, see if they are free to meet us at The Ocean Spray, my treat." Fiona had not yet sampled the food there, but she knew people came from miles around to eat at the famous and very expensive restaurant.

"That's a great idea." She left him standing on the terrace. "I'll call her and start getting ready. Come over in an hour."

Brenda quickly accepted the invitation since Adam had the evening off. Fiona told her to be ready in an hour—"dress up!"—and hurried into her tiny bathroom. When Ethan arrived, Fiona was waiting, dressed in her simple black sheath and wearing pearls at her throat and ears.

Ethan had wondered belatedly if he should have told her that the restaurant required dress attire, but he saw she already knew that. He whistled quietly. "That's quite a change from the cleaning lady I found in my room yesterday."

"Oh, you didn't like the way your cleaning lady looked?" she asked archly.

"Well, I might have reacted differently had I found something this delightful by my bed."

Fiona blushed, and found herself wondering exactly how he might have reacted. But he was leading her to the door, locking it behind them. Then he walked her to his Jeep, a newer model than the one which was in the garage for her use, and they drove to the village. "Those shoes aren't made for walking," he said, glancing at her high-heeled strappy sandals.

Adam looked almost as good in his suit and tie as Ethan did, but there was a certain way Ethan carried himself, an elegant confidence, which made him stand out. He wasn't handsome, not in the classical sense, but he was the most attractive man she had ever known. She tried not to stare at him, but she knew she wasn't being very successful when she constantly caught him also staring at her. Even though Adam and Brenda were wrapped up in each other, they couldn't help but become conscious of the growing relationship between their friends.

Though their day had been spent comfortably together, Ethan and Fiona now felt more tense in each other's presence. It was dark, and they were in a romantic setting surrounded almost exclusively by couples. The conversation was not as easy as it had been that day, but Brenda and Adam kept things from getting awkward. They laughed together, helped themselves to tidbits of food from one another's plates, and talked disjointed nonsense. They shared a bottle of good wine, not enough to blame for their behavior, but enough to relax them. One couple was plainly already in love, and it was clear to everyone, except the two involved, that the other couple was well on their way.

Ethan gave Brenda a quick hug when they parted in the parking lot by Adam's big crew cab truck. Fiona was surprised by Adam's hug. Then Brenda reached toward her. "Grab him, honey, he's smitten!" With a grin, she let Adam help her up onto the running board.

"I'll get the painting to you," Ethan called to Brenda. "And I'll do another tomorrow."

Brenda gave him a thumbs up.

"I promise to try to do a little painting in New York, too."

Brenda smiled approvingly and nodded as the truck pulled out and headed back into the village.

Ethan held the door open for Fiona, and they drove slowly, silently through the quiet town. They said nothing when they passed

Adam's truck which was parked in front of the co-op. Two figures were intertwined in front of the door.

Ethan looked away from the couple who were obviously having a long good-night, and into Fiona's eyes. It was dark in the Jeep, but she knew he could see what she was thinking—or, at least, he ought to feel it. She realized she was holding her breath, and she forced herself to breathe deeply, but the sound only made Ethan look at her again.

They walked to her cottage, the space between them wide enough that they would not accidentally touch. When they arrived at her door, they still had not said a word. He pulled her toward him slowly after he turned the key in the lock and pushed the door slightly open. She told herself she should move away—it would be easy, his hold was so light—but she didn't. When he finally kissed her, she knew why she hadn't. She was, at long last, where she belonged.

They stood there for a long minute even after they vaguely heard the ringing of the phone and finally recognized what it was. Fiona did not answer it. She stood back and let Ethan pick it up.

"Ethan Shane." His voice was rough, and he cleared his throat.

The voice on the other end was his father's. He sounded a little amused. "I won't ask why I finally got you at this number rather than the one in the main house," he said. "But your boss called me when he couldn't reach you. They need you back in New York, as quickly as possible."

Ethan's eyes stayed on Fiona's face. "Since you didn't ask, Dad, I won't tell you," he said wryly. "I'll give Jennings a call and be on the road within half an hour."

"We'll talk soon. Drive carefully, son." After a brief pause, he added, "Be very careful, son."

"Will do. I'll see you Thanksgiving, if possible." Ethan hung up the phone and walked toward Fiona.

"I have to leave now. I'm needed in New York."

"Now? It's late, and you got up early this morning. You'll be on the road all night." She didn't want him to go for many reasons, but she definitely thought he should stay until morning.

"Duty calls," he said. "This time duty's timing is unusually bad, but I have to go, nonetheless." She was glad when he again took her gently into his arms. "Don't worry, I do quite well on little sleep. I am, unfortunately, used to it." He bent toward her, kissing her again before he let her go.

"Remember that," he said. "We'll finish that up when I return, Thanksgiving with any luck at all." He turned back to smile at her from the door. "Get that painting down to Brenda when it dries, will you? Tell her I'll try to get some small ones done and ship them to her." And he was gone.

Ten minutes later, there was the beep of a horn, and the Jeep lights disappeared down around the house. He was gone, but he would be back eventually. And what would she, a married woman with a husband in the same Mafia he was investigating, do when he returned?

* * *

Ethan called occasionally, but their conversations were not as comfortable as they had been when they were together. He seemed different when he was in New York. There he was the attorney, a persona she did not know; in Seafair, he was the artist. And he had so little time, so much on his mind, that his attention did not seem to really be centered on her. That made her feel hurt, unsure. She didn't realize that Ethan hated phones, that he had always been uncomfortable talking on them. When he said he had to work the Thanksgiving holiday, she thought he probably just didn't want to see her and had most likely changed his mind about her.

She tried to avoid his calls after that. But she had to talk to him when he phoned from the office on Thanksgiving Day, just as they were finishing the meal she had helped Margaret and Libby prepare. She had been surprised when Keith Shane, a warm and funny man who seemed as calm and steady as his wife was artsy and flighty, produced two perfect pumpkin pies.

"He bakes wonderful desserts," his mother said. "We had a cook years ago who taught him. But he can't boil an egg."

"Who would choose to eat an egg rather than a pie?" her son asked reasonably.

When the phone rang, Libby answered it, bemoaning to her son that he had had to stay in the city. She then passed it to her husband who chatted for a minute before handing it to his mother. After Tom Shane talked to his grandson, he unexpectedly gave the phone to Fiona. His keen eyes studied her, his eyebrows raised quizzically.

"Happy Thanksgiving, Fiona."

"Happy Thanksgiving," she responded. She stared at the floor, conscious of the four sets of eyes which were all trained on her face. She could feel the color creeping up from her neck.

"I'm sorry I wasn't able to get home, and you no doubt realized that I don't do well on the phone. But we will continue where we left off when I get there. I promise." She felt her face grow hotter, as though everyone could hear what he was saying. "I told the boss I'm quitting if I don't get to come home for Christmas."

She couldn't think of anything to say, not in front of the rapt audience which would hear every word.

"Do you hear me, Fiona?"

"Yes."

"They're all listening?"

"Yes."

He laughed. "Okay. But you understand what I mean, right?"

"Yes."

It wasn't what he wanted her to say, but it was apparently the best he was going to get. "Have things changed, Fiona?"

He sounded less confident than she had ever heard him. Even though she was embarrassed, she didn't want to do anything to make him uneasy with her.

"No." Why couldn't she make more than monosyllabic conversation? Then she thought of something to say. "Have you done any paintings for the shop?" She was relieved she had thought to ask the question.

He was pleased to hear an actual sentence from her. "Yes, I shipped off seven yesterday. They're all small, mostly cityscapes. But I think you'll like them."

"Good."

He sighed. This wasn't very satisfactory, and he didn't think it was going to get any better.

"Well, Happy Thanksgiving, Fiona, and I'll see you as soon as I can."

"Happy Thanksgiving, Ethan. I'll tell Brenda the paintings are on their way."

There was a pause before he hung up, but he said nothing more than a quiet good-bye. She knew he wanted her to say more, but she'd done the best she could.

"He's sending paintings for the shop," she said to the listeners. Then she picked up her fork and aimed it at her empty plate.

The conversation finally began again, but she was oblivious, playing over and over again in her mind what Ethan had said. *We will continue where we left off.*

She should leave before she saw him again, she told herself. But she knew she wouldn't.

* * *

All the Shanes headed back to Washington, D.C. the Tuesday after Thanksgiving. Margaret and Libby insisted on doing laundry before they departed, leaving only the cleaning for Fiona. By Thursday, she was trekking down to the co-op shop in the village.

Brenda was always glad to see her, but this time she practically pulled her through the door and into the shop. "I hope you're not just visiting," she said breathlessly, looking behind her at the woman she'd left standing in front of a case, trying to decide which pair of turquoise earrings to purchase. "We've been running as fast as we can every day since last Friday. I was going to call you as soon as I had time to see if you wanted to come in. I was going to *beg* you if necessary!"

"Sure, I'll help the lady over there." Fiona inclined her head toward the young woman who was impatiently tapping on the counter at the back of the shop.

"Thanks," Brenda threw over her shoulder as she rushed back to her customer.

By the time Fiona's customer decided the hand-carved Noah's Ark was a necessity for her own collection, but that the cost of it meant she had to choose smaller carved animals for her nephews than she wanted—and Fiona helped her find ones which made up in intricacy and personality what they lacked in size—there were two more shoppers wanting assistance. She couldn't help being amused that both purchased merchandise for themselves which was priced higher than the items they bought as gifts.

After two hours of quickly-paced sales, the shop was suddenly quiet. Fiona shook her head in wonder at Brenda as she returned to the sales floor after taking a much-needed break to the ladies' room. "Do you know, I didn't have a single customer who didn't buy something for herself? And they all spent more on their own things than on the gifts they bought."

"I know; I couldn't believe it the first year I worked here. But now I know to try to find out what *they* like, not what their friends or family like, and that's where we make the big sales."

"At this rate, I'm afraid we'll run out of inventory."

"No, we should be fine. We don't keep a lot in stock here, but all the crafters know to have things stockpiled at home. We try to keep enough on hand for a couple of days and call them when we need more." Brenda started adding things from drawers as she spoke.

"Of course, we've sold two of Ethan's paintings already, so that leaves only five to last until Christmas. And I'm emailing digital photos of those tonight to a lady in Minnesota who wants to choose one for her husband's present."

"I sold four of the ships in bottles." Fiona checked the drawers at the bottom of the case and found ten more bottles. She pulled out four and filled in the space on the shelf. "I don't know if the Shane men have one of these. If not, they'd make a nice gift."

"I'm sure they don't. Libby said last summer that she'd like to get Keith and Tom a replica of their sailboat, but she never mentioned it again." She looked toward the door where a man and woman were about to make the bell chime yet again. "We could order a couple if you want."

She turned to smile at the newcomers. There was nothing in her voice or expression that revealed she was tired, and that she was standing on feet which were beginning to ache. "Hi! Welcome to the Seafair Co-Op Shop. There's something here for everyone!" The little speech sounded as fresh as it had the first time she recited it that morning.

Two middle-aged women came in soon after, and Fiona was so busy with them, she didn't see the teenage couple stroll in. She heard Brenda say, "We'll be with you in a few minutes," but didn't take the time to see to whom she was speaking.

She wrapped the hand-blown vase for the gray-haired woman, and then the pottery jug for her henna-haired companion, only vaguely listening to what was going on around her. Brenda offered to help the young couple as her customers left, but they declined her assistance. Then a man came in alone, and Brenda led him to where the hand-hooked rugs were displayed.

"Oh, Ricky, I love these!" The girl's voice had a definite Brooklyn accent.

"You already bought stuff at that shop yesterday." The young man's voice had an accent, too, but it was one she recognized, one which made her catch her breath as she sank behind the counter. She tugged a drawer open, wondering how long she could rummage around in it, if she could stay out of sight until Brenda's customer left so the teenagers would ask her for help.

"How do you think you could get that big basket home on a motorcycle?"

"They ship! See the sign over there?"

"Two hundred bucks for a basket, they should hand deliver it!"

"It's not two hundred, Ricky, it's just $185." Her tone was taking on a slight whine. Fiona's heart was beating in double time, and she took deep breaths to calm herself.

I look like Fiona, not Emilia. I am Fiona. She could hear the murmur of voices across the room. The man was going to buy a rug, but Brenda was doing her best to guide him toward the purchase of a more expensive one. It was true what she was saying, that the more valuable rug was a better investment, but right then Fiona wished Brenda were not quite as adept a salesperson as she was. *Come wait on these customers*, she silently pled, but her friend was not reading her mind.

Footsteps moved away, and she thought she was safe until she heard again, "Ricky!" It was a definite whine now. The footsteps stopped. Lighter feet moved quickly. She could hear leather rubbing against leather.

"Ricky." The female voice was soft now, a silly little-girl wheedling sound.

"I'm hungry," the male voice growled. "We'll come back after we eat."

Again there was the slight squeak of leather. "You promise?" The tone was meant to be sexy.

"Yeah." His response was grudging.

The footsteps moved away together, the door chime sounded, and Fiona stood up. Her feet and legs were beginning to cramp, so she held one up and then the other, shaking them in turn.

Brenda and the man were approaching the cash register, a big vintage brass one Adam and Brenda had found at a sale in New Hampshire shortly before the shop opened. The man was carrying the more expensive rug, and Brenda was smiling with triumph.

As soon as the man left, and before the potential group of customers outside could come in, Fiona spoke quickly. "I have to run up to Cliff House," she lied. "I think I left the dryer on."

"It would have turned off by now." Brenda looked quizzical.

"But haven't you heard that they sometimes don't turn off and catch on fire?"

"No…"

"Oh, it can happen." Her tone and expression were earnest, and she was moving away as she spoke. She could tell Brenda thought her behavior odd, but she didn't care at the moment. "I'll make us sandwiches for lunch while I'm there, and then stay until closing after I get back."

"All right." But Brenda didn't sound as if Fiona's leaving was really all right. She, too, saw the group on the sidewalk. They were studying the window display with interest.

"See you!" Fiona fled.

She was walking briskly toward the edge of the village when she heard, "It would have taken us hours to get our food in there! Like I said, let's go to the café."

"But the restaurant was so much nicer. And warmer." That petulant voice again. They were crossing the street in front of her.

She put her head down and moved doggedly ahead. She nearly

fell when the unseen hand grasped her arm, forcing her to a stop.

"Fiona! It *is* you, isn't it?" Enrico bent down to allow his young, almost-pretty face to look closely into hers.

She slowly raised her head. It wasn't difficult to look confused.

"They found part of Emilia's driver's license and part of—uh," he realized what he had been about to say was bound to upset her, so he quickly rephrased it. "They identified Jim, but there was nothing of yours." His hold relaxed slightly. "How did you make it out alive? What the hell are you doing here?"

She ignored the second question. "I had left to go to the travel agent's." The lie came easily; she had rehearsed it so often it almost seemed true by now.

"Why didn't you let us know?"

"I guess I was in shock. I just didn't know what to do, I was so upset. I left New York and kept going."

"But to not let your family know…"

"Emilia and I were very close, but your parents…" She shrugged, and he nodded. Her behavior had been strange, but a lot of strange things had happened in the recent past.

"Well, I'm glad you survived." For just a moment, he was the little boy she and her cousin had adored until his parents' spoiling turned him into a selfish brat whom they avoided. He looked as though he wanted to hug her, but he held her hand tightly for a moment instead. Even someone as self-involved as Enrico could see how fragile she was. She was grateful that he did not ask any more questions, but just to be safe, she added, "Please don't tell anyone I'm here. I found a place to live and just settled in. I need time to get used to things. It's quiet and peaceful here." He nodded, looking closely at her again, and she felt he could be trusted not to give her away. There was no reason for him to tell anyone, and she wondered if he might not forget the whole incident by the time he'd returned to New York. Enrico was not famous for his interest in anyone other than himself.

"Ricky, we might as well buy the basket now." His attention had been away from his girlfriend longer than she would tolerate. "Then we can start back after we leave the café."

"Yeah, sure." He didn't even glance at her. He was looking at the small hand which he held. Fiona pulled her hand back, moving slightly away from him. She didn't care if her behavior seemed odd. It might be to her advantage if he thought she was at the point of cracking up. "I'll look you up if I get back here again."

"I have to make a new life," she said. *I want you to leave me alone*, she meant.

He nodded. "Well, uh, good luck. Maybe I'll see you again."

"Maybe."

Then he was moving to join his girlfriend at the shop door. It was going to cost him to erase that peeved expression from her face, Fiona guessed.

She grabbed two sandwiches at the café counter, and was out before Enrico and his companion left the co-op shop. She watched from a souvenir store as they entered the café themselves, then she returned to the co-op.

"Halfway home, I remembered I did turn the dryer off, so I came back and picked up lunch at the café for us."

Brenda obviously thought there was something strange going on, but she asked no questions. She was a true friend, Fiona thought, and she hoped she would one day be able to explain everything to her.

More customers came in then. Their sandwiches were cold by the time they were able to pause and eat.

* * *

Fiona didn't think Enrico would mention seeing her to his parents. If he did, they did not make any effort to contact her.

But phone calls between Washington, D.C. and Seafair were plentiful. Holiday decorations at Cliff House were always extravagant, and Fiona was trying to follow the instructions from Libby and Margaret, word for word.

She worked in the shop nearly every day, and she worked in one or the other of the houses, too. Only her little cottage was left to her own devices, and she had the most fun there.

The huge quantity of molded wax ornaments and wax head dolls—Mrs. Weissmueller made them as beautiful as any to be found in the Christmas markets of Germany—was quickly disappearing when she decided to decorate her three-foot reproduction goose feather tree (made by Mrs. Weissmueller's two daughters) with them. She also found old mercury glass bead garland in one of the antique shops. The small tree topper angel, also created by Mrs. Weissmueller, fit perfectly. She added a few small pinecones and a string of lights, and the tree was complete.

Of the many wreaths in the shop, Fiona could not decide which she wanted until a new crafter brought in half a dozen, hoping to be accepted in the co-op. One was just what Fiona needed, a pinecone and glass icicle combination with tiny beaded ornaments added. She hoped she wouldn't offend Libby by not buying one of her wreaths, but they were almost gone from the shop anyway.

Working in the shop not only filled her days and let her spend time with Brenda, but she also was getting to know her village neighbors. Mrs. Haddington came to the shop often, sometimes purchasing something small, but more for the company than anything.

The ships in bottles for the elder Shane men were delivered the week before Christmas. Although the ships were identical, marvelous copies of the actual sailboat they both so enjoyed, the backgrounds were different. One showed the cliffs and lighthouse in the distance, the other the charming village.

Fiona found a vintage tatted doily in Mrs. Wilson's antique store. The price was outrageous, but she couldn't resist it for Margaret. For Libby, she chose a Victorian pillow with ornate ribbon embroidery. And she managed to purchase the rather expensive ruby earrings Brenda loved—she'd seen her friend's face when she thought a snippy woman from New Jersey was going to buy them—one day when one of the high school girls was working. She bought a scrimshaw tie bar for Adam; he had to dress up occasionally and wear something other than boots!

But she couldn't think of what to give Ethan, and his gift was the most important. She was still puzzling over the possible choices when it came to her. It took some calling to several stores in New York before she located just what she wanted. Then she asked Buck Terrance to make her a sign. Her instructions were precise, and she was pleased with the results.

All the packages were wrapped and tucked under her tree the night Ethan called. "I'm taking off," he said. "I'll be there the 23rd."

"Yes!"

She could hear the smile in his voice. "My boss isn't happy; he thinks that check I get every two weeks buys me heart and soul, but I want to see you."

"Yes!"

"I guess *you* are looking forward to seeing *me*?" He was laughing now. His voice sounded tired, but he was pleased with her reaction.

"Yes!" And she was laughing, too.

There wasn't anything more to say. Not tonight.

"Goodnight, sweetheart."

"Yes," she whispered, and giggled like a teenager. He was still laughing until she heard the dial tone. She slowly hung up, too.

Just a little happiness, is that too much to ask? She could have answered her own question, but she chose not to. Ethan was coming for Christmas. They would have Christmas, at least.

SECOND ACT

Antonio Scarpellini leaned back in the burgundy leather chair behind the massive oak desk. He was relaxing in the wood-paneled office which was his favorite room. The view through the window which overlooked the entrance drive was hazy, as though a pea-souper had rolled in, but the fog was actually dense smoke from the half dozen cigars which he had smoked since he lit the first one several hours ago.

Cigars were a habit "The Torch" had acquired from his father-in-law. The cigars had brought him much more pleasure than the daughter Gianni Bellini had, for all intents and purposes, sold him. Scarpellini smoked his expensive Cuban cigars, which he smuggled into the country along with other, even more illegal goods, the way he did everything—to excess. Gianni could make a cigar last all day, sometimes two; Antonio routinely smoked as many as three dozen a week.

Cigars and women…Scarpellini considered the merits of each. He had quite fancied the coolly reserved, pretty daughter whom Bellini had blatantly dangled in his face in order to get more of a foothold in The Torch's crime family. Bellini, he had known at the time, wanted to leave his beloved son a powerful legacy. He had been more than willing to sacrifice his daughter to achieve his goal.

Antonio, however, believed he was in a position to gain more than he gave away in the deal. He had told his friend, Dom, his only truly trusted ally, that his instincts told him Emilia was the embodiment of the sage's adage that "still waters run deep."

Dom's reaction had been a sound which could only be described as a guffaw. "You got enough experience to know, boss."

"My experience is incredibly varied." They both laughed in a way that would have turned Emilia's stomach had she been there to hear.

Antonio and Dominic O'Neill had been friends since their initial shared recess at parochial school when Dom first found himself the subject of derision because of his surname. There was parochial school, and then there was the *Italian* parochial school where all the students' names ended in vowels. All except Dominic O'Neill's. His mother had been born and raised in the neighborhood. A devout Catholic, she had demanded marriage after getting pregnant by one of the Irish thugs whose business occasionally meshed with her father's.

The bold interloper disappeared shortly before his wife told her parents the reason for their elopement. Perhaps that news would have guaranteed Dom's father's survival, or at least increased the length of his life, but no one doubted who was responsible for his "desertion" of his family.

Luisa O'Neill had surprised everyone, particularly her father, when she insisted on keeping her married name, and that her son be a junior. Dominic's birth certificate actually carried the name "Donald," but the nuns had refused to call him by something so heathen. He was "Don" to his mother, and "Dom" to everyone else.

The slight, wiry boy had ears which would have been too large for a big man's face, but which totally overwhelmed his. His nose was also too generous, drawing attention away from his remarkably beautiful blue eyes with their thick black lashes.

But he was lacking only in looks, not in loyalty. And he never forgot the boy who stood up for him when others were taunting and threatening.

Dom didn't know that Antonio's actions had been motivated, as they often were through the years, by boredom. He didn't enjoy the status quo, but craved excitement. It was amusing, challenging, to face down the other boys on the playground. Besides, his father was a powerful Mafia leader—he had yet to learn there were more powerful ones— and the lesson he had learned best was that no action of his would ever cause him to suffer a consequence. It was also to Antonio's advantage to have a loyal friend. He enjoyed the genuine adoration, and more importantly, Dom was someone whom he could trust. That was a quality to be valued above all others.

"Tony, honey, can I show you my new hairdo?" The door to the office opened slowly, so it could quickly be closed if his response was the often-shouted, "Get out of here!"

But thinking of his wife, who had turned out to be colder than her cool attitude, made him feel what might have passed for insecurity in a less confident man. His ego needed a shot of female attention.

"Yeah," he growled. "Let's see how I'm spending my money."

Millie Mae Carter had been born a brunette, had still been a brunette when he met her several months ago, but her hair had lightened considerably when she returned from her trip to the "boowty pawrerler" (as she drawled it) the previous week. Her southern accent was so artificially pronounced, he suspected her birthplace was actually nearer to the Bronx than the deep south. She certainly was no southern belle. But she amused him, she flattered him, and she left when he told her to leave. Right now she was happy he had let her into his room, and she smiled as she approached him through the smoke, waving her hand as subtly as she could to clear the way.

"It's blonde."

"Do you like it?"

"Turn around."

It was too elaborate, too light, but he had a taste for the trashy as well as the elegant. "It suits you."

She took it as a compliment, and turned to look at him, her smile wide with pleasure. "Oh, I knew you would like it. I think it's so classy!" She was well-pleased with herself.

Classy was not what she was, but Antonio was becoming bored

with her ignorance, and he saw a familiar car coming through his gate, one of the very few which were allowed to enter without the guard having to contact him for permission.

"Tony?" Her voice was beginning to grate on his nerves. "I was thinking…" When he said nothing, she continued, speaking quickly so she could say it all before he interrupted. "Do you think I could do a little redecorating? I mean, this place needs a little color, it's kind of dowdy, don't you think? I mean your wife's gone, and I'm not plain and boring like her. I think we need to jazz it up…"

He could stand no more, and he didn't want this silly broad here when his visitor came in. "Enough!" He spoke with so much power, the smoke cleared momentarily in front of him. "Go upstairs, play Barbie Doll with all those clothes I've bought you, but get the hell out of here and don't come back down until I call you."

She fled.

He was sitting back in his chair, feet on the leather blotter on top of his desk and blowing precise smoke rings as his father-in-law had taught him to do, when Gianni Bellini came into the room. Antonio did not stand up to greet him.

"You don't knock?"

Gianni paused briefly before crossing the room to approach the desk. "I apologize. I did not think it necessary to knock at my daughter's home." But Gianni was anything but apologetic. He was so sure of himself, Antonio felt his blood begin to boil. It was a joke between he and Dom that when his blood boiled, someone else got burned.

"Your daughter doesn't live here anymore. Your daughter is dead."

Gianni was briefly taken aback. His grief, when shown the partial driver's license which had been found less than a block from the enormous crater downtown, had been admittedly minimal, but it had been his wife who uttered the damning words, "Thank God it wasn't Enrico's!" after fearfully glancing at the remains.

Enrico had been on one of his many motorcycle trips. He had taken off the first time the day after his 16th birthday. That first time, they did not hear from him for three weeks. For the last year, that had been his way of life, and they did not question it. They had not questioned his refusal to go back to school, either. They all knew his "career" did not require formal education. Besides, there was nothing they could have done to control him.

He had left early on the morning of September 11, and they had been frantically worried he might have visited friends in Manhattan before hitting the road. When they were told someone wanted to talk to them about evidence found near the World Trade Center, they had held their breath in fear for their only son. The thought that the evidence might be related to their daughter, whom they and their son-in-law had not seen in days, did not occur to either of them.

For his part, Antonio had almost thought himself in love with his wife at one time. True, he had been ready to rid himself of her if she had not produced an heir soon, but it annoyed him that something which was his, which belonged to him, was of so little importance to Gianni and Maria, particularly since Gianni had bartered her as something valuable. Thinking of this, he decided to address the situation immediately.

"I will marry again, Gianni. My son will be my heir, not your son." He knew he had hit the mark when Gianni flushed. He had no intention of telling his father-in-law he had learned from the mistake he made in marrying Emilia. He had given Gianni power, and Gianni's daughter his name, asking only a son in return. But only he had kept the bargain; both Gianni and Emilia had cheated him.

Antonio had no intention of marrying until the woman—and she must be Italian, unlike that simpering woman upstairs—was pregnant. And the child must be a son. He would hold all the cards now.

"I gave you power, Papa," Antonio said softly. "You are rich, you are successful, because of me."

Gianni was now smiling and nodding, misunderstanding his son-in-law's quiet tones and seemingly affectionate name for him.

Antonio's feet crashed onto the floor as he lurched forward. He leaned across the desk, dislodging miscellaneous papers and a heavy brass paperweight which made a muffled sound on the thick carpet before rolling silently away. He gripped his hands together, slamming them repeatedly against the leather to stress the words spitting from his lips.

"You're through, *Papa*. You go back to your narrow kingdom with your little group of sniveling thugs who scare little people. I'm not sharing any more. There's no reason for me to give you a thing. *And don't ever come to my home again!*"

Gianni's face was livid, veins throbbing in his neck, and he lost his temper. "How dare you! You forget how much I know. I have proof!"

Antonio's voice became disconcertingly calm, almost soothing. "Proof? You have proof you could use against me?" He smiled. "Where is this proof?"

"I'm the only one who knows." As soon as he said the words, Gianni knew he had made a mistake.

But oddly, Antonio did not react as Gianni expected him to. He merely sat back in his chair and silently studied his guest. "Leave me, Gianni," he finally ordered. "It's over."

He turned away in his chair, gazing out over the side yard where water splashing from a fountain into a marble pool glimmered in the afternoon sun. The garden, he thought absently, was still beautiful with its late autumn colors.

Of course, the relationship between the two men was not quite over.

* * *

Ethan was studying information from an undercover agent who was imbedded in the Mafia. He had been part of the Merconi family for nearly three years. Ethan wondered when a slipup might get him caught. Would he one day be caught in a situation where he himself was expected to kill someone? He was a paper pusher for the family, using the accounting skills which had earned him a place in the FBI, but no one in the Mafia could stay away from violence forever. Ethan couldn't help thinking the guy's days were numbered.

Maybe that was his problem, Ethan thought. People in his line of work were usually ultra-responsible types who felt they had to save the world, or they were adrenaline junkies who lived for the next thrill, the next close call. He found the constant exposure to the underbelly of society depressing. He was by nature an artist, not a prosecutor. Too bad he was so skilled at his job.

The phone at his elbow jangled. "Shane," he answered.

"Ethan?" His mother's voice was high pitched, as though she was under stress. "Oh, Ethan, we can't go home for Christmas, we have to stay in D.C."

"What are you talking about? Congress recessed, and everyone has already gone home. I thought you were there, or at least on your way, by now."

"No…" There was muffled conversation in the background, and then his mother started talking again. "I can't explain on the phone, but I just wanted to call and tell you to plan to come down here for Christmas."

He hesitated before he responded. "That would leave Fiona all alone."

"She could come, too."

"There's…ah," he cleared his throat, wanting to tell her enough to make her understand his decision, but not wanting to tell her everything. "Ah, there's something we promised to do for friends on Christmas Eve."

"What? Who?" Libby might be unhappy about not being able to go home for Christmas, but her curiosity was piqued by this information.

"I've been sworn to secrecy."

"Ethan!"

"Mom, I'm not going to tell you what it is, and I have to go to Maine for Christmas. I hope you understand."

"Just a minute." More muffled conversation, his father's voice in the background followed by tones which must have been his grandmother's. Then, "If you insist on going to Maine, Gran and I are going to bring you your presents. We're coming to New York tomorrow. We'll meet you for lunch."

"Tomorrow? For just the day?"

"Yes, your father says we can get an early train and then return tomorrow evening."

"Lunch it is. Name the place."

The restaurant she named was a small one, not fancy, and certainly not one where they could expect to meet anyone they knew. But it was one they had visited on trips to New York in his teen years, when they often made weekend jaunts to the city for a couple of days of theatre and culture.

* * *

The next morning he was in the office before seven, intent on getting enough work done to justify the long lunch he planned to take. There was nothing extraordinary in the information he was reading from the Merconi family agent. He wished the man would turn up something which would enable them to start indictments and get the agent out. Not likely, judging by the careful way they were currently playing their cards.

He sighed. The door to his office closed softly, and Ethan looked up into his colleague's grim face. He'd never seen Sam Cunningham smile. The man was slightly under average height, slightly under average weight, and his belly had begun to slightly show the effects of too many hours at a desk, too many fast food meals, in the last couple of years.

Sam had worn the same crewcut for fifty years, since he was a boy of eight. His clothes never seemed to have been pressed, and he usually looked as though he needed a shave, but his light blue eyes revealed the intelligence of the man whose quick mind had helped catch and prosecute some of the most notorious criminals in the last quarter century. He was a legend, but he had paid a personal price for his accomplishments.

Cunningham had grown up on a farm in eastern Iowa, the son and grandson of farmers. He had decided to go to college when he read about the Scopes Trial as a boy, and he had done so on scholarships and supported by the high school sweetheart he married a week after they graduated from Sullivan County High School. She continued to work when he went on to law school.

Her loyalty was finally rewarded when he graduated first in his class and took a job as assistant prosecutor in their home county. Sam told her she would never have to work outside the home again, and—even better—they could now have the baby they had put off for a half dozen years.

Melissa Lee was born eight months after Sam received his law degree. That was when his life and Linda's began to go in different directions.

When Melissa was barely four months old, a murder was committed in Sullivan County. There wasn't a great deal of evidence in the case, but what there was all pointed to one man. That one man had killed before, but had been acquitted because of the sloppy prosecution by Sam's predecessor. Sam was determined he would not escape justice this time. That was the first time the weight of responsibility fell fully on his shoulders. Each subsequent case added more until he seemed to be carrying the entire burden of saving the world.

Cunningham began to acquire a reputation. When a hitchhiker

broke into two homes in two days, killing an elderly couple in one, and a family of four in the other, the case made national news, and so did Sam's brilliant work prosecuting him. Sam was offered a job in New York when Melissa was 16, and her brother, Michael, was 12.

Linda was a country girl, Michael wanted to be farmer and had begun breeding cattle, and Melissa was active in school and church. She was the lead cheerleader, the first chair flute, FFA vice president. They all voted against leaving Iowa, but Sam took the job anyway. Then the day before they were to leave their farm, Michael was seriously injured in a tractor accident.

Sam stayed two days longer, until he was told his son would survive—although he would always walk with a cane—and then he left for his new job, his new and greater responsibility. His family did not go with him.

He was still surprised when Linda divorced him two years later, and he was even more surprised when she married a boyhood friend of his within six months.

His children visited him a couple of times in New York, but they didn't like the city. After a while, they didn't have anything to say to him. Finally, they just declined his offers to fly them there.

He occasionally went back to Iowa, but it seemed strange that another man lived in his house, on his farm, with his family. When Melissa married, there was a crisis in an important case. Sam didn't make it to her wedding, and her stepfather walked her down the aisle. She never forgave her father for that.

Now there was a multitude of grievances for his children to hold against him. He had never even met the woman Michael married last year. He had seen Melissa's daughters, Mandy and Megan, only twice, and they were now five and nine. Melissa's third child was due any day.

Joe Linman, Linda's second husband, had died a year ago from lung cancer. Sam's secretary had sent flowers in his name, just as she reminded him about his children's and grandchildren's birthdays.

Sam had married again, too. The woman had been fourteen years younger, in love with the limelight more than the man. She had bought him new, more expensive clothes, most of which he still owned and wore. Most importantly, she had agreed to having no children. Sam knew he was not a success as a father.

Three years into the marriage, however, she decided being recognized in swanky restaurants was not enough. She wanted a baby, and she wanted a husband who would take her on a vacation, go to the theatre, *talk* to her. Her requests were not unreasonable, but it was clear they would not be met. Sam went through another divorce. Now he knew he was never going to be a success as a husband. But he was still a damn good prosecutor, so that was what he did. That was all he did.

Now Sam sank into the chair across from Ethan's desk. It had been years since he had had a farmer's tan, or any tan at all. The strong muscles he had developed working as a young man were now due to a somewhat disciplined schedule which usually allowed two or three hour-long sessions per week in a gym. That was his life—the office, the courthouse, and the gym.

"Look at this, Shane." Cunningham threw a file down on top of the open one on Ethan's desk. "There's something going on with The Torch. Antonio's wife—Gianni's daughter—was killed in one of the towers, and Tony demoted his father- in-law shortly thereafter. Word is the old man is nervous because he has some evidence on Antonio. And, get this, Gianni got mad at the way Tony treated him and, like a dumbass, *told* Antonio he had the evidence. He threatened him with it."

"He's a dead man." After all, Ethan thought, the implication was obvious.

Sam was silent for a moment, then shook his head. "You know,

Shane, I've been putting bad guys in jail for thirty years. But there are as many criminals out there now as there were when I started, maybe more. I've been divorced twice, don't know my kids, don't know my grandkids, have no life." He gazed out the window, his eyes going past Ethan's head.

"You know, I had the greatest wife," he continued. "Put me through college, law school, waited to have a baby." He rubbed his hand tiredly down his face. "She called last night and invited me for Christmas. She said I needed to be with my family. She said they needed to get to know me, feel they were important to me."

Ethan was surprised at his friend's tone and did not interrupt. Sam's eyes moved to meet his. "They always were important to me, that's the kicker. That's why I worked so hard to get the bad guys, so they would be safe, so other families could be safe. I didn't want glory, I wanted justice."

"I don't know that we can accomplish what is needed, Sam. Sometimes I think we just have to be content with what we're able to do."

"You're a smart kid, Shane." Cunningham slumped into the chair, once again lost in thought.

After a moment, Sam glanced at the folder, and Ethan opened it. Gianni Bellini was an attractive, if quite over-weight, middle-aged man with receding hair and a mustache so thin it appeared to have been penciled on his upper lip. His aquiline nose and full lips gave him a foreign air. His wife, Maria, was plump, with luminous dark eyes and a delicate nose. There was a streak of gray in her otherwise raven hair. He read the descriptions; appendectomy scar, and knife wound on Gianni, birthmark on Maria's right calf.

"There's info about the daughter and son, too." Sam had been silently watching him. "Uh, Shane, I'm sorry I yakked so much. I don't talk about my personal life, but I guess that call last night, and the fact that I didn't sleep much, knocked me a little off center. I'm tired of the noise. I find myself thinking of the quiet in the country. I couldn't wait to leave the farm, but now I miss it in my old age." His smile was self-conscious.

Ethan glanced up at the older man, wanting to reassure him somehow. "Understandable," he said. "I'm not much for cities myself." He returned his attention to the file, and was about to look at the next page when his phone rang. Cunningham made no move to leave.

"We're on our way to the restaurant." Margaret's voice was overly loud. "Can you hear me? This is that new cell phone your father forced on me."

"I can hear you, and I'm on my way." Ethan closed the folder and stood up. "I'll get to this later," he promised. "Right now I have a date with two beautiful ladies."

Sam's eyebrows rose. "Maybe I should come with you."

Ethan's answer was uncharacteristically impulsive. "No, where you need to go is Iowa. For the entire Christmas and New Year holiday. And while you're there, think about the fact that thirty years is a long time."

He smiled as he passed Cunningham on his way to the door, briefly clasping the older man's shoulder. Sam scratched his head. He liked that boy, had liked him the minute he met him, but he had a feeling he wouldn't be staying too long. He didn't think the younger man would be as tardy as he had been in figuring out what was important in life.

That was the problem. Unlike Shane, whom Sam knew really thought of himself as an artist, Sam was only an attorney. That was his sole identity. Was it too late for him to learn to be anything else? He'd failed as a husband and a father. Could he learn to be a grandfather?

He picked up the phone and called the first airline he thought of. It didn't fly into Des Moines, but the cheery voice gave him the name and number of a couple which did. He dialed before he could talk himself out of it. He was 58, he could retire now if he wanted. He'd made a dent in crime, but even he had to realize he couldn't save the world.

And he was very, very lonely.

The rate to fly during the holiday on short notice was so high he whistled, but he booked it. Then he dialed the number which had once been his own.

"Linda, if the offer's still good, I'm coming home for Christmas." He said it in a rush, before she could even say hello.

There was no response for a long time. He nearly panicked, thinking she was trying to think of a way to tell him not to come, but he could hear the smile in her voice when she finally spoke. "The offer's still good. It's been good for the last 16 years."

Now he couldn't think of what else to say. Would it be like this the entire time he was there? He hoped not. He hoped they would finally relax in one another's company and be the way they had been years ago. He had to try.

"I'll rent a car at the airport."

"I'll have the lights on."

* * *

His mother and grandmother were seated when Ethan arrived at Mario's. It was a small restaurant, only about a dozen tables, and they had snared one of the two in the enormous bay window. From there they had seen his approach. Now Libby waved at him as though he couldn't see them the moment he walked through the door.

After kissing them both, he sat on the opposite side of the table, facing them. A large shopping bag was on the chair next to his. They ordered from memory, without menus.

"We wish we could change your mind and talk you into coming

to Washington for Christmas," Libby began. "Fiona could close the house for a few days and come, too."

"Remember, Mom, I told you we promised to do something on Christmas Eve. It's not something where we can call and say, 'Sorry, can't make it.'"

"I can't imagine what it is you have to do in Seafair during Christmas."

"And I can't tell you."

"Oh, for heaven's sake…why is it so secretive?"

"Mom…"

Margaret interrupted. "Libby, don't put the boy on the spot. It could even be that we'll end up in Seafair ourselves. We don't know how long we'll have to stay in Washington."

Libby looked at her. "Keith said he had the meeting with…"

"Libby!"

Her daughter-in-law sighed. "No one could hear me."

"*I* could hear you; Ethan could hear you." They stopped speaking as the waiter arrived with their meals.

"I can't imagine why you can't know," Libby resumed as soon as the waiter had gone.

Ethan was firm. "If it's not to be told, that means us, too. But I don't understand why Dad has to stay in Washington when the rest of Congress has left."

Libby leaned toward him. "I don't know much more, but I know there are several members still in Washington. They're simply not advertising the fact. And I know your father has a secret meeting on Christmas Day. Now why would they pick Christmas Day?"

"Because no one would expect it?" Ethan shrugged. "I don't know, but that would be my guess. They don't want anyone to find out they're meeting or what the subject, findings, and/or decisions are. How many reporters are working Christmas Day? How many informants? How many lobbyists? If you want to keep it secret, do it when everyone else isn't working, particularly if they think you aren't working either. Christmas would be the day to pick."

"But I can't imagine why your Dad and a few others only." Margaret had been drawn into the mystery in spite of herself.

"Maybe because he's a retired Naval Intelligence officer. I bet I could come up with the names of the others who are going to be with him." Ethan saw his mother's eager expression and wished he had not said that last sentence.

"Who?" Two female voices spoke in unison.

"Senator Bonadicci and Representative Williams who both used to be in Special Forces, Representative Berry who also was in Naval Intelligence, Representative Jones who retired from the CIA, Senator Douglas who was with the FBI for twenty years or so, and probably Senator Clark who everyone knows was in Viet Nam, but few know what he did there."

"What?" The same surprised, eager duet.

"I don't really know either. I just know Dad said once that he knew that group and they confer occasionally, though usually unofficially. He wouldn't answer my questions about what they did. Doesn't that tell you something?"

"Well, they're a bunch of middle-aged men, some almost elderly, and I can't imagine what they can do about fighting radical cowards who sneak around our own country," Margaret said.

"They're not using their brawn, Gran," Ethan responded, "although I think Dad might not be happy with your lack of confidence in his physical abilities. The old guy's in pretty good shape."

Margaret dismissively waved her hand through the air. "He may be in good shape for a 57-year-old man, but he *is* a 57-year-old man."

"With a very bright, experienced, and crafty brain. That's what, I expect, they need from him."

Libby looked out the window for a minute. Everyone was warmly dressed, many carrying packages. One small woman looked as though she might sink under the many boxes and bags she carried. Following his mother's glance, Ethan also saw the woman and hoped the items she toted were light in spite of their size. Surely she was nearly home?

Another woman passed by, holding the hands of two pretty little girls identically dressed in red velvet coats with matching hats tied under their chins. Each child carried a gift bag in her hand. They were as perfectly balanced as the previous woman had not been. They appeared happy and full of Christmas cheer despite the blustering weather. It was almost Christmas Day, and the very air was different than it was at any other time of the year. In spite of the tragedy of three months ago, maybe because of it, people were making an effort to enjoy the season.

"I don't know what is going on," Libby finally sighed. "I just know I overheard him talking on the phone about meeting with someone else. That person's name told me the meeting is very important. I mean, if he's coming to this country on Christmas…"

"Mom, no national security leaks, please. You'll get Dad into some very hot water."

"Well, as I was going to say—I'm not going to leave your father alone at Christmas. We have been apart on too many Christmases, the one he was in Viet Nam and three when he was at sea, and I said we'd never again be apart if there was anything I could do."

"I understand, Mom. I agree." Ethan clasped her hand. "If you can come up to Seafair, fine. If not, we'll call on Christmas and tell you what we did on Christmas Eve."

"That might be quite interesting," Margaret said, almost under her breath.

Ethan flushed, "What did you say, Gran?" But he had heard, and he had trouble meeting her challenging look.

"Well, I really don't understand why your Christmas Eve plans can't be delayed, but I guess you're old enough to make your own decisions," Libby didn't sound sure at all.

"I should think." Ethan's voice was wry.

Margaret interrupted. "Your gifts are in that bag. Fiona's are, too. It's fortunate we hadn't bought something enormous for either of you."

"I guess your gifts are going to be late. Fiona told me the ones she bought you are wrapped and under her tree, and my gifts aren't easily portable."

"That will give us something to look forward to, then." Libby was trying very hard to be cheerful.

"Thanks for understanding, Mom."

They finished the delicious food, the rest of their conversation light. When Ethan glanced at his watch, saying he needed to get back to the office, they also rose to leave.

"We're looking for some stocking stuffers, nothing of consequence," Margaret said, bundling her coat tightly about her and walking through the door Ethan held open. "We're just having fun shopping."

Ethan was lucky, being able to quickly hail a cab. "Merry Christmas, darlings," he said, hugging them each in turn. "I love you."

"I love you, son," Libby blinked back tears. "Merry Christmas."

"We'll get there if we can for as much of the Christmas week as possible," Margaret assured him. She stood on tiptoe to kiss him again. "Love you, Tanny." She didn't often call him by his childhood nickname, and her use of it now told him she, too, was feeling emotional about them all not being together for Christmas.

He pulled the taxi door open, then turned back to smile and wave at them. They waved back. Then the cab pulled out into New York traffic, and they disappeared from view.

* * *

"Get some things packed, Maria," Gianni ordered. "We're going away."

"A Christmas trip?" She looked incredulous. "Gianni, our daughter just died three months ago. I think our Christmas should be quiet this year." Maria spoke out of a sense of duty rather than remaining sorrow.

"Maria, we are not celebrating, we are getting away. I have gotten together every cent I could get my hands on, and we are leaving New York."

"Why?" She was beginning to feel alarmed.

"Antonio has changed." He had thought about what he would say to her, but there was no way to tell her why he was afraid of their son-in-law. He and Maria had never really discussed what he did for a living. That was not unusual; the Mafia men pretended to be businessmen, and their wives pretended to be married to successful business owners. It was a convenient arrangement with which everyone was more comfortable.

"Antonio has taken away my position," he continued. "With Emilia gone, he is withdrawing his support of me."

For the first time, Maria spoke frankly to her husband. "Do you mean you are going back to working by yourself, as you did before Emilia and Antonio married, or do you mean we are in danger?" She didn't mind that her home, until two years ago, had been more modest than those of many of her friends; she and Enrico could adjust their lifestyles downward if necessary. But Gianni's perspiring face and shaking hands told her there was more than a reduction in their income facing them.

Gianni swallowed hard. He started to speak, but nothing came out. Again he swallowed, then took a deep breath. "I got angry," he said, barely whispering. "I told him I could prove things against him."

"Oh, Mother Mary…" Maria gasped and put her hands up to cover her mouth.

"He didn't threaten or yell at me." Gianni couldn't think how to explain how frightening Antonio had been. "He was just so cold, Maria, very calm and cold."

"Where can we go? Do you really have information about him? Where is it?"

Gianni was shaking his lowered head. "I will tell you nothing except we must go, and we must not be found." He faced her, and his soft, pudgy fingers bit into her arms. "Pack what you can get into a car. We are leaving as soon as it is dark."

A footstep startled them both. "Who's leaving?" They simultaneously sighed with relief to see Enrico, dressed in his black leather motorcycle jacket and pants, in the doorway.

Gianni sent Maria on her way, then talked earnestly to his son. When he finished his brief explanation, Enrico remained with his head bowed, seemingly studying his eel skin boots.

"Antonio called me today, Papa," he said when he finally spoke, his words carefully chosen. "He told me to get out of the house before midnight."

Gianni took a deep breath. "Then I must trust you to do something, my son." He quickly told him what he needed him to do, and why.

Less than an hour later, Enrico carried the last suitcases and mementoes to his SUV, kissed his white-faced parents good-bye, and drove to a garage owned by a friend who knew nothing of his family's background. Then he got on his motorcycle and disappeared, heading west on the small roads which showed up as the thinnest lines on the pocket atlas he carried.

His parents were driving south, on similar roads, in a 12-year-old car which no one would expect to carry a man who had once been powerful in the Mafia. In six months, they had agreed, they would call Enrico's friend at his garage, and Enrico would leave a message so his parents could find him. They would wait six months to discover whether any remnant of their family was still alive.

* * *

The Torch arrived at his in-laws' home precisely at midnight. He was accompanied by his assistants who carried the materials he needed to practice his craft. He rarely visited the scene himself, and when he did his men did not splash gasoline around, making it obvious to fire inspectors that a house or business had been destroyed by an arsonist. His methods were usually more subtle, but this time he wanted everyone to know what had happened, and what would happen to anyone else who threatened him.

The house was vacant. That fact was immediately apparent to him. Lights had been left on, a television was blaring, but he knew with the keen senses which had kept him alive that his prey had fled.

His sense of tidiness made him go through the house, turning off the lights and TV. With a look of distaste, he decided to leave the messy kitchen alone and walked briskly back out to his car.

His assistants followed, confused. "Leave the house," he barked. "It's not the house I want, it's that disloyal, ungrateful, spineless snake." He got into his car, barking orders.

Had Enrico tipped his parents off? If so, he would also pay. Typically, Antonio had considered all possibilities. He had thought his brother-in-law greedy enough, smart enough, to be loyal to him, but in case he was wrong... well, he had not risen to his current position without learning to look at situations from all the angles.

* * *

When they stopped in the tiny town in Pennsylvania's coal country, Gianni felt safe. No one had followed him, he was sure. He fell across the sagging bed in the cheap hotel and was instantly asleep.

Maria quietly opened the door and went outside. The smell of coal clung to the night air. The town had looked poor when they drove through, but then coal dust on houses did detract from their beauty. She had never been to Pennsylvania, never been anywhere really. Gianni had traveled, there had been money even before Antonio for all the things Gianni wanted.

When there was lots of money, there was that apartment in Manhattan, where he had kept his girlfriend for the past five years. He didn't know she knew about Liza Stephens. Maria was much smarter, however, and much angrier than her husband realized. But then he had made little effort to get to know her in the last 21 years.

She wandered into the motel office. A tired, wrinkled woman looked as though she had mummified there, she was so lifeless. She answered Maria's one question, and made no comment when Maria thanked her.

Around on the other side of the building, Maria found the old-fashioned phone booth. She already missed her beloved son. She had told the woman she was going to call him.

She dialed the number she had been given, spoke briefly, and hung up. Then she started walking again, away from the buildings. It wasn't long before the car arrived, just minutes after the light went off in the small living area which adjoined the shabby office. It parked well down the road. They were dressed in black, invisible in the moonless darkness. They were inside, then back out, in minutes. Under their arms they carried her suitcases. They ran with her to the car which was crudely hidden under the low branches of an old tree on the sparsely traveled road.

"He didn't know we were there. That's why we was so fast." The man, a large flunky with whom she was only vaguely familiar, was taking his mask off as he reported to her. "We knocked him out with one blow, maybe even killed him just like that." He snapped his fingers, but seemed somewhat disappointed.

The run had winded her, and her heart was beating hard from the excitement. All those years of servitude, she was thinking. All those years... but she was still young, and she had money now, money which she could spend as she pleased. The man thought she was not speaking because she could not get her breath, but he was wrong.

Her mind was full of plans as he pulled the car over, angling so they could easily turn in their seats and see back from where they had come. The flames were already visible, and as they watched they went higher, the sky now alight with their glow.

"Good job, good job," the driver muttered under his breath. Then he pulled back on the road before taking an abrupt turn in another direction when they heard the scream of an emergency vehicle.

They wound around for hours, Maria too tired and excited to rest. When, at daylight, they drove through a fast food restaurant, Maria ordered two breakfasts.

"All torn up, ain't ya?" the driver said sarcastically. He exited the restaurant and passed through the town to a picnic area. They got out to stretch their legs, and Maria went into the primitive toilet.

She was washing her hands when she heard a bar slip across the door. Icy cold fear and understanding swept through her body.

The flames began immediately, all over the dry wood of the small building. She began to scream. She tried vainly to reach the lone, high window. She clawed at the door, threw her body against it with such force that she fell backward to the floor, stunned. After only a minute she had to gasp and cough for air. It was not long before the black smoke became black oblivion.

The car drove away quickly, but not so quickly as to attract attention. That was a mistake made by too many criminals, but not by anyone who worked for Antonio.

They took another quick turn, leaving the road which they had traveled. They would work their way to the main road, then the interstate, before dumping the car in Jersey.

"Shame for that good food to go to waste." The driver gestured to Maria's uneaten breakfasts. "I don't like sausage, reminds me too much of..." He grinned. "Well, never mind. Give me the ham and scrambled eggs."

"Sausage's good with me," his buddy replied. "I ain't squeamish."

RESURRECTION

"Do we have any more packing tape?" Terri Leland looked up from the large box she had packed. A strip of tape held the top closed, but more was needed to make the package safe for shipping.

"I think we've used all the tape we had out, but there's another big container in the storage room." Brenda folded bubble wrap around the lamp which had been fashioned from a vintage cigar tin. They sold a lot of the tin litho lamps, and the ones made from cigar or gasoline tins were particularly popular as gifts for men's offices. They had mailed two dozen in the last week alone.

Terri was disappearing into the storage area when Brenda called an afterthought behind her. "Bruce brought in a box last weekend, so there may not be any left in there after all. If not, the last two boxes are in the loft. I put them on the dining room table."

"What *isn't* on the dining room table?" Fiona asked.

"Not much," Brenda replied cheerfully. At this time of year, Brenda's living area was more of a second storage room than her home.

"I can't believe all the orders we've filled," Fiona said. "It was almost a relief to have the walk-in traffic slow down so much when it began to snow. Otherwise, I can't imagine how we would have taken care of all the mail orders."

Brenda expertly pulled the tape dispenser across the box and then attached a label. "Oops, I should have double checked the order before I closed the box," she said, squinting at the sheet of paper beside her on the floor. "That's what happens when you don't keep to the routine."

"Shame on you, taking time to eat," Fiona pretended to scold. "After all these years of practice, you should be able to work nonstop from the day after Thanksgiving until December 23rd."

"Thank goodness the 23rd is our last day to ship," Brenda sighed. "That gives me exactly one and one half day to finish up my own Christmas." She returned her attention to the order form. "Let's see, the tin lamp, three pints of strawberry preserves, a pound each of chocolate and maple nut fudge, an antique hankie sachet, and a small shell wreath. Yep, I remember packing all of that."

Fiona pushed her package aside and picked up the next order form. Four wreaths, that would be easy. She now knew how to pack them so they could almost be guaranteed to arrive safely.

Terri's sister, Kerri, leaned in the door. "I'm almost out of preserves," she said. "I can't call Mrs. Cadberry, because the phone starts ringing…" She left hurriedly as it rang yet again.

"I'll call Mrs. Cadberry." Terri tossed the box of tape she carried onto the work table and picked up Brenda's cell phone.

Fiona and Brenda continued packing, talking softly. What had initially taken Fiona twenty minutes to pack now took less than half that time, but there were still a couple of dozen orders to pack before they left tonight, and it was almost seven o'clock. Promptly at seven, at least, the order phone would be turned off.

"She says she has half a dozen strawberry and nine blackberry at home," Terri reported. "And she thinks there may be as many as a dozen apple butter."

"Any apricot butter?" Brenda checked some ornate beaded earrings before placing them in a gold gift box.

"I didn't think to ask, but I can call back." Terri rummaged around on the shelves behind her. "We have three here, but I don't know how many are out on the floor."

"Whoever goes out there next can check. We'll probably be fine."

Kerri was looking stressed when she next came into the room.

"Why is it the last call is always the doozey?" She went to the shelf and took two of the apricot butter. "This lady wants two baskets, just the right size to hold a jar each of apricot butter, apple butter, blackberry preserves, strawberry preserves, *and*" she rolled her eyes dramatically, "she didn't want to pay more than $25 for the baskets! She didn't mind that the preserves are $12.50 a pint, but a handmade basket shouldn't cost over $25." She shook her head. "She was very specific about the embroidered doilies she wanted in each basket, made me describe at least fifteen in minute detail and didn't question their prices, but she wants a cheap basket."

"So are you just mailing her the doilies and jars?"

"Oh, no. I described basket after basket, too, lots of baskets! I tried to find them as small as possible, as inexpensive as possible." She leaned against the door. "She kept saying they sounded too small, too oddly shaped, whatever. She was looking at the sizes and styles in the catalogue, saying, 'Is that the one on such and such page; is that the middle-size one?' Then she suddenly said, 'I like the big one on the bottom row of page 26, get me two of those.'"

Fiona had no idea which basket was on the bottom row of page 26, but Brenda burst into laughter. Fiona looked at her quizzically. Terri and Kerri were now laughing, too.

It was Terri who explained what was so funny. "That's our most expensive basket," she giggled. "It costs $225! We only sell half a dozen or so a year."

Kerri finished her story between gales of laughter. "And then she had to buy more things to fill them up, lots more things! Her daughters' Christmases are costing their mom over $600 each...and she started out wanting to buy a $25 basket!" She could still hear the sisters' merriment when they went into the next room. It took them quite a while to locate all the items for the baskets and pack them for shipping.

"I think we're all so tired, we're getting giddy," Brenda said. "I fell onto the bed last night and didn't wake up until 2am. Then I took a bath and went back to bed, under the covers that time."

"We're almost finished." Fiona picked up another order. It was for only two items. No challenge there. "I can't believe how organized you are, Brenda."

"Gotta be." Brenda, too, started on another order. "This close to Christmas, we have two types of orders, the ones for people who waited until the last minute and are now in a panic and need to get everything at once, or the ones for people who want an extra gift or two or remember someone they forgot."

"But the thing that amazes me is how you have an alternate list made for every item," Fiona said. "If we run out of scrimshaw tie tacks, the list says to offer them a key ring and vice versa."

"And if we run out of both, suggest a knife." Brenda rarely needed to look at the list, she knew it so well. "Believe me, that list brings in 20 per cent or more of our sales in the last week or two. If someone wants scrimshaw, try to get them scrimshaw; if they want a man's unique or quality gift, find one even if their first choice is sold out. Remember, they want to buy, you just need to find them something appropriate."

"Well, I was proud of myself when I convinced the woman in Nebraska that a shell mirror would be just as nice as a shell wreath, since we didn't have any more wreaths in the large size she wanted."

"Yes, but those mirrors are about the worse thing we have to pack!" Brenda said. "You have gotten the hang of the system, though."

Mr. Cadberry's dried apple face appeared in the window of the back door. Brenda rushed to let him in from the cold.

"The missus says I was to brung these." He walked slowly to the table and unloaded a box which contained various preserves and butters. It was clear his arthritis was bothering him when he turned to go. "I ain't gettin' 'round too good, but she's busy gettin' Christmas 'gather for the grandkids, sos I says I'd come in town.

'Course, she ain't no night time driver no ways."

"Thank you so much." Brenda set the jars into rows. "And thank Mrs. Cadberry for us. Her things are so popular, we always sell out."

The old man's face broke into a proud smile. "She's a good 'un, for sure."

"That she is, Mr. Cadberry," Fiona smiled. "You be careful driving home."

"Oh, I been driving in the snow since I was ten," he said. "Don't yous worry none aboot me. But yous be sure an' lock this here door." He firmly closed the door behind him, and Fiona obediently locked it.

They wrapped quickly and efficiently, double checking the contents of each package before applying the labels. Before long, Terri and Kerri said good-bye and left to walk the two blocks to their home. They must have called their boyfriends, because Jason Royce and Brett Haversham were standing outside the door when Brenda closed it behind them.

"Only one more night like this," Brenda remarked. "I think I'm getting too old to do this another year."

"Oh, I've had fun!" Fiona said. "Did I tell you Ethan is supposed to get here the day after tomorrow?"

"Once or twice," her friend wryly responded. "That relationship seems to have become very serious very quickly."

Fiona's face didn't mirror Brenda's smile. She was excited about Ethan spending Christmas with her, but she knew she shouldn't be. She shouldn't feel this way about Ethan when she was married. A little voice kept telling her that no one knew she was married, and that she had a right to be happy. But another, more persistent, voice told her to adhere to her values. Her values were far different than one might have expected from the daughter of a smalltime Mafia leader and the wife of a notorious Mafia boss. And that small word, she thought, was the key. Wife.

"Ethan's mom wanted him to go to D.C. for Christmas," Fiona said. She was tired of arguing with herself, she'd been doing it for weeks. "But he told her he'd promised to be here."

"Do you think she suspects what we're doing?" Brenda asked with alarm. Brenda, Fiona had come to realize, was personally a very shy girl. She was warm and friendly to customers, but that was her facade. The real Brenda was quite retiring. While most girls wanted the pomp of a formal, elaborate wedding, the very thought made Brenda shudder. She preferred to be quietly married with only Fiona as her attendant.

Despite the fact that they had seen each other infrequently during the last ten years or so, Adam and Ethan had been good friends when they played football together in high school ("Adam was the hero they carried off the field on their shoulders," Ethan had insisted. "I was the guy eating dirt."). Ethan had been touched when Adam asked him to stand up with him at his wedding.

"You're sure you don't want a big wedding, or even just a small one?" Fiona absently counted the stack of orders. Eight more, only two of which were large. "I enjoyed…" She had been about to say, "I enjoyed my wedding, if not my marriage," but caught herself just in time, she hoped, although Brenda gave her a curious look.

"I enjoyed helping a friend plan hers," Fiona corrected too quickly. Brenda continued to study her silently but said nothing for a few minutes.

"Maybe if my parents were still alive, I don't know." Brenda turned away and opened yet another roll of tape. "I just think it sounds romantic to be married with our friends there with us, in front of the fireplace at the Seafair Inn. And then a honeymoon in a lighthouse! What could be better?"

"It does sound lovely," Fiona agreed. "And without the stress and expense of a big production."

"Just us and you and Ethan."

"Ethan and I are honored."

"Well, I can't imagine having anyone other than you with me. I feel as though I've known you all my life." Brenda reached for another order form. The writing on it was mercifully brief. "You know everything about me, and I know everything about you."

Not quite, Fiona thought. Her friend's honesty made her feel guilty. She wished she could confide in her, but she didn't dare.

"You're the best friend I've ever had," she said instead. *Except for my cousin*, she silently added.

"Well, thank you!" Brenda smiled widely. "I hope things work out for you and Ethan, but I'd hate for you to move to New York."

"I will not move to New York!" Fiona's tone was a little too adamant.

"Well, maybe Ethan will come home to Seafair." Brenda sounded hopeful. "We sold every painting of his. I think he could make a living as an artist."

"Maybe." Fiona had thought the same thing. But would that really be the best thing for her? She had grown to love the little town and its friendly inhabitants who had taken her in so quickly. She felt so at home here, but it might not be so comfortable if she had to see Ethan every day. And she certainly could never marry him." I think he's good enough."

"That gallery manager thought so, I guess. She left her card for us to give him."

"Yes, I'm excited about telling him that." In spite of her fears, Fiona smiled at the thought of delivering such good news.

They were silent for a few moments, checking their merchandise. Then Fiona went to the shop to look for a couple of items. She found the last hand-knitted afghan, the next-to-last wedding ring quilt, and picked out the handsomest carved horse she could find. Then she jumped, almost dropping her bundles, when someone rapped on the door.

When she whirled around, she saw a face pressed against the

glass, the nose flattened so that the features were distorted. Her heart seemed to stop a moment before finding its rhythm again when she realized it was Ethan. Dignified Ethan Shane was standing in the cold of a winter's night, comically squashing his aristocratic nose so that it left a smudge on the frosty glass.

Fiona set the armful of gifts on the counter and rushed to open the door. "Ethan!" She didn't think about keeping her distance from him. Instead she threw herself into his arms, and was rewarded with a long-awaited kiss.

"You nearly scared me to death," she managed to gasp, but she couldn't make herself sound angry.

"I'm sorry," he murmured, but he didn't sound the least bit contrite. "You were working so hard, I thought you needed to lighten up a bit, have a laugh."

"You're right." She gave him a squeeze. "We need to have more fun." She looked up at his square-jawed face from the safety of his arms. "I don't think either of us has had enough fun in our lives."

"Well, we're definitely going to have fun this Christmas," he promised her.

"I wish your famiily could come home." She could imagine how unhappy Libby was not to be able to spend Christmas with her only child. "Do you know why they couldn't leave Washington?"

"Not really. And I didn't ask." He released her and stood back. She understood that she was not to tread further in that particular direction.

"You've really been selling, haven't you?" It was obvious that he wished to change the subject. He turned slowly, looking at the sparsely filled shelves and cabinets. "How many of my paintings are still here?"

"None. We sold the last one a week ago."

"Really? I have a tidy little sum coming at the end of the month then, don't I?"

"You do, indeed." Taking his hand, Fiona pulled him into the next room. With a whoop, Brenda rushed to hug the newcomer.

"Where's the business card, Brenda?" Fiona searched the board where a multitude of business cards were thumbtacked.

"Not there, I stashed it upstairs so it wouldn't get lost."

"In your loft?" Fiona started to laugh. "Brenda, an elephant could get lost in your loft!"

"Please!" her friend responded with mock indignation. Then she ran up the stairs. She was back again almost immediately, the card held victoriously in her extended fingers.

When she handed it to Ethan, he looked confused. "It's a gallery, Ethan. The woman manages a gallery in New York."

"So?"

Brenda spoke slowly, as though explaining something to a child whose mind was hopelessly muddled. "She saw your paintings, and she loved them. She wants to talk to you about exhibiting in the gallery she manages. Who knows? Maybe you could have a private show!"

"Did she say that?"

Fiona jumped into the conversation. "Well, not about a private show, but she definitely is interested in selling your work. Isn't a private show the next step?"

"A very big step," he said, but his eyes were shining.

"Maybe you'll get rich and famous." Brenda was enthusiastic, but Ethan calmed her with his answer.

"Maybe I can someday make a living painting. That would be enough."

Lights flashed across the small parking area behind the building where Mr. Cadberry had been a couple of hours earlier. But this time the driver was Adam. Brenda greeted him with a warm hug and kiss.

"I'm on my dinner break," Adam said, smiling over Brenda's smooth blond cap of hair at the other couple. "I saw your car, Ethan. Glad you made it up early from the city."

"Couldn't wait to leave."

"Maybe you shouldn't go back."

"I wish."

Brenda interrupted. "Come upstairs, everybody, we'll get a bite to eat and something to drink."

It was easy to persuade Fiona to put off packing the last three boxes until the next day. Depsite the rush of orders that evening, the calls had been less frequent today than yesterday, and they expected them to be a little slower tomorrow.

They cleared off the remaining mess on Brenda's table. It was actually less cluttered than it had been, because most of the stored items had been toted downstairs and used. Then they made coffee and warmed up the chili Brenda had found time to make at some point during that busy day.

Fiona looked around her. She couldn't remember ever being this happy with anyone else except her cousin and Jim. Even with their company, she had felt alone, not part of a couple. It was much nicer to be with Ethan, two couples who were friends.

When Adam checked his watch and then left quickly, kissing his soon-to-be bride soundly on his way out, Fiona and Ethan also rose. "Get some rest, Bren, I'll be here in the morning."

"No hurry, Terri and Kerri are bringing Jason and Brett to help tomorrow in the morning. Then it will be we four girls again in the afternoon."

"If you let me sleep in, I'll help in the afternoon," Ethan offered.

"You're on!" Brenda accepted his offer gratefully.

They walked to the back door, and Brenda let them out. Her cat, which had disappeared hours earlier in the boxes, strolled out and past them, headed up the stairs to bed.

"Goodnight, Yolanda," Brenda called after her. The faintest switch of a tail was the feline's only response. Brenda hugged Fiona and then Ethan. "I'll see you in the afternoon."

"We'll bring a pizza for lunch," Ethan offered.

"Yum-m! That would be wonderful!"

Ethan steadied Fiona on the icy pavement as they approached the Jeep, and closed her door behind her before entering his own car. "I'll follow you home."

She drove slowly. She was not an experienced driver in the bad weather, and she took her time whenever she took the Jeep to the village. She still preferred to walk, but not when it was late at night. They pulled into the garage, side by side. She hopped to the ground before he could get out of his car and come around to hers.

"Do you want some tea or coffee?" She was anxious to get inside. It was really cold on the cliffs when they stepped out of the protection of the garage, and she couldn't wait to get to the warmth of her cottage. She didn't worry about the weather, because a generator was there to back up if wind, snow, or ice knocked out the electricity.

"Tea would do nicely as a start." He took her gloved hand and shorted his stride to hers. She liked that. On the few occasions when they had gone out together, Antonio had always walked away from her, leaving her rudely in his wake...but she didn't want to think about Antonio, didn't want to remember he existed.

They hung their coats on the hooks by the door and turned on only a single lamp before going into the kitchen. Wanting to avoid the glare of the bright overhead light, Fiona switched on the tall, narrow lamp which sat on one end of the small sideboard. It still seemed too dim, so she also turned on the light over the stove. She pulled out her varied selection of tea bags, some gourmet, and placed them in the center of the table.

"Cream or sugar?" She was suddenly self-conscious in the intimacy of the small cottage, and found she couldn't meet his eyes.

"No, thanks." He sounded amused, and she glanced up at him.

"I'm not going to bite you, Little Red Riding Hood," he said gently.

"Are you saying you're the Big Bad Wolf?"

"I'm anything but a wolf," he said, his tone now serious. "I don't casually chase after beautiful girls."

"Are you chasing me?"

"If you were to run, I would certainly give chase. But you haven't seemed inclined to flee, at least not until the last few minutes."

"Things are going too fast. Everything seemed to happen immediately. I guess I'm…" She searched for the word, finally settling for, "confused."

"By what?" he queried patiently.

He was multi-faceted, she decided. The cool, intellectual pragmatist lawyer versus the romantic, impulsive artist. He fascinated her. She might even be in love with him.

He spoke again before she could collect her thoughts to answer him. "I was prepared to mistrust you, even dislike you, but I knew the moment I saw you that you were special. And I couldn't wait to get back here and get to know you better."

He walked toward her, slowly, giving her the chance to move away if she chose. "Now I feel as though I've known you all my life. And I can't imagine not knowing you the rest of my life."

You were right to mistrust me, she knew she should say the words, but she didn't. *I'm nothing like you think I am, nothing like you want me to be.* She wished she were; she could be, if only she were not trapped in a marriage and a past she had not wanted.

His slightly long face was serious, and she realized he was afraid he would say or do the wrong thing and lose her. It was his vulnerability, the earnest yearning in his eyes, which made her forget all her misgivings, all her plans to avoid a relationship with him which she knew, even as she moved toward him, was doomed.

He wasn't a threat, he wasn't dangerous. He was her safe haven. And she was going to let him shelter her from the storms of her life as long as she could.

* * *

She awoke in the night because she was too warm. Fuzzily, she thought that was strange, because she often had to wear socks at night to ward off the chill. She rubbed her bare feet together. Where were her socks?

She was suddenly wide awake. She remembered in an instant why she was so warm, and why she hadn't thought about putting on socks—or anything else—before she went to bed. Ethan was snoring lightly beside her. She crept out from under his arm, freezing in place momentarily when he murmured something unintelligible, then slowly slid out of bed until she was standing, shivering in the cold room.

Br-r-r! She grabbed the warm robe draped across the footboard and snuggled into it. It wasn't as warm as Ethan, but it was safer. She rummaged around in the dark and finally located her nightgown. It was flannel, and she would melt if she wore it back to bed. Maybe she should curl up in the living room?

She was being silly, she decided. It was too late to act outraged and innocent. Nothing would be accomplished by anger or remorse. Last night she had decided not to worry about the future, at least not until she had to. She was going to grab what happiness she could.

She did quietly open a drawer and pull out a light summer nightgown before climbing back into the bed. She drew up the heavy quilt. There. The temperature should be just right now. She snuggled back into the curve of Ethan's body, and his arm pulled her closer, but he didn't wake up.

It was a few minutes before she dozed off. She had never slept with someone before. Her cousin had not spent the night at her home, because her uncle Sean had been afraid to let her visit there. He had heard too many tales, mostly true, about Mafia violence. When she stayed at their house, her cousin had twin beds in her room. Mercifully Antonio had followed a routine, alternately visiting her room once or twice each week, never staying longer than was absolutely necessary. She had also followed a routine, closing her eyes and pretending she was somewhere else as soon as he entered her door.

* * *

The dawn coming through the lace curtains awakened them slowly. Fiona sleepily wondered for a moment why she hadn't closed the inside shutters; then she remembered why she had been too preoccupied to weatherproof the room the previous night. The reason sat up and then smiled down at her.

"Hi." His eyes were studying hers, trying to see what her mood was this morning. "I'm afraid I totally crashed last night. I was dog tired."

She tried not to look as embarrassed and self-conscious as she felt. She concentrated on showing her happiness. He looked relieved when she smiled. "You didn't act tired," she said pertly and climbed out of bed. His eyebrows rose when he saw the nightgown, but he said nothing.

Pulling on her robe, she headed for the bathroom. "I'll be out in a minute, and it will be all yours," she threw over her shoulder. When she emerged several minutes later, he entered the bathroom, shutting the door as she had. He brushed his teeth and looked at the disheveled man in the mirror. He still looked tired, but he felt wonderful. This was the girl, he told himself. This was the one. He'd known it immediately.

Fiona was back in bed when he reentered the bedroom. The covers were up around her chin, and her hair gleamed in the early morning light. "It's only six," she said. "I'm not ready to get up, are you?"

"I'm not sleepy," he replied. "But I'm planning on coming back to bed." He leaned over to kiss her. She smelled minty. He climbed in beside her, aware of her momentary stiffness. But when he kissed her again, she began to relax, finally pulling him closer to her. Now he could faintly smell the floral scent which she wore.

"Roses? Lilacs?" He murmured the question against her throat. She didn't understand. "What?" He seemed to be talking about gardens, a subject which did not interest her at the moment.

"Your perfume. What flowers are in it?"

"I don't know, it's called 'Bouquet,' I think."

"I like it. I'll buy you the largest bottle they make when I get back to New York."

She laughed. "You do that. But right now..." She grasped his face in her hands and pulled his head up so she could see his face. "Right now," she whispered again, but she didn't finish what she had meant to say. Instead she reached up and kissed him.

* * *

They called and ordered a pizza before leaving to go to the co-op. Her Jeep stayed in the garage, as they both climbed into Ethan's larger SUV. Fiona went into the shop and Ethan walked over to pick up the pizza after parking the car.

"Hi." Brenda glanced up when Fiona closed the door, making the chime ring merrily. She had been wrapping yet another package, but her busy hands stopped their movement as she regarded her friend with frank interest.

"Well..." She drew the syllable out.

"Well, what?" Fiona looked away from Brenda's questioning gaze.

"Just well it's obvious something has happened," Brenda said. "You look radiant this morning."

Fiona glanced pointedly at her watch. "It isn't morning, it's a quarter after noon."

"Whatever." Brenda smiled knowingly. "You don't have to tell me anything, say nary a word, but I know. Protest if you will, but you can't fool ole Bren."

Fiona's sigh was exaggerated. "I didn't think I could. You read me like a book."

"And the book is growing more interesting by the day," Brenda said smugly.

Ethan appeared, the aroma of hot pizza swirling about him. "Pizza anyone?" He called out loudly enough for the girls, who were working in the back room, to hear.

They had an impromptu pizza party, interrupted only twice by the phone. It looked as though they would be able to leave early today.

There was a flurry of orders around five that evening, however, and Terri and Kerri's boyfriends were enlisted to help once more when they arrived to take the girls home. With all of them scurrying, they had the boxes packed by seven o'clock when the store closed. Now as soon as the customer who had arrived at ten minutes till seven finished her leisurely shopping, they would be able to go.

"Slim pickins," the portly woman complained in a pronounced southern accent, eyeing the shelves and cases.

"Yes, we've been very busy, both with customers in the shop and telephone orders," Brenda said cheerily, making a face at Fiona when the woman bent over to examine the sole remaining quilt. "You should have come in earlier. The place was packed with wonderful things, and we had even more in storage."

"I didn't have time. My husband and I just moved up here to be near our son and his wife. He married a girl from Maine. One of our grandchildren is sick, so they need our help." She picked up the quilt and walked over to place it on the counter. "We can't believe how cold it is."

"It does get cold," Ethan agreed. "Where are you from?"

"Alabama, the very southern tip of Alabama. I miss it already."

"I imagine so."

She smiled pleasantly at him, appreciating his friendliness, and Fiona and Brenda exchanged a sheepish glance. The poor woman had pulled up stakes, going to a cold region when she would rather be at home, in order to help her son and daughter-in-law.

"How old are your grandchildren?" Brenda was trying to make up for her earlier lack of friendliness. "Maybe we can suggest something for them."

"Hayleigh's four, and she loves animals and plush toys. Max is six and wants to someday own a ranch." The woman beamed as she talked about her grandchildren. "The baby doesn't need anything to play with. He was three months premature when he was born in November. We don't know when, or even if, he will come home. Sonny and Patty will probably spend most of the day at the hospital, but I'm cooking Christmas dinner anyway. The children deserve to have Christmas."

"Oh, I'm so sorry." Brenda's soft side was now apparent. "How about this fabric Noah's Ark for your granddaughter? It has eight sets of animals."

The woman looked it over, smiled, and nodded. Then she saw the carved wooden animals on the next shelf. The detail in them was amazing, and she picked one up and examined it. "I think these will be perfect for Max," she said. "I'll take a horse, a cow, a sheep, and a pig." Then she spotted the dogs. "One of the dogs, too," she added, picking up the largest in the group.

"Let's see, the quilt is for Patty and Sonny." She checked off people using her fingers. "I think one of those hand-knitted sweaters would be perfect for my husband if you have one in extra large—he's eaten my biscuits for too many years! That should do it."

"Are you sure that's everything?" Brenda asked.

There were fat stuffed toys, their features sewn on in wonderful detail, by the register. They had had several dozen before Thanksgiving, but now only a few were left.

The woman silently looked at the toys before she replied. She slowly reached for a blue calico bear, and added it to her pile of purchases. "For Baby Jack," she said quietly.

Fiona felt tears sting her eyes. The woman who had so annoyed them by her late arrival and tart comments was trying to deal with the grief of having a grandchild who was quite possibly dying. Additionally she was watching her son and his wife suffer, but she was trying to make Christmas as happy for them as she could. "Would you like for us to gift wrap these?" There was usually an additional charge for that service, but Fiona knew Brenda wouldn't mind her offering.

"That would be such a help!" The woman's smile again lit up her tired face. "I'm afraid my husband isn't much help decorating or cooking, so I'm going to be busy tomorrow. Thank goodness he's wonderful with the children."

They wrapped each package with special care, chatting with the discouraged woman. She didn't see Brenda place red foil around the beautiful antique lace pillow and place it into the bag. She had sneaked a look at the woman's charge card to get her name, Sally Callahan, so she could write it on her gift.

As she left, Mrs. Callahan turned back to wish them "Merry Christmas." She looked less stressed than she had when she arrived, and she promised to come back.

"She was nice," Brenda said as she turned from locking up. "I feel bad that I was so crabby."

"We were all annoyed when she came in so late," Fiona responded. "But she was happy when she left."

"Well, I couldn't bear to think of her not having a gift…"

"I saw you putting that pillow into her bag," Fiona said. "And we would usually have charged $3 for wrapping each of those presents."

"I hope she has a better Christmas than it sounds as though she will."

"I do, too." Fiona gazed at the darkness outside. The day had started out so happily. Now she just felt sad. "When she picked up that toy for the baby, I could have cried."

There was a short silence, before Ethan spoke up.

"You did what you could. Her grandchildren will enjoy their Christmas, which will make her enjoy hers, they will eat her dinner which will no doubt be delicious, and the stressed parents will sleep peacefully under their warm quilt." He put his arm around Fiona before reaching to put the other around Brenda. "And, please God, Baby Jack will grow up to be so healthy and active that he exhausts everyone."

Fiona sighed. "Amen."

* * *

Adam arranged his dinner break so he could spend the time with them at the café. They told him about Mrs. Callahan, and they discussed the wedding, now only two days away.

"I can't believe we only have three more hours in the shop before we close tomorrow for Christmas," Brenda sighed gratefully. "Of course, we'll have any orders that come in by noon to pack, but we should get the last of them to the post office by two or so, and then we're through."

"By the time the shop reopens in March, you'll be ready to go again," Fiona assured her.

"Oh yes, that break of almost three months is enough for me. But I do get a lot done. It's fun when everyone brings in the new things and we put the store together again in the spring, Fiona. I'm glad you'll be here to help me this year."

Would she? Fiona said nothing, but she doubted it.

Shortly thereafter, they parted. Brenda walked back to her loft, Adam got back into his car marked "Seafair Village," and Ethan and Fiona drove home to her cottage.

Ethan unlocked the door, and they removed their coats and went into the kitchen as though they had done this together for years. Fiona adjusted the thermostat upwards a couple of degrees. Ethan began to boil water in the teakettle. They sat together at the table, sipping tea and talking quietly, until Ethan announced he was going to start a fire in the living room fireplace.

"That's a good idea." Fiona, too, left the warmth of the little kitchen. "I'm going to take a quick shower and get into my robe."

"And *that* is a good idea," Ethan leered comically at her.

"I'm going to have to cut off your vitamins," she threatened.

"Don't take them, don't need them," he shot back. "But on second thought, maybe I should start. I'll have to keep you busy while the shop is closed this winter."

"That will be difficult, since you'll be in New York." Her voice floated back to him from the bedroom.

He looked after her, thinking. Then he pulled the business card from his wallet. Maybe he'd give that gallery owner a call, he mused. The check from his sales at the shop was substantial. If he could sell that many paintings every month, get well-known enough to demand higher prices... Thoughtfully he bent to make the fire.

By the time Fiona returned, the room was warmed by the heat from the flames, and Ethan had thrown pillows on the floor. He pulled her to him gently, kissed the top of her damp head, then silently left the room. Moments later, she heard the shower begin.

He was back in minutes, wrapped in his own terrycloth robe, his mussed hair going every which way. "A little wine, I think," he said, and went into the kitchen to pour them each a glass. He handed one to Fiona before joining her on the pillows.

"I love this cottage." He sipped his wine while gazing around the room, small and intimate in the dim firelight.

"It's so cozy," Fiona agreed. "It's like being right on the beach, even when there's snow outside." She sipped from her own wineglass. "Of course, I love shells anywhere, and this house has plenty of them."

They leaned against one another, watching the flames. When their glasses were empty, Ethan took hers and placed it with his on the hearth. He turned so they were facing one another. "I want to say it, even though I'm sure you know it, Fiona. I'm not the kind of guy who has casual affairs. I'm kind of idealistic, I guess, and I've had women tell me I'm too dull and serious. Well, I know one thing—I'm very serious about you." He took a deep breath. "As a matter of fact, I'm in love with you." His eyes studied her own. "And that's the very first time I've said that in my life."

"You aren't dull at all!" Fiona responded indignantly, focusing first on the slur against Ethan. How dare anyone tell this warm, romantic man that he was dull. She couldn't imagine ever being bored by him.

She paused for a moment, aware that he was waiting expectantly for her reaction to the revealing words he had spoken. Again, she silenced the voice inside demanding that she tell him the truth now, before things went any further. The truth seemed so ugly, unwanted and out of place in a moment so romantic as this.

"I like the fact that you're serious." She touched his face gently. "Particularly that you are serious about me." She kissed him lightly. "Because I am most definitely serious about you."

He smiled widely. He really has a beautiful smile, she thought as he took her hand from his face, looking down at it in his own, much larger one. He traced the scar with one finger, very lightly. Then he pulled her closer, closer, until she could no longer see the flickering flames.

Sometime in the night, she stirred because she was cold. "Shush," Ethan's voice whispered, and a thick quilt was tucked around her. "I'll have the fire going again in a few minutes." But she was contentedly asleep before the fire again warmed the room.

* * *

In the morning, familiar as a long-married couple, they rushed to eat and get ready in order to reach the shop before nine. Brenda was on the phone when they entered, taking a customer's frantic order, and that set the tone for the entire morning as they took one call, packed the order quickly, and were ready for the next. Against all their expectations, they were able to take their final shipment to the post office before one.

They spent the afternoon and evening with Adam and Brenda. Adam had begun his week's vacation, and they finished off the last of the chili and played a competitive game of Trivial Pursuit. It was late when Brenda showed them to the door. "Four-thirty tomorrow," she called out to them excitedly. They waved back.

They again shared a glass of wine after Ethan started a small fire. But Fiona headed for the shower shortly thereafter. It was colder tonight, and a hot shower followed by slipping between cool sheets sounded very inviting.

She had just adjusted the temperature when she heard Ethan's voice. "You're wasting water, woman! You should share it!" She laughed and pulled the curtain slightly aside. Ethan stepped in, shielding her from the sudden blast of cold air.

She knew this happiness couldn't last, but she was happy right now, today, she thought as she ducked under the stream of water to rinse shampoo from her hair. Ethan had scrubbed her head, piling foaming soap thickly like a crown.

We're happy and together today, she told herself, even if today might be all they had.

* * *

Fiona slipped up the stairs to the loft half an hour early, leaving the two men in the shop nervously fingering their ties.

"Bren?" She called ahead as she entered the expansive loft. "Where are you?"

"Over here." Brenda's voice was muffled. Her head appeared then, peeking over the bed. "I know I bought those shoes, I've even paid the credit card bill for them already, but I'm darned if I can find them."

"Let me help." Fiona dropped to her knees on the other side of the bed and began to pull out boxes. There were boxes of fabric, boxes of beads, boxes of ribbon, and boxes of shells of every shape and size. But there was not a single box of shoes.

"Where do you keep your other shoes?" Fiona looked across the rumpled bed at her friend.

"In the closet, but I already looked there. I only have three pairs besides the ones I bought for the wedding."

"Only three pairs?" Had Brenda known it, Fiona's expensive upbringing showed in the question. There had been four pairs of shoes in Fiona's luggage, and she had bought a few more since she came to Seafair.

"Hate shoes." Brenda looked around the loft, trying to think where she could have stashed the elusive shoes.

"You don't think we mailed them to someone, do you?" Fiona was half serious.

Brenda frowned, thinking just that. They had been here, she remembered. And one or the other of the kids had come up to get ribbon or tape...that was it! She went to the top of the stairs and called down to her nervous groom. "Adam! Would you look in the storage room for a shoebox? I think it's under another box filled with tape."

Adam soon called up that he had found them, but it was Ethan who brought the box to the top of the stairs. Brenda slipped on the pretty high heels, and brushed at her knees. Her dress was the palest shell pink, lacy and full in the skirt.

"You look beautiful," Fiona assured her. She was remembering her own wedding day, the bridal attendants gathered around her, a Manhattan hairdresser arranging her elaborate hairdo, the wedding consultant issuing orders. This seemed more real. For a moment she envied Brenda her simple, quiet wedding, which could take place today without any shadow of deceit or fear.

The feeling continued as she watched Adam's eyes light up when he saw his bride descend the stairs. Ethan was watching her, smiling proudly at how pretty she was in her own emerald green dress of watered silk.

The wedding ceremony was short, the warmth from the massive fireplace circling around them. Someone from the inn took a few pictures, then the two couples ate dinner together in the elegant dining room before the bridal couple left to travel the few miles to their lighthouse honeymoon.

Fiona and Ethan stood, hands clasped between them, and watched the truck disappear from view. Fiona sighed. "I've been to weddings which cost more than a house, but none as nice as theirs."

Very rarely did Fiona say anything about her life before coming to Seafair, and some caution prevented Ethan from inquiring further, but he had to agree with her observation. "It was nice, what a wedding should be—no big production to impress, just a simple ceremony with friends before God."

He turned her toward him. "We could do it, too. I could get Judge Robins to give us a special license, and we could get married tomorrow."

"Brenda would kill us, not to mention your mother and grandmother." She felt her heart begin to beat erratically, and knew she had to stall for time without putting him off or sounding as though she didn't love the idea as much as he did. He was just going too quickly. She didn't want it to end before it had to, but he might force her to leave if she couldn't dissuade him from pursuing what seemed to be the natural conclusion to their relationship.

She shivered. "It's cold out here, Ethan." She put her arm around his waist and leaned into him. "Let's go home and warm up."

* * *

On Christmas morning, most of the presents under Fiona's little tree were for people who had yet to arrive: Ethan's parents and grandparents. She had already delivered her gift to Mrs. Haddington, and the lighthouse honeymoon had been Brenda and Adam's wedding/Christmas present from her and Ethan.

There would be another gift waiting for them in the loft when they returned. Fiona had bought the queen size brass bed Brenda had drooled over in the antique store and a new mattress and box springs to replace the sagging set Brenda insisted were fine, but Fiona couldn't imagine supporting Adam's considerable weight. Fiona still had almost all the money she had brought with her from New York.

Ethan started another fire before they sat down on the carpet in front of the tree to open the few gifts which were there. They had stayed in bed until late, snuggled together as carols played on the radio. Then they called Washington, and shared quick Christmas greetings all around, before Keith had to say good-bye and head off to his meeting. Now they sat on the pillows by the tree.

Fiona opened Libby's package and exclaimed over the beautiful hand-knit sweater. Margaret's gift was a delicate cameo brooch which could also be hung on a chain as a pendant.

Ethan received a cashmere sweater from his mother, as well as a silk tie. His grandmother gave him an antique enameled gold tie bar.

"Open my gifts to you, Ethan." She handed him a large box.

He pulled off the ribbon and tore away the paper excitedly to reveal a dozen tubes of the azure paint. "Perfect!" He laughed, but he was touched that she'd remembered he used so much of that particular color.

The next gift made him laugh even harder. He pulled the navy wool beret out of the box and perched it precariously on his thick hair. "Now that makes me a real painter," he declared. "I just need to make a trip to Paris and find my own little place on the Left Bank to paint."

The next gift was a smoothly sanded wooden sign. "Ethan Shane, Artist" it said in elegant lettering. He held it silently, smiled at her, and set it beside the paint. His final gift was an album filled with photos of the village, the sea, the marina, and the cliffs. They were taken in all kinds of light and from multiple angles. The front and back of the album were made of burl wood.

"So you can paint Seafair wherever you are," she told him quietly.

He said nothing, turning page after page until he had looked at every one. "This is perhaps the most thoughtful gift I have ever received," he finally said. "Thank you, thank you very much." He leaned across her pile of presents to softly kiss her.

He had only one gift for her, but she gasped when she saw it and tears filled her eyes. "Oh, Ethan…" It was so beautiful, and she desperately wanted to keep it, but she knew she couldn't.

"It's a gift," he said firmly. "It's not an engagement ring. It was my great-grandmother's, and Gran gave it to me years ago. She told me it was to give to my true love." He wiped the tears which were now slowly falling from her eyes. "You are my true love, so it belongs to you. No matter what happens to us, it's yours."

The square cut diamond was large, but not overly so. The setting was lacy filigree, and it was just the kind of ring Fiona would have chosen for herself. Of course the idea of receiving a ring from Ethan had crossed her mind before, possibly more than she wanted to admit, but she hadn't realized how much she wanted this until now, when it was happening. She couldn't keep it, and to have such a beautiful thing presented to her with all the love it represented, only to have to refuse it, was torture. Whatever he said, it couldn't be anything but an engagement ring. "I can't take it," she protested, shaking her head back and forth.

"Yes, you can. It belongs to you, I knew I would give it to you that night when I waited for you on the terrace." She looked up, surprised. "I couldn't give it to anyone else, Fiona." Unresisting, she let him put it on her finger and wasn't the least surprised when it fit.

The remainder of the day was lazy and relaxed, and Ethan never saw how Fiona slipped between a state of euphoric happiness and intense dread. They ate dinner with Mrs. Haddington, who repeatedly exclaimed over the beautiful crystal epergne Fiona gave her. It was dusk when they returned home. After Ethan started the fire, they sipped champagne in the quiet room.

"Thank you for the most wonderful Christmas I've ever had, Ethan." Fiona smiled at him. She knew it would be their only one together, but she had made a decision not to let that knowledge ruin tonight.

"Thank you for my most wonderful Christmas, darling." He saluted her with his flute.

They were in bed before ten o'clock, the ring still sparkling on Fiona's left hand. "It was perfect," Fiona murmured against his shoulder, where her head lay safely cradled.

* * *

Fiona was buttering her toast when the phone rang the next morning. She grabbed it with one crumby hand. "Hello?"

Libby's voice sang through the line. Fiona turned the receiver slightly away from her ear, so Ethan could also hear. "Hi, Fiona! We're almost to Seafair. We'll be there in half an hour or so. I called the house, but Ethan didn't answer. I guess he's in the shower."

"Probably so," Fiona managed with only the briefest of guilty pauses.

"See you in a little while." Libby called a cheery good-bye and hung up.

"Whew! I'd better run next door." Ethan hugged her close. "Bye, darling."

She clung to him when he would have pulled away. "They'll stay after you leave; we'll have to be careful now."

"Maybe not." He lifted her chin up with his finger. "If I do leave before them, I promise to come back soon."

She nodded, but couldn't help the tears in her eyes. "I miss you already."

"I love you." He hugged her again, then grabbed his coat and flew across the snow to the back door of the big house.

* * *

Fiona watched from the window as Keith parked the car outside the garage and everyone climbed out. Ethan had gone outside to greet them. They looked energetic for people who had driven most of the night. And she realized they were surprisingly dear to her. She felt as if she hadn't seen them in too long a time. His grandparents walked toward their own cottage, pulling a wheeled bags behind them. Libby turned to say something to Ethan before she went inside her own house.

"Of course, it's really none of my business, but if I were you, I would have made more than the one set of footprints in the snow," Keith said quietly to his son.

Ethan turned to follow his father's gaze. The snow between the garage and cottage was packed by multiple tracks, but only one led from Fiona's door to the terrace. "Worked in intelligence, sir?" he asked with a shameless grin.

"One learns to observe the obvious. And you have made the situation very obvious. I don't suppose you thought to splash water about in the shower or muss your bed a bit?"

"I guess I don't have a criminal mind."

"You mother, however, does." Keith adjusted the suitcases, and led the way to the house. "Try to get upstairs before she does."

Ethan followed him and went upstairs with some of the bags. He dropped the suitcases in his parents' room and then went into his. He rumpled the bed slightly, then ran the water in the sink and splashed it on the inside of the shower curtain and on the wall and faucet.

"Ethan?" Libby called from the open door of his bedroom. He flushed the toilet to explain his presence in the bathroom, then reentered the bedroom.

Libby was smoothing the coverlet. He was glad he had thought to make an impression in the pillow, because Libby pulled it out to fluff it.

"Have you been busy?" his mother asked innocently, moving casually in the direction of his bathroom. She looked into the mirror to fuss with her hair, noting his razor on the edge of the sink. He saw her glance, and was proud of that little touch. He'd pulled it out of his bag at the last minute. He couldn't help grinning when Libby casually straightened the shower curtain, managing to feel the lining of it as she did so. She peeked quickly inside and saw the splashes of water.

"Fiona and I both helped out at the co-op. I actually enjoyed it."

"Were the sales as good as last year?" She walked back into his room and perched on the bed.

"Better. There was very little left by the time we mailed the last packages on the 23rd." He sat in the single chair. "You don't seem tired for people who drove all night."

"We left yesterday afternoon and stopped early last night," Libby explained. "Then your dad had us up and moving before six this morning. I feel great now, but I imagine I'll want to go to bed early."

"I've gotten caught up on my sleep," Ethan said truthfully. "I didn't realize how tired I was until I stopped working the 12 and 14-hour days."

"I hope it won't be so busy when you go back."

"Probably will be," he shrugged. "But I've decided I'm going to take more time off in the future. Life's too short to work all the time. We could work 25 hours a day and never get it all done."

"You're very good at what you do." His mother's voice was gentle. "I'm sorry you don't particularly like it."

"It feels good when we get someone dangerous off the street, but that isn't often enough." Ethan looked at his feet before continuing. "Did you know they sold all my paintings at the shop? A woman who manages a gallery in New York left her business card. She told Fiona and Brenda she wants to talk to me about selling some of my paintings."

"That would be wonderful!" Libby was cautious, not wanting to appear to push Ethan either way.

"Libby!" Keith's voice carried through the house. "Fiona's here, and she's brought Christmas with her."

Ethan and his mother joined the others in the kitchen where coffee was being poured into mugs. Fragrant breakfast rolls were just coming out of the warming oven.

"Grab your mugs and plates, and let's go in to the tree and open our presents," Margaret ordered them.

They moved into the living room and found places to sit. "The decorations are perfect, Fiona," Libby said. "I'm sorry you worked so hard to have us not even come home until after Christmas."

"We'll have to have a big New Year's celebration," Margaret said by way of consolation, and they all agreed. "By the way, what was it you two had to do on Christmas Eve?"

"Stand up with Adam and Brenda when they were married," Ethan answered.

"Married? I didn't even know they were seriously dating!" Libby exclaimed. "See, Keith, I miss out on everything when we go to Washington!"

"Most people would find Washington more interesting than Seafair." Her husband did not try to hide his amusement.

"That's because they don't live here," Libby snapped back. "I missed the wedding, and I didn't give them a gift."

"You couldn't very well know to buy a gift if you didn't know they were getting married," Keith said patiently. "You can go shopping for one tomorrow."

"I'll go with you, Lib," Margaret said. "I'll need to get something, too."

Fiona passed around the gifts then, and they all exclaimed over her thoughtfulness. Keith seemed particularly pleased with the model of his sailboat.

"This is going to be right on my desk in my Senate office," he promised her. "Then I'll be able to remember why I'm working so hard for my home state."

"And you'll know why you want to retire after this term," Libby reminded him.

"We'll talk about that as the time gets nearer, sweetheart."

"Well, I'm casting my vote now."

He laughed and turned to study his father's similar model. "I'll put this on my mantel," the elder man said. "I don't have a Senate office, and I'm very grateful for that."

"Agreed." Margaret nodded vigorously. "I can't wait until we all move back to Seafair permanently."

The banter went on as Fiona sat back and observed the family. She caught Ethan looking pointedly at her hand where the ring had been. She smiled at him, but shook her head slightly, letting him know she wasn't ready for the others to see it on her finger.

Margaret yawned as they sat talking, and Fiona took the opportunity to leave. "You're all tired after your trip, and I've been busy at the shop. I think I'll go back to the cottage unless there's something you need me to do."

"Nothing at all," Libby said. "The house looks lovely, Fiona. Why don't you have dinner with us tonight? Margaret said something about making stew."

"If I wake up from my nap in time." Margaret was heading toward the door to go to her own house. "We can always order pizza if we're all too lazy to cook." Her hand waggled over her shoulder. "Bye."

Her husband followed her out, and Libby headed up the stairs as Fiona shrugged into her coat.

Ethan poured another cup of coffee and stood at the kitchen window, watching Fiona trudge through the snow. He sat down at the table when her door closed behind her.

Keith stacked plates from the living room in the sink, then made another trip to get the mugs. He also filled his cup again and joined his son in the kind of direct, simple conversation men have.

"So is it serious? Fiona seems to be the kind of girl a man marries."

"Fiona is that kind of girl."

"So it is serious."

"Very."

"Good." They sat for a while in companionable silence. "Not thinking of doing something like Brenda and Adam, are you?"

"No, I value my life too much to deny Mom and Gran a wedding."

"Right. They'd have your head on a platter."

They talked for another hour in the quiet house. Then Keith joined his wife in their room, and Ethan went to his own.

The room which had been his all his life, whenever they visited or lived at Cliff House, seemed strange now. He missed the cozy little rooms in the cottage, but he knew that was really because he missed Fiona's quiet presence and the awareness that, even if she was in another room, she was still near.

A sudden chill swept through him, a sense of foreboding. He nervously laughed at himself. His life was the best it had ever been right now. It couldn't get much better.

He listlessly took a book from the shelves and began to read where it fell open. It was one of the mystery novels he had enjoyed as a boy. It held his attention for only a few minutes now. He left the chair in favor of the bed and fell almost instantly asleep. His dreams were all of Fiona.

* * *

Fiona turned on the television to fill some of the void in the cottage since Ethan was no longer there. The weather information droned on, then she caught bits and pieces of the news as she moved about in the kitchen, making herself a cup of tea.

"...thought to be the remains of Gianni Bellini, a suspected organized crime figure. His wife's body was found, badly burned, in a roadside restroom across the state." She heard only a high buzzing in her ears as the commentator continued to talk, and pictures flashed across the screen. There were photographs of her parents, even a wedding picture—where had they obtained that? Then a picture of a burned motel cabin and another of the rest area.

They had been burned to death. Burning had always been Antonio's method of choice.

She felt numb first, followed immediately by sadness which was not quite grief. She couldn't cry. The people in the pictures were her parents, but they were really strangers she had decided to remove from her life long before they died.

She watched the television, seeing the reports and photographs again and again. She wondered with detachment what they had done to incur Antonio's wrath, as it did not occur to her that their deaths could be the responsibility of anyone other than Antonio. She was not horrified at the manner of their dying any more than she would have been if they had been strangers. Briefly she wondered where her brother was, and it was as this crossed her mind that she heard Ethan pounding on her door.

"Are you all right?" Ethan noted her pale, strained face.

She nodded. "I don't feel very well for some reason or another," she managed to say, but her voice was raspy.

"I think you have a cold." He laid his hand against her forehead. "No fever."

"I'll be fine." She didn't feel like talking, even to him.

"I just came over to tell you good-bye. I have to go back to New York, something has happened. There's been a Mafia double murder—something we might be interested in."

"Oh, no," she said in dismay, and Ethan took it as disappointment at his departure. Fiona couldn't believe he was going back to New York to investigate her parents' murders. It was just too bizarre. She was having a hard time taking it all in.

"I'll be back as soon as I can." He pulled her to him and whispered in her ear. "I love you."

"I love you, too," she responded dazedly, though he seemed not to notice her distracted state.

"I'll remember that." His eyes shone, then he kissed her and was gone.

That night she had the dream again, where she struggled with her father over the dollhouse. Only this time he finally handed it to her and stepped back. He stood several feet away, looking at her, his face so sad she began to cry and tried to give the dollhouse back to him. He shook his head...and then just faded away.

She awakened because her pillow was wet. Tears were still pouring from her eyes, tears for the years of being unloved, ignored, and unhappy, and tears because there now was no chance to make it right.

* * *

Fiona was glad Ethan's parents were there after he left. They all slid back into their comfortable patterns, Fiona helping in the house, but with plenty of freedom to go to the village and visit the newly married couple when they returned from their honeymoon.

Brenda and Adam were invited to Cliff House for New Year's Eve, when Margaret and Libby gave them their wedding gift. They had decided to go together to purchase a beautiful Waterford lamp, and Brenda's excited reaction showed they had made a good choice.

"Did Fiona tell you about the antique bed she bought us?" Brenda asked the older women. "Complete with mattress and springs."

"That was a very generous gift." Libby's quick mind was working, Fiona could tell.

"I have no expenses to speak of," Fiona casually stated. "And I had quite a bit of savings when I came here. I decided the bed was just the gift for Bren. She loved it when we saw it in the store." She paused briefly before continuing, "Do you have photos of the lighthouse and your room there?" She hoped her effort to change the subject wasn't too obvious.

"I'm picking them up tomorrow. Oh, Fiona, it was perfect. Thank you..." Fiona imperceptibly shook her head, but Brenda understood and stopped before she told Libby and Margaret that the honeymoon, too, had been provided by Fiona with help from Ethan. "I can't believe you found that lighthouse and told us about it," she finished gracefully.

"That would be a unique place for a visit." Libby had not seen the subtle exchange. "Maybe Keith and I will go there for a second honeymoon."

"You and Keith have already had a second honeymoon," Margaret reminded her dryly. "And a third, and a fourth..."

"Multiple honeymoons are better than multiple divorces!" Libby shot back, and Margaret nodded in agreement.

Fiona couldn't help laughing at the repartee. "I've missed you two," she said, and honestly meant it. But it had been nice to be alone with Ethan, and she missed him even more.

* * *

Enrico saw the news on a hotel television in Florida. He had traveled a circuitous route, finally making his way to sunshine and the beach.

So his parents were dead. He'd always been on good terms with Antonio. Maybe it was time to go back and claim his place in the family.

"Come on, Ricky! The waves are perfect today!" The redhead in the very revealing bikini did not enter the room. After two weeks with her, Enrico knew she was loathe to miss even a minute of the daylight. By the time she was thirty, he expected she'd look like someone's leather handbag, but right now, she looked very good. With his fake ID, he was officially 22, and he had been partying hard.

"I'll be right out." The girl obediently disappeared at his unspoken request, but he remained seated on the end of the bed, watching the reporter show photos of the places where his parents had died. He wondered why they hadn't been together, but doubted he'd ever know.

He'd tried. He'd taken a big risk in warning them to get out. But maybe Antonio could be convinced they'd fled because of Antonio's meeting with Gianni. Surely Antonio realized Gianni would have known he'd made a mistake? It was plausible to assume that Gianni fled without any outside warning.

He'd think about it and decide what to do. But right now, Lulu was waiting. With her looks and body, she wouldn't have trouble replacing him, if he ignored her.

He grabbed his gaudy beach towel and then ran for the sand. He was just in time. Two guys were standing beside Lulu's beach chair, but they backed off when he greeted them coolly. He had hinted to Lulu that he was tight with the Mafia, and she thought it was exciting to mention his "connection" to the men who flocked around her. With his dark good looks, it was easy for people to believe. It was often convenient, and he liked the power it gave him. Yes, he decided, he would soon go back to New York and reconnect with his brother-in-law.

THIRD ACT

The urgent request for Ethan's return to the office had been due to a break in a case on which he and Sam, along with myriad others on staff and in the FBI and ATF, had been working. The case had been at a stalemate when Ethan first arrived in New York, but he had been pulled into it almost immediately.

There were those rare days when you awakened just as you did every other day, ate the same breakfast, more or less, and then had something happen which changed your life irrevocably. Ethan had one of those his fourth day in the New York office.

The phone on the office secretary's cluttered desk rang repeatedly, and no one answered it. He didn't know where her backup was, the girl who usually came in from files, but he walked out to the vacant desk and picked up the phone. The woman's voice on the other end of the line was an informant whom he knew to be reputable and reliable, and she had information which made him sink down onto the cluttered surface of the desk, oblivious to the ballpoint pen which was marking his trousers. She told him who had been responsible for two high-profile murders in the Mafia, as well as the death of an undercover agent. She told him whom to contact for the proof, and more importantly, what they could do to induce him to talk.

Ethan had responded immediately, and once he had dealt with this new source, the woman refused thereafter to talk to anyone but him. From their first contact until the informant was placed in protective custody, Ethan was at his side. The young attorney was shoved into the limelight.

He had done very well in Boston too, well enough that his name was known by those in the upper levels of federal law enforcement agencies. That, too, had been something of a fluke. He'd been given what appeared to be a minor case to prosecute, but the investigation into the accused had uncovered major ties to the IRA's presence in the United States. The whole office had been busy, but Assistant United States Attorney Kendall had been assigned the case once it broke and began to expand.

Of course, he had been miffed that his work would largely be credited to someone else, but he accepted the inevitable. Then Kendall and another AUSA who also outranked Ethan were killed in a private plane crash on their way back from a trip to New York. Ethan had offered to go—the trip was to collect what they hoped would be pertinent evidence—but his offer had been declined.

The cause of the crash was still under investigation when the case became his. Over the course of a year he had built a perfectly balanced tower of evidence which he presented piece by piece. The first suspect was declared guilty and removed from the federal courthouse in an armored vehicle by way of an underground entrance. Several others were under indictment. AUSA Shane was a household name, at least in Bostonian legal circles.

Ethan had been ready to roll up his shirtsleeves and go to work on the subsequent cases when he was asked to transfer to New York, and his cases were handed to a couple of prosecutors who had assisted him. He was comfortable with that—the evidence was all there, all they needed to do was present it—and he liked the fact that he was moving to a city which could provide him with even more challenging, rewarding work. Even so, he had been awed by the twisting tentacles of the Mafia case into which he was unexpectedly thrown.

It was like doing a genealogy chart, he imagined. The marriages, feuds, murders, disappearances, and alliances were all important to know. Missing a tiny fact could make the entire picture go askew, and cause them to overlook an important nugget of evidence.

Sam and Ethan had somehow recognized one another as kindred spirits. Before his arrival, Ethan had heard about the workaholic without a personal life who lived in a barely furnished studio, but he was surprised when he met him. The man was not cold; he was insulated, because that was the only way he could survive. Like Ethan himself, his talents had drawn him into a career in which he excelled, but which was slowly destroying his sensitive soul.

Others might keep their distance from Sam, but Ethan felt comfortable talking to his superior. When he reached the office in the early hours of the morning after he left Seafair, he immediately approached Sam's office door. It was ajar, so Ethan pushed his way in.

"Hey, Sam, how was the holiday?"

"Good and bad." His solemn face smiled, but the smile changed into a half-grimace as he unloaded on Ethan. "Linda was great—always has been—the boy was fine, if a little distant. The grandkids were wonderful, but the girl..." He shook his head. "She's never going to forgive me, I guess, and I can't really fault her. I mean, a dad who doesn't make it to your wedding..."

It was clear that Sam had been sitting alone thinking about his past. "Guess you'll just have to keep plugging away," Ethan said, hoping that would be a helpful response.

"Maybe there's too much time that's passed, too much water under the bridge." He shuffled files aimlessly. "This is the only thing I'm good at. Guess that's why I'm here and not living on a farm." He looked out the grimy window. "But I gotta tell you, kid, I loved waking up and looking out over that clean, quiet land. Didn't hear a siren, a car horn, or a gunshot for days."

"Take it one day at a time, Sam. At least you have Linda on your side."

"Guess I've always had that, even when I didn't appreciate her."

He opened a thick file, pulled out a page of paper, then reinserted the paper and reclosed the file.

He looked up again at Ethan. "Funny thing happened when I was there. I got up in the night to go to the bathroom—you know, at my age, a guy never makes it through the entire night—and I automatically opened the door to my and Linda's old bedroom when I came back. She woke up and kinda laughed, but it sure as hell felt funny staying in what used to be my house but sleeping in the guest room."

"Maybe you'll make it back to the master bedroom if you play your cards right and have a little patience. You've earned retirement, Sam."

"I'm ready for it. I didn't want to come back. Even with my daughter barely civil to me, I wanted to stay."

"I didn't want to leave Seafair, either."

Sam sighed. "Well, we're both here for the present, and there's all hell breaking loose. If we get some of this taken care of, maybe I'll retire in the spring." Sam glanced at the stack of folders. "Maybe by Christmas, anyway." He grinned and Ethan took off, waving over his shoulder.

The file which had been on his desk when he left to meet his mother and grandmother for the pre-Christmas lunch was still there. This case was minor compared to the one they were pulling together now, but he glanced through it anyway. Once he became immersed in the procedure for prosecuting the big case—discussing strategy, lining up the order of witnesses for the most effectiveness, deciding who would be responsible for what part of the case—he would be out of touch with what was going on in the rest of the world. He didn't like the feeling, but that level of concentration was required.

As he had thought, this was the case of the small potatoes Mafia guy and his wife being killed in Pennsylvania. This would have to be shelved for now, but he couldn't resist glancing into it before putting it away indefinitely. There had to be a reason they died hundreds of miles apart, he knew. The fact that The Torch was their son-in-law certainly pointed the finger in his direction, but Antonio Scarpellini had been known to kill before without leaving enough evidence to convict him.

This Bellini guy had profited greatly while associated with The Torch. But it looked as though the relationship had started to deteriorate after the Bellini daughter was killed when the towers collapsed. A niece and her husband had also apparently been killed. An obituary with a photograph from a small town newspaper had been faxed to them, but it was fuzzy and he didn't take time to read it. Had the older man been nervous that he'd lost his connection to power? Had he tried too hard to maintain it?

Bellini had a young son, he noted. Dropped out of parochial school, spent a lot of money. Looked like he, too, was tight with The Torch. The boy was still alive, as far as anyone knew, whereabouts unknown. There was a picture of him paperclipped to the back on the short page with his data. He looked older than his stated age of 17. Living hard would do that to you. Ethan noted absently that the boy had an appendectomy scar and another scar, across his left cheek from a bicycle accident when he was six.

There was little information about the daughter. Not surprising, Ethan mused. She was probably no more than a bargaining chip between her husband and her father, used by the one to get more power by association with the other. She carried a scar on her right hand.

He was unclipping her photo when Sam appeared at the door. "We're going to have federal security on this case. Several of us are in the line of fire."

"We'll be fine." All the same, it wasn't a bad idea.

* * *

There were a lot of them working on the case, and they were all working long hours, so it was coming together nicely. They had gone over it again and again, and they were certain that they had as watertight a case as was possible. They were trying to move quickly, because both of the men being held were very powerful and prominent businessmen. They did not kid themselves that they were totally secure, even with their suspects in jail.

Ethan had awakened at three that morning with an idea for presenting a key piece of evidence. He'd gone to his computer and typed out a page, then been unable to go back to sleep. He'd sat in the room, drinking coffee and gazing at his untouched easel. He hadn't been able to use the photos in the album Fiona had made him. He had barely had time for a quick call to her cottage two days ago.

He was again swept into the swift current of the prosecution as soon as he entered the office before seven that morning. He took the page he had written that morning in to Sam, noting a stack of unopened mail on the older man's desk. On top was a card-shaped envelope, and the address was written in a feminine hand.

Ethan picked it up, noting the return address. "Hey, Sam, here's something from your daughter." He held it out, but Sam did not look up from the thick folder he was studying.

"Sam!"

"Huh?"

"This looks like it's from your daughter."

Sam's head jerked up, and he grabbed the envelope from Ethan's hand. Without another word, he made a ragged opening with his index finger.

It was a card. He read it, closed it, then read it again. Then he closed it a second time and held it out to Ethan.

"Happy Birthday, Dad." Ethan looked up. "It's your birthday?"

"Naw, read the rest."

"From your daughter," was the simple message inside. But

Melissa Lee had added, "I know it's not your birthday, but I'm trying to make up for the ones I missed. At least you never forgot to call on mine." And it was signed, "Love from your daughter."

"Hey, that's right up there with getting the bad guys."

"No, it's better than getting the bad guys. I just took a lot of years to realize that." Sam flipped some pages in his Rolodex, then dialed the phone with quick jabs. Ethan dropped his page of paper on the desk and started to back out of the office.

"Hi, sweetheart, I got your card," Sam began tentatively as Ethan closed the door behind him. "I can't tell you how much it meant to me…"

Ethan went to his own office. He pulled the business card out of his wallet, dialed the phone, and asked the secretary who answered for the manager. A click was followed by a throaty voice.

"I'm Ethan Shane," he said. There was a moment of silence when he could almost see the busy woman trying to recall where and when she had heard his name.

"I sell paintings through the co-op shop in Seafair, Maine."

"Oh, yes!" She sounded much friendlier now. "Lovely paintings. I'd like to talk to you about exhibiting here. Could you ship two or three to me?"

"Actually, I live in New York. But I don't have any paintings at the moment, except those hanging in the family homes in Seafair."

"Well, try to get at least a couple to me. Even small ones would be a start. Aren't you painting now?"

"I'm a federal prosecutor," he explained. "I haven't had much time for painting lately."

"With your talent, you must make time." She spoke emphatically. "Get those paintings to me." And the phone went dead.

He hung up and replaced the card, then retrieved it again. He dialed his parents' number and was relieved that his father answered. They spoke briefly, Ethan relating his conversation with the woman at the gallery.

"That sounds wonderful, son!" Keith was beginning to feel uneasy about his son's profession. He'd skated on the Boston deal, but this current one looked really dangerous to him. Besides, he knew his son was an artist at heart. "I'll talk your mother into releasing at least a couple of paintings, and we'll have Fiona and Brenda get them packed and mailed." Ethan quickly gave him the address, then told his father he had to go.

There was work to be done before he and Sam would be able to review their lives. They couldn't afford any mistakes.

* * *

Ethan had a wonderful idea shortly after hanging up the phone. Fiona hadn't been away from Maine in months and he really wasn't too happy about shipping his paintings (or so he told himself). Hurriedly, he redialed his father.

"Look, Dad, I think it might be a good idea for Fiona to deliver the paintings herself. She could use a break away from Maine and I don't really like to ship the paintings. She could get them here more quickly, too."

"And you could manage an evening off to take her to dinner, maybe the theatre?" Keith's amusement was obvious in his tone of voice.

"I could certainly try. At the very least, she could get a day or two of city life, do a little shopping."

"How thoughtful of you." Keith sounded as though he was restraining his laughter with only the utmost effort. "Wait a minute, son." He turned away from the receiver, but Ethan could hear him talking to someone about Ethan's suggestion.

"Your mom says that's an excellent idea. She thinks Fiona deserves a break. So give her a call and see if you can use your persuasive talents to talk her into visiting you."

"Not visiting me, Dad. She's delivering my paintings and taking a couple of days off."

"Sure. Tell yourself that." Keith was laughing as the connection ended.

Ethan was grinning himself as he dialed the number of Fiona's cottage. There was no answer, so he next tried his parent's house. Fiona picked up on the second ring.

"Hey, lady, how about a little vacation?"

"Ethan! Are you coming up to Seafair?"

"No, you're coming to New York. I need some paintings and Dad and I agree you should be the delivery person. You can come down in the Jeep and spend a couple of days with me. I *promise* to take you to dinner, and I'll try for an evening at the theatre. At the very least, we'll be together."

"I can't leave, I'm supposed to house-sit."

"I talked to Dad. He and Mom agree you are due a few days off. Brenda and Adam can go by the house once a day and check that everything is okay."

She wanted to see Ethan, and two or three days with him sounded heavenly, but she felt a chill when she contemplated going back to New York. "Oh, Ethan…"

"You have to come. Dad said so, and you know there are not many people in the country who would dare defy him."

"Except your mother and grandmother!" As always, his rare playfulness won her over. New York was enormous, there was no reason for her to be afraid to go there.

"Wrap up the paintings, pack a suitcase, and leave in the morning. Got a pen and paper? I'll give you directions to my apartment building and you can park in the lot there."

"I'm ready." She quickly wrote down the instructions he gave with succinct efficiency which changed to affectionate murmurings when they said good-bye. Ethan sounded excited, and she couldn't help but feel some excitement herself.

* * *

Fiona awakened early and didn't even try to go back to sleep. In the predawn hours, she carefully loaded the paintings into the Jeep and threw her suitcase onto the seat beside her. She hung up the padded hanger from which draped the slinky dress Brenda had convinced her to buy when the small, but very elegant women's shop in Seafair held its after-Christmas sale. The neckline was high, the sleeves long, the skirt below the knee, but it was the fit which showed the quality of the dress—and Fiona's curves. Brenda didn't know she had only been able to talk Fiona into the purchase because of the color. It was the azure blue of the sea, the hue which Ethan so loved.

There was snow on some of the roads, so the going was slow for a portion of her journey. Part of the way, she was able to drive the speed limit, but she didn't want to arrive earlier than late in the evening, so Fiona took her time. As she approached Manhattan, she briefly consulted the notes she had written from Ethan's instructions. Then she drove, without making a single incorrect turn, to his apartment.

The concierge had been told to expect her. He smiled warmly when she strolled into the lobby, the paintings under her arms, and rushed to assist her.

"Miss Patrick?" A cart appeared out of nowhere, and he carefully situated the paintings on it before turning back to Fiona. "I'm Reggie. If you'll tell me where your car is, I'll get your suitcases."

"Oh, thank you!" Fiona's gently shook the cramps from her arms. "It's in the second row, the Jeep." She held out the keys.

"I'll be right back, and then I'll take you up to Mr. Shane's apartment." The man was gone and back in little more than a minute. Then he led Fiona onto an elevator and they sped upward. After opening the door across from the elevator, Reggie handed the key to Fiona. "Mr. Shane said to make sure you have a key so you can come and go as you please."

"Thank you, Reggie." Fiona was fumbling in her purse when he returned from placing the items on the cart in the single bedroom.

"You're welcome, Miss Patrick," he smiled broadly. "Mr. Shane's taken care of everything." And he left before she could offer a tip.

Alone again, Fiona wandered about the small living space. It was attractive in a mass-arranged way, the placement of each piece of furniture and picture rigidly observing the basic rules of decorating without the odd chair or memento which would have given the rooms personal charm. She was sure that if she looked into every other suite of rooms on that floor, perhaps in the entire apartment hotel, they would have the identical arrangment. She hoped at least the palette of colors would be different. She couldn't imagine Ethan, an artist, living in rooms which contained only neutral browns and beiges.

The kitchen was tiny, and the bedroom was large enough only for the king-size bed and dresser. So Fiona was surprised to see that the bathroom was actually quite large. There was a big shower and an even bigger tub. Looking at the jets on the sides of the tub, her tired body began to imagine how good it would feel to sit in hot water and feel the swirling around her.

She opened her suitcase, quickly stuffing some items into the empty drawer she found in the dresser and hanging up the rest. Reggie had hung her dress in the closet. Carrying a silk gown and robe into the bathroom, and leaving only a single lamp on in the bedroom, she started to fill the tub. Before it was half filled, she climbed in, sliding down into the soothing liquid.

Fiona was half asleep in the shadows of the darkened room when she heard the sound of a closing door. She hoped the intruder was Ethan, because she really didn't think she could summon the energy to evade a burglar. There was only the faint light from the shaded lamp to illuminate Ethan's rugged features when he peeked around and saw her.

"Well, my dream come true, a sea nymph to greet me when I come home!" His voice was warm and low.

"Just a tired country bumpkin from the backwoods of Maine, sir, come to do your bidding."

"Come to do my bidding? Well, that's an intriguing offer!"

Fiona could feel herself blushing. "I didn't mean *that*! I meant I brought your paintings, as you asked me to do."

Ethan was pulling off his tie and unbuttoning his shirt. He scraped his loafers off, rubbing the expensive leather of the toe against the heel of the other shoe. "Oh, we both know the paintings could have been shipped safely and quickly enough." His voice was almost without inflection and very, very soft. "We both know why I wanted you to come." His belt buckle clattered against the tile floor. "We both know why you agreed to come."

The level of the water rose as he settled into the enormous tub. "Um-m-m, do you know I've never been in this tub before?"

She was no longer sleepy. Her eyes opened and she looked into his own smoldering gaze. "You always use the shower?" Her voice was so quiet, no one else could have heard her even if they had been in the same room.

"Just the shower." His hand floated through the water to rest—very lightly—on her shoulder. "Although even the shower, now that I look at it with you here, might have its attractions. It's a *very large* shower, did you notice?"

* * *

They were sitting together on the wide, surprisingly comfortable sofa, wrapped in matching robes of soft terrycloth when it occurred to Fiona that she had not eaten since noon and it was now after

10pm. She sat up, lifting her head from Ethan's shoulder, to look at him.

"Have you had dinner, Ethan?"

"I had a late lunch. Are you hungry?" He stood up and walked toward the kitchette. "I can scramble eggs, make a toasted cheese or offer you a frozen dinner, although that will take awhile. Or," he glanced over his shoulder with a smile, "we could order room service."

"Room service," Fiona said without hesitation.

"Don't like my cooking skills, huh?" Ethan reached for the Room Service menu.

"I think you are truly the most *skilled* man in the world," she answered saucily. "But nothing in your cooking repertoire appeals to me at the moment."

He chuckled, told her he thought he'd order a club sandwich with a piece of pie and handed the menu to her. "I'll try to think of something which will *appeal* to you…later," he said.

They were being silly, she knew, but she liked being silly with Ethan. And she liked that he was able to drop his serious, oh-so-earnest-federal-prosecutor personna with her. "I'll have the shrimp salad," she said, then watched as he dialed the phone and ordered, fascinated with his long, strong fingers and the way his thick eyelashes shadowed his strong cheekbones as he spoke.

"What's so interesting?" He replaced the receiver and turned back toward her.

"You," she answered honestly. "I like to look at you. You have beautiful hands, wonderful cheekbones, and eyelashes which would make a model envious."

"Hm-m-m, never thought of myself as handsome."

"Not handsome," she countered, then grinned when he bristled in mock anger. "Better than handsome. You're interesting, extremely attractive, and exciting."

"And *you* are beautiful." He leaned toward her, and only a knock at the door several minutes later could separate them.

* * *

It was late in the morning when Fiona finally forced herself from the rumpled bed. She only vaguely remembered Ethan's goodbye kiss on the back of her neck and his quiet assurance that he had hung the 'Do Not Disturb' sign on their door. She supposed it was too late now to expect maid service, so she made the bed herself and wandered over to the little kitchen.

Right now, scrambled eggs sounded good, and their appeal increased when she noticed two types of cheese in the refrigerator. She whipped up three, added cubes of both cheeses, then pulled a chair to the window so she could look outside while she ate. New York seemed almost foreign to her after all her months away. Maine was home now. But she enjoyed observing the traffic and pedestrians rushing about below. And she could get a fairly good view of Central Park when she moved her chair a little to the right.

She had no intention of going out today. If Ethan was able to leave the office in time, she supposed they would go out to dinner. Otherwise, room service would be fine with her. Just being with Ethan was all she wanted.

Ethan did, indeed, get away early—although few people would consider an eleven-hour workday short. He had arrived shortly after eight, a little late for him, and locked his office door behind him just before seven that evening. He breezed into the apartment with a smile on his face.

"Want to go out to dinner, Honey?" His voice roused her from the sofa where she had been napping, an old movie on the television providing background noise.

"Whatever you want to do." She stood up as he reached her,

hugging him back and welcoming his enthusiastic kiss.

"I saw the pretty dress," he smiled down at her, holding her close. "I want to show you off before you return to the woods without me."

"Hardly the woods," she corrected him. "I'm a sea nymph, remember? I live by the ocean."

"Oh, yes, I must have confused you with someone else. Must have been a wood fairy in my past."

"Then stay out of the woods, sir, because you belong by the ocean."

He sighed. "I do, indeed. I wish I could live there." But he smiled again as he pulled free. "A quick shower, a white shirt and an evening suit, and I'll be ready to go."

He turned at the door. "Care to join me?"

"Then we'd be back to room service for dinner." She made a face at him.

"If I didn't want to see you in that dress…" His voice floated back and she soon heard the shower turn on. She went into the bedroom to check her makeup and get ready.

Ethan reentered the bedroom, wrapped in the terry robe, minutes after the water stopped. Fiona pivoted to meet his gaze.

"Wow! I may change my mind. I'm not sure I want anyone else to see you in that dress!" He stood there, staring.

"You like?"

"Oh, yeah, lady, I like!" He headed toward her, but she laughed and evaded him.

"I'm hungry, Ethan. Get ready." With effort, she made her voice sound stern. She left him there, fleeing to the safety of the living room.

* * *

"I called Chez Pierre." Ethan held Fiona's hand as their elevator descended. He had fastened the velvet cape snuggly around her before they left the apartment, giving her a quick kiss. She couldn't remember when she had felt so safe, so cared for, so happy. "Does French food sound good to you? If not, we can go somewhere else."

"That sounds fine." She had been there, but only a couple of times, and the food was excellent. It was the type of restaurant where Ethan's evening clothes and her beautiful dress would be expected attire.

Reggie commented that they made a handsome couple as he hailed a taxi. "Have a good evening," he called as he closed the door of the car, and Fiona waved to him.

"You are devastatingly good-looking tonight," she said as she turned back to look at her escort. "You look quite distinquished."

"And *you* look very beautiful." Ethan's arm pulled her back so she rested against his side. "Your hair's a little shorter, isn't it? And I like the eye makeup." He peered down into her face.

"It's fun to dress up and play with makeup sometimes."

"Do you miss the city?"

"No," she answered honestly. "I like being here with you, but I prefer Seafair. And I love my tiny cottage."

"Would you be willing to live here for me?"

She was afraid where the conversation might be leading. Under normal circumstances, she would have been willing to leave Seafair for Ethan, but she knew she would never be safe in New York. It was only a matter of time until she ran into someone she knew, someone who knew her. And there were a lot more people who knew Emilia than Fiona. Almost anyone she met would assume she was Emilia, and she wasn't sure she would be able to act convincingly enough to keep suspicions from reaching her husband.

Her husband. Ethan's question might be leading up to another, more dangerous one. If he asked her to marry him, what could she say?

"Please, no serious questions tonight, Ethan." She hoped her expression and her tone of voice were as carefree as she was attempting to appear. "Let's just have fun tonight. You are long overdue for fun."

"I always have fun with you." But he didn't persue whatever he had intended to ask.

The taxi pulled up in front of a building of quiet elegance. The facade was subdued with a green and gold striped awning leading to massive oak doors with a single *fleur de lis* carved on each. But the interior was much grander, with tall, full flower arrangements on side tables, mirrored walls of beveled glass, Impressionist paintings, and small bouquets on the diners' tables flanked by candles in crystal holders. Everything sparkled in the light cast by the heavy crystal candeliers.

They were escorted to a secluded table on the raised floor near the tall windows overlooking Rockefeller Center and far from the kitchen. It was not a table offered to just anyone, Fiona realized. Ethan was obviously known here.

At the same time, Ethan was wondering with whom Fiona had dined at Chez Pierre. He had noticed that she didn't seem overwhelmed by the opulence of the place as everyone was on their first visit. His overly-developed instincts told him with certainty that she had eaten there. When he had mentioned Chez Pierre, it had been evident that she knew about it. But that hadn't surprised him. Most people who lived in Manhattan, or socialized there, were aware of the very famous restaurant.

He felt the smallest tinge of suspicion. Fiona had obviously been accustomed to 'living high' as Margaret liked to call it. Where was her family? Who were they? And why had she fled to Maine?

He was asking himself the same questions he had asked his mother and grandmother when they first told him about her. And now he had an additional question or two. Why didn't Fiona ever speak to, or of, her family? And how did she have so much money at the age of 20? He suddenly remembered something that had niggled at the back of his mind for months. His mother had told him

Fiona had never held a job. *So where had her money come from?*

"Ethan?" Fiona leaned across the table, a look of concern on her beautiful face. He looked into her dark eyes and saw only love there, no hint of guile or dishonesty. Ethan had met more than his share of criminals, some of them incredibly crafty, but he had never met any who could portray Fiona's level of sincerity and innocence. Despite the dull knell of warning bells, he was willing to believe that she loved him. He was willing to bet his heart on it.

"Ethan?" Fiona repeated. He forced himself to smile, half ashamed that he could even doubt Fiona's goodness. There had to be plausible answers to his questions. She would give them to him eventually.

"I've only known Ethan the artist," Fiona murmured, "but I think I was maybe getting a glimpse of Ethan the prosecutor?"

"I'm sorry," he apologized as he took her small hand in his. He didn't say he was mostly sorry for his thoughts. "I promised to leave my job early tonight, didn't I? It's not much good to leave the office if I take the worries with me."

"I prefer Ethan the painter," she said. "I think you must be a formidable attorney!"

"So they say," but he was smiling then. "I don't think you'll ever need to fear me, though."

A shadow was in her eyes for just a moment before the softness returned. "I hope not." He would have believed she was serious if he hadn't known that she couldn't possibly be.

The waiter appeared, and Ethan ordered for them, including a bottle of good wine. The next two hours were blissfully spent in quiet conversation as they enjoyed the food and drink as well as one another's company.

They were quiet in the taxi which returned them to the apartment. Reggie opened the door with a greeting when they arrived. They smiled and murmured a good evening as they walked past him.

"Now that's a couple in love if I ever saw one," Reggie remarked to the longtime resident who had been visiting with him, a lonely widower who often paused to chat on his way in or out of the building.

"Yep, I hear he's a big wheel prosecutor, but he looks plain smitten with that little girl," Hal Drewer replied. "Remember being young and in love, Reggie?"

"I remember being young," Reggie answered. "But I don't have to remember being in love, 'cause I still am. I'm just plain crazy about that sassy little wife of mine!"

"How long you been married, Reggie?" The older man looked mildly surprised.

"Thirty-seven years, ever since I was 19."

"That's somethin,' Reggie."

* * *

"I meant to suggest a carriage ride after dinner," Ethan remembered as the elevator sped toward their floor. "Do you want to take one? Reggie could get us a another taxi."

"No, it's late," Fiona said. "And you'll be up early tomorrow, no matter how little sleep you get tonight." She glanced coyly up at him through her lashes.

"All I do when you're not here is work and sleep," Ethan said, dropping a kiss on her smooth, shining hair. "I can get by on very little sleep for several days, longer if I can talk you into staying."

"I guess I need to go back tomorrow." Fiona sighed.

"Not tomorrow."

"Your mother or grandmother might call. I'm supposed to be house sitting."

"They know you were bringing the pictures to me. Dad was going to tell them *he* suggested you do it, so they would get here quickly."

He was also planning to mention that you hadn't been away from Seafair in five months."

"So Keith knows about us?"

"Strongly suspects," Ethan answered. "Actually, I'm sure he knows, but he hasn't asked any questions and I haven't volunteered any information. My mother and grandmother may still see me as a toddler, but Dad has no such illusions."

"So your father knows you are usually romantically involved with one girl or another?" She knew it was a silly question which implied an insecurity she really didn't feel about him.

He tipped her chin up so he could look into her eyes. His were somber as he spoke. "Dad knows I'm romantically involved with *you.* And he knows I'm not a frivolous guy who chases anything in skirts." He pulled her close. "Dad probably realizes I'm in love with you."

He started to kiss her, but pulled back with a grin. "So are you sure you don't want to be serious? Because it just occurred to me that Dad might be more certain of my feelings for you than you are!"

She didn't know how to answer without possibly falling into the quagmire of a marriage proposal. She was saved by the door gliding open.

"Ethan!" She remembered something as they entered the stiff decor of the living room. "You forgot to take the pictures to the gallery!"

"You can do that for me tomorrow, hm-m-m?"

"But I need to get back. Libby and Margaret aren't going to believe it took me four days and three nights to deliver a few paintings to New York!"

"Trust Dad to run interference," Ethan soothed her worries. "The day after tomorrow will be soon enough," he guided her toward the bedroom. "The day after tomorrow will be *too* soon."

Within minutes, Fiona forgot she was worried about her employers discovering how long she had stayed in New York with

Ethan. She was willing to leave that possible problem to Keith.

* * *

Fiona was vaguely aware of the sound of the alarm the next morning. When Ethan came into the bedroom from the shower, she could hear him dressing, but her eyes preferred to stay shut. She couldn't believe how blissful she felt. She and Ethan belonged together. Right now, she wasn't going to allow herself to dwell on the fact that their being together was impossible.

"Are you awake, lazy girl?"

"The romance is over," she responded, barely lifting her eyelids. "I was the sea nymph, a beauty, etc. etc., and now—so quickly!—I am reduced to the title of 'lazy girl.'"

"Ah, well, you couldn't expect to fool me forever." He was surprised to see Fiona's eyes fly open in what almost appeared to be alarm. But the alarm, if that was what it had been, quickly vanished. "I was bound to figure out that you were lazy if you refuse to ever leave the bed," he finished.

"Actually I thought I'd go to the gallery. Those paintings really do need to be delivered before I leave, and then I thought I might do a little shopping."

"Good idea," Ethan pulled on his cashmere coat. "I'll be back as soon as I can. Want me to make reservations some place swanky?"

"I only brought the one dress."

"Ah, I could never grow tired of you in that azure blue dress."

"I'll wear it for you in the cottage the next time you come to Seafair," she promised lightly. "We did the elegant dining thing last night, don't you have a little neighborhood restaurant which you like to visit?"

"Not neighborhood, but there is a restaurant my family has loved for years. The food's really good."

"Sounds perfect."

"Casual dress. We'll go as soon as I break the chains that hold me to my desk, okay?"

"I'll be waiting for you."

* * *

The paintings caused great excitement at the gallery. Fiona met the assistant to the manager, a slight young man who was somewhat overly effusive, but likeable. He lost no time in mounting the paintings on the wall in prime locations.

"Tell him to send more as soon as he can." The words followed Fiona as she exited through the door.

Ethan might someday be able to make a living painting, Fiona thought as she headed toward Bloomingdale's. He might be lucky enough to have that particular dream come true. If only his dream which included her wasn't impossible…

She found several things to purchase as she made her way through the shopping district. She had retrieved her sunglasses from the glove compartment of the car, and her hair was newly dyed, so she felt little fear. But she found herself looking quickly around whenever she was in a crowd. At her final stop, Tiffany's, she chose a pair of sterling earrings for Brenda. Then she returned to the apartment.

Fiona took a shower and dressed in a calf-length skirt of softly swirling fine black wool and a pink cashmere sweater. She applied a little more makeup than she usually wore, remembering Ethan had admired her eyes the evening before. Then she sat down to wait.

The phone soon rang. "Honey, would you mind taking a taxi and meeting me?" Ethan asked. "I have to make a call before I leave, then I'm only a few blocks away from the restaurant. If you don't mind my wearing my work clothes, we'll save a lot of time if you leave now."

"I think you'll be passable in work clothes," she answered. "It's not as though you left here wearing overalls and work boots this morning."

"I'm a little rumpled, though," he said. "And there's an ink mark on my cuff."

"Oh, dear, maybe I'll pretend I don't know you then," she laughed. "I'm on my way."

"Thanks, darlin.'"

"Don't get caught up in that call and forget me."

"Oh, honey, there's no way I could ever forget you. I promise you that!" He was chuckling as he hung up the phone.

Without her sunglasses, she felt very exposed and vulnerable. But, as the restaurant came into sight, Fiona was also feeling the familiar excitement that anticipating a meeting with Ethan always caused. The taxi driver opened the door for her and she had her foot nearly on the pavement when she recognized the man exiting the building next to where she was to go. She lunged back into the cab, unaware of the man who watched from the table in the deep window.

"Drive around the block!" She hissed at the startled driver. "Hurry! Get out of here!"

The man ran around the car and they took off, only to be mired in traffic at the far corner. But the man who had so frightened Fiona, her husband's righthand man, had been walking in the other direction when they sped past. She was sure he hadn't seen her.

It took several minutes to make the trip around the block, but the taxi driver asked no questions. And he was very grateful for the generous tip she gave him.

* * *

Ethan was standing by the table in the window, quite close to the entrance, when Fiona rushed into the restaurant. Being outside, on the sidewalk, made her feel vulnerable.

"What happened?" Ethan brushed her lips in an almost-kiss. "I saw you getting out of the taxi nearly ten minutes ago, and then you jumped back in and the taxi sped off."

"Oh, I was sure I'd given the driver the wrong address," she lied quickly. "I didn't remember the restaurant's name, and I thought we were at the wrong one. Then I found where I'd written the address down, and this was the right place after all."

She laughed shakily. "I feel silly now. I'm sorry if I worried you." She sounded as though she were lying, she thought. But Ethan let the subject drop. He probably knew she was lying, but couldn't imagine why, she decided. Or else he *did* believe her to be a silly dimwit.

"Our table is over here," Ethan pulled her with him toward the window. "I met my mother and grandmother here before Christmas, and this is the table they always like to get. They say they enjoy watching the people going by."

What if someone walked by and saw her sitting there? Fiona's throat seemed to close up at the possibility.

"I really don't like for people to gawk at me in a window, Ethan. I'd feel like a mannequin on display sitting there. Do you think we could possibly have another table, one that is away from the window?"

Ethan looked at her quizzically. He thought her behavior odd, she knew. She hoped he didn't think it suspicious. It was only a matter of time until everything blew up between them, but she didn't want it to be now, not yet. Even as she thought that, she knew it wouldn't be any better if he discovered the truth in the future. She would always be wishing for just another day with him. And the last day had to arrive sometime. It was inevitable.

"Just a minute." Ethan pulled away and approached a very rotund man who was swathed in a pristine apron. He looked up at Ethan with a wide grin, listened to his request, then shrugged and regretfully shook his head. After a few more words, Ethan returned to where Fiona stood, sheltered by a coat rack by the door.

"They are completely full tonight, Fiona. I called and ask that Carlo hold the table for us, and that's the only one he has available." She felt like a petulant brat. Oh, well, what did it matter if someone saw her? She was going to lose Ethan and she might also lose her life. She was getting weary of being afraid all the time. "I'm sorry to be so difficult, Ethan." Resolutely, she headed toward the big bay window. "I'm sure this will be fine."

"Are you sure? We could go somewhere else." He followed her and held out her chair even as he spoke.

"Not when Carlo held your favorite table for you. It would be awfully rude of us to leave and Libby and Margaret would never forgive me if I made him angry!" She laughed, trying to lighten the mood.

She saw the confusion in Ethan's eyes as he studied her. But he didn't ask any more questions.

"This will be okay?" Carlos was at her elbow.

"Yes, I'm sorry if I caused any problems." Fiona smiled up at the anxious man, putting all the warmth and charm she could into her expression. "I've never sat in the window before, but now that I've thought about it, I'm sure I'll like watching the people walk by."

Carlos's smile was worth the effort it was costing her to conquer her fear. "Good, good. There are some very interesting people in this neighborhood." With a little bow which was unexpectedly graceful, he left.

"I think I'm just a little strange tonight, thinking about having to leave tomorrow, Ethan." The words were true, but they also were ones which might allay his suspicions.

"I've thought about that all day, too." Ethan's wary look disappeared. "You in Maine and me in New York isn't the ideal situation."

"It will all work out," she managed to smile, but she was thinking that the way it was going to work out wasn't going to be nearly as satisfactory as the present situation.

The mood was better the rest of the evening. And Fiona, who had turned her chair slightly so she wasn't fully visible, actually ate every bite of the delicious lasagna which Carlos served them himself.

"Thank you so much, Carlos." She shook his hand as they prepared to leave. "The food was delicious, the service was wonderful, and I may only eat in restaurants with window tables from now on!"

Carlos's hand was surprisingly strong. "Come again, I am so happy you enjoyed the evening. Please come again." He was nodding and smiling as Ethan escorted her to the waiting taxi which he had called.

"See, it wasn't so bad, was it?" he asked when they were settled into the back seat of the car.

"No, I forgot all those people outside, because I was fascinated with you."

"You were fascinated with the food, not me! I've never seen you put away so much food!"

"Oh, I was a pig, hm-m-m? You were chowing down, too."

"I admit, I'd weigh a ton if I indulged at Carlos's too often. I'm weak and I can't resist temptation." The cab was at his apartment building and he jumped out and reached back to assist her.

"You can't? I'll have to remember that." She laughed up at him.

"You already knew that." He bent to whisper in her ear as they passed Reggie. They both waved at the concierge, but they were too occupied with one another to speak.

They snuggled in the elevator and then rushed through the living room and into the bedroom as soon as Ethan pulled the key from the lock.

"What were you saying about that shower?" Having kicked off her shoes just inside the door, Fiona was hopping about, trying to pull off her stockings.

"I can't really tell you about the shower. It's wonderful attributes require that you *experience* it, a shower tour so to speak." His jacket and belt were already on the easy chair and the rest of his clothing was quickly being discarded.

"A shower tour? What an original idea." Fiona was on her way to the bathroom. She looked over her shoulder. "Come on slowpoke, you're the one who knows all the points of interest on this tour."

"Believe me, the tour is going to include points of interest I've never seen myself in that shower." Ethan caught up with her and pulled her in behind him, closing the heavy glass door. They were both laughing as the warm water cascaded over them.

* * *

Ethan was half an hour early to work the next morning. Fiona had awakened at five, and she wanted to be on her way by six, but he used his considerable skills of persuasion to convince her to stay a little longer.

He finally kissed her one last time before he closed the door of the Jeep. When she pulled out of the garage, he watched until the car's taillights were no longer visible in the morning gloom. He didn't want to return to the apartment for breakfast. He realized he wouldn't ever be able to go there without wishing Fiona was waiting to welcome him. And there was a strange sense of dread, a sadness, that settled in him as he headed toward the office.

Fiona, meanwhile, was swamped by a similar grief. Would these days be the last she and Ethan would spend together? Tears slid from her eyes, but she determindedly kept driving. She was helpless to control what was going to happen. There was a certain relief in finally admitting that much.

* * *

By March the prosecution felt their case was coming together. They were about to make a very big hole in organized crime leadership. With the defendants in jail and bond denied by the federal judge, the effects were already being felt in the city and its boroughs.

One quiet evening, Ethan and Sam took a rare break and joined two other prosecutors for dinner. The restaurant was near the office, a small place with small windows, but out of habit they requested a table at the back anyway. It didn't hurt to be safe.

The food was good, better than Ethan had tasted in a long time. Fast food gulped hurriedly down was the norm for him lately, but the case was firming up nicely, and soon he and Sam would be able to pass more responsibilities on to the less experienced attorneys in their office. It would be a relief to place the major case on his mental backburner, at least until the trial began. He was looking forward to resuming work on the lower-profile Bellini case.

They had a quiet and enjoyable meal punctuated with laughter and, though it was not the custom, they actually talked about things other than work. Sitting in the warm little restaurant tucked away from the street, Ethan thought he would never have known he was in New York City, and felt as though he could have been in a small town anywhere in the country, away from all the bustle and stress. With a slight pang he realized how badly he missed Seafair.

Ethan and Sam left together, their co-workers wishing them a goodnight at the door and walking briskly in the other direction. They went slowly together through the cool evening, speaking rarely, and Ethan slowed his pace just a little to match the older man's. Ethan was still thinking of Seafair, and when Sam spoke it was of the rural life he missed, echoing Ethan's thoughts.

Ethan returned home full of affection for his mentor and hopeful they would both find some peace when this trial had ended. He knew it was time for him to slow down, and, when he finally climbed into bed, his attorney mind was putting together arguments to convince Sam to retire.

He overslept the next morning, which was something he never did. When he awoke to see bright sun filling his room, he leaped out of bed with a curse, jumped in the shower, and was at his office half an hour later. Rushing through the door, he was amused to see that apparently Sam had slept deeply too, as his office was still closed, and his secretary had not yet heard from him.

"Better give him a wake-up call," Ethan laughed as he passed her.

At noon, Judith, an office page, was sent to Sam's apartment because he wasn't answering his phone or his pager. At first Ethan had been reluctant to pull out all the stops in finding Sam, since his boss deserved the rest, but it was so unlike Sam to come in late that Ethan was becoming concerned.

Sam's secretary tapped lightly on Ethan's door before entering. "Judith called and said she didn't get any answer at his apartment. The doorman saw him come home last night and is pretty sure he didn't go out again."

Ethan was trying to be reasonable. He fervently hoped Sam had left in the middle of the night and boarded a plane home. "We'll give it a little more time," he said, but his increasing worry made him unable to focus on his work that afternoon. More messages were sent to Sam's pager, with no response.

At six o'clock, the police retrieved a key from Sam's superintendent and entered his apartment. Sam was in an armchair in the living room, still seated where he had collapsed the previous night when he felt the pain in his chest as he came through the door. One shoe was off, and his tie had been loosened. That had been all he had time to do. Ethan was waiting downstairs and was given the news by the ranking officer. The grief he felt was sharp and deep. Ethan walked out into the brisk evening breeze. Sam had not boarded a plane as he had hoped, but he had definitely gone home.

* * *

The Shanes were out at dinner when Keith's cell phone rang insistently. They were treating Adam and Brenda, as well as Fiona, to seafood at a restaurant up the coast from Seafair. Their after dinner coffee was just being served when Keith stepped outside to take the call. When he returned to the table to give them the news of Sam's death, his face was sober. Libby was dismayed, but Adam and Brenda had only heard Sam's name in passing. Only Fiona knew how unhappy Ethan would be now.

Keith took a deep breath. "He's really upset. They'd become good friends. He said he'd been trying to get Sam to retire." He looked around for the waiter, suddenly anxious to get home.

"Can I pay you?" he asked the hovering maitre d'. Keith took care of the check quickly, and they exited the restaurant into the quiet evening.

Fiona was uncertain as to whether she should call, though she wanted very much to comfort Ethan. Her phone rang before dawn the next morning. "I can't talk long. I just wanted to hear your voice."

"I'm sorry about Sam." She was unsure what she should say, though a great deal was on her mind. She had little experience with this kind of situation, and she hadn't seen Ethan in weeks. "Get some rest, please, Ethan. If you need something, please let me know."

"I love you. I just need to know you're there."

Those words restored her faith. Until then, she was beginning to wonder if Ethan's feelings might have changed in the time they had been apart. It had been hard for her to accept that his job was so demanding.

"I love you too, Ethan," she said with all the feeling she could put into it.

Then he said a quick goodbye and was gone.

Later in the morning, the phone rang again. This time it was Libby. "Ethan called to say he's doing fine," she dutifully reported.

Fiona didn't tell her he had called her before calling them. "Thank you, Libby."

Libby told her to stop by later if she wanted, and they said goodbye.

* * *

Over the course of the next two weeks, Ethan was able to finalize most of what needed to be done before his colleagues could take over the case. He only took a break long enough to accompany Sam's body on its journey back to the midwest, where he met Linda and Sam's children. The night before the funeral, he talked with Linda until nearly dawn. He found her to be a kind, intelligent woman, and he mourned Sam's loss even more than Linda's and his own. Immediately after the funeral he returned to New York, where he went back to work with a vengeance. His single goal was to tie up the loose ends of this case as quickly as was humanly possible.

Ethan felt as though he hadn't slept in a week, and he had rarely stopped work long enough for a real meal, but by the first of April he finished what needed to be done, and he didn't want to think about this case ever again. He was more interested in a message from the gallery manager. She had sold the two paintings his father had wrestled from his mother and grandmother (neither had been willing to give up more), and wanted at least another half dozen. Of course, Libby and Margaret wanted the blank walls in their houses refilled.

There was the Bellini case to look into. But first he was going home.

* * *

Enrico summoned up the courage to call Antonio from Florida. "Come on home," his brother-in-law said. "I can always use a good man."

He hated to leave the beach and the beautiful companions he had so enjoyed, but Enrico liked to spend money, and he was running out. The best and easiest way that he knew to earn more was to work for Antonio.

When he stopped his Harley in the circle driveway, having had the iron gates opened as soon as he approached, Enrico felt strange. The last time he had been here, his sister had been mistress of the house. Now she was...well, he knew where she was, but no one else did. He tucked that knowledge away, to be used sometime when it might prove handy.

"Enrico!" Antonio beckoned to him from his study, and greeted him more warmly than he had hoped. "How have you been? You disappeared after I told you to leave your parents' home."

"I believe you when you say something."

"Yes, but I was disturbed that your parents also left. Did they have an idea about my plans?" He held his head to one side, smiling slightly.

Cold rippled up Enrico's spine as he recognized the look in Antonio's eyes. He willed himself to speak clearly and calmly, to look as though he was telling the truth. "They were packing to go when I stopped in to get some things. Papa said he had told you he had information he could give the feds about you. He knew he shouldn't have lost his temper and said that." All of those words were truthful.

"So you didn't warn them." It wasn't really a question.

"No. I swear it, Antonio." Now he was telling lies. This meeting wasn't going the way he had thought it would.

"What kind of son doesn't warn his parents they are about to be killed?" Antonio wondered aloud. The odd smile was still there. "Do you know about the information Gianni had? Do you know where he kept it?"

"No, I didn't even know it existed until he told me that night."

"But he didn't tell you where it was? That night, when he knew he was in danger of dying, he didn't pass this valuable information to you?"

"No, Antonio, I swear it…no." He couldn't control the strain in his voice, but he was telling the truth. His father hadn't told him what the information was, but he had told him what to hide in case The Torch destroyed their house. He had taken it back just yesterday evening, driving the family car to the garage and returning the contents to the rooms where they belonged. The value of most of the items he'd been told to rescue was obvious. There was only the one thing which it seemed silly to bother to save.

"I must be honest, boy, I am bothered by your lack of loyalty to your parents."

What could he say? If he admitted he'd told his father he knew Antonio was up to something, he was doomed. But now Antonio faulted him for not trying to save his parents.

"I don't know how I could ever trust you. How could I know you would be loyal to me? I can only judge you by your actions, and you have shown a lamentable lack of this necessary quality in the past."

"I'd be loyal to you, Antonio." He was feeling desperate. His brother-in-law was cruelly playing with him, and he was frantically trying to think of a way to save himself, for he knew his fate was about to be decided.

"Look, Antonio, I know something you need to know." He would give Antonio the one thing that should convince him of his allegiance.

The man flicked ashes from his cigar into the Murano glass ashtray, and looked up with a quizzical expression. Enrico could see he was getting bored. His own time was running out.

"Emilia is alive. She wasn't killed in the attack on the Twin Towers." The words came out in a rush, the last almost gasped as Antonio came around the desk, grasped him by the collar, and nearly pulled him off his feet.

"What the hell are you talking about?" His voice was deathly quiet, all the more emphatic for the restraint it conveyed. "Where is she?"

"In Seafair, Maine. She works in a craft shop there."

Antonio glared into his face, then released him and stepped back. "Dominic!" His second-in-command instantly appeared.

"This little rat has no loyalty. He is not worthy of being a member of our family." He sneered at the shaking boy who was reaching for him. "Find a pair of concrete boots to fit him."

He turned and walked to the window, pulling the heavy drapes aside so they did not block his view of the spring garden. But he did not see the early flowers, he did not even hear his brother-in-law's frantic pleas, because he was planning what he would do to his faithless wife.

RIPTIDE

As April brought a touch of green to the landscape of Maine, Ethan gratefully took a leave of absence from his job and traveled homeward. He had painted only two small landscapes from the photographs Fiona had made for him, both immediately after his return from Sam's funeral. It had felt good to simply concentrate on beauty. Debora Foxe, the gallery manager, had seemed very pleased with them and was eager to advance their working relationship.

With spring making inroads against the stubborn chill of winter, Ethan wanted to get a last glimpse of the snow against the rough seas, and convey the almost silver gray of daybreak before it dissolved into vibrant hues of rose and peach. He had felt too raw to be able to resume his life with his family after the death of Sam and the grittiness of his work, but the soothing act of recreating life on canvas had somehow been a balm.

He went into the office on the way out of town. He parked his car in the employees' lot. It was filled with painting paraphernalia and clothing. He could stay in Maine, if he chose to do so, and he had to admit that thought was prominent in his mind. He'd have to arrange to have his few mementoes and the trunk in which they were stored shipped, but none of his furniture, dishes, or miscellaneous belongings meant anything to him. For all he cared, the super could donate them to charity.

He was ready to settle down, take a chance on making a living as a painter, get married to Fiona. They could stay in the cottage until they were financially able to either enlarge it (he smiled at the thought of children) or buy something else—although he couldn't imagine not living on the cliff. The cliff had, quite literally, been the rock in his life. When they traveled while his father was in the Navy, they had known it was there, waiting for them. It was home.

He talked to the attorneys about cases. Those who had begun work on the Bellini case reported that the FBI case agent was now sure that The Torch had, for whatever reason, ordered the deaths of his in-laws. There was new information that Enrico had been in Florida, but had returned to New York and then immediately disappeared again. A usually reliable source claimed he had been seen visiting his brother-in-law. Were the two partners in killing the Bellinis? Or had Antonio finished off the heir of the family, too?

Right now, Ethan didn't much care. He might have to come back, but this case wouldn't be his. Someone else was going to get any glory gleaned from dousing The Torch. It was like sweating with effort to hoist a sail and then seeing it fill with air, becoming incredibly graceful as it turned to and fro with the wind. Crime had been a weight on his soul, but now he felt freed.

He made only a single quick stop on his way home. He slowed down to a crawl as he neared the co-op. He was trying to determine if Fiona was in the shop, but he couldn't tell if the quick glimpse he caught of someone disappearing into the storage room was her or not. Just in case, he parked farther down the street and walked back. He had been thinking of this moment for months, but he was surprised at how excited he was, both to be home and at the prospect of seeing Fiona again. His heart was pounding in his chest as he approached the shop.

She was there. She had just carried in a large box of linens and was methodically arranging them on a shelf.

"Tomorrow, Brenda, you can mess with these things," she called to the woman who was tugging an enormous crate into the shop. "By the time I try this position and that position, everything needs to be ironed again."

Brenda had opened her mouth to respond when she saw Ethan about to come through the door. He held his finger to his mouth, and she hurriedly looked away, but she couldn't keep the smile from her face.

"You think it's funny that I'm totally incapable of folding and stacking?" Fiona demanded in mock anger. "Remember you're the one who absolutely cannot get a picture wire caught on the wall hook."

"I don't need to hang pictures," Brenda smoothly replied. "I'm not the one who's going to marry a painter."

"I'm not..." But Ethan had softly closed the door after reaching up to muffle the chime, and now leaned over to brush a light kiss onto the nape of her neck.

Fiona jumped so violently she smacked him in the nose, and he yelped and put up a hand to protect his face. She whirled around and stared in amazement at the beloved visage which was contorted with pain.

"Ethan! Oh no, I'm so sorry." She stood on tiptoe to hug and kiss him.

"Ouch!" He angled his face to the side. "I think it may take some maneuvering to kiss me now. I thought you'd be happy to see me." But his eyes were laughing down at her.

"I'll be more careful next time." She was smiling broadly, and kissed him again, carefully avoiding his nose.

"I like a girl who is inventive," he murmured.

"I like a guy who doesn't mind if I show him who's boss."

"Then, lady, you sure enough have met your dream man."

She pulled his head down for another kiss. "I think I have."

"Uh-humm!" Brenda loudly cleared her throat several times before they remembered her presence.

"Hi, Brenda," Ethan smiled over Fiona's shoulder.

"'Lo, Ethan." She looked radiant, prettier than before if that were possible. "I guess this means I'm losing my best helper for the rest of the day."

The store had opened the weekend before, but the shelves still needed a lot more stocking because a late storm had delayed delivery on some of the merchandise. Fiona knew her friend needed her assistance, but she wanted to leave right way and spend the day with Ethan.

"I wanted to paint before I lose the light today. The demanding Miss Foxe is nipping at my heels, wanting more and more paintings." Ethan smiled down at the girl in his arms. "Right now, however, my good intentions are rapidly dissolving."

"Miss Foxe is demanding paintings because she is selling paintings." Fiona loosened her hold on him. "Go paint. I'll finish here and then see you soon." She struck a provocative pose and added in an exaggerated sultry voice, "I'll see you ver-r-ry soon."

He sighed regret and left her there with Brenda. Fiona returned to her task, but her efforts were even less proficient than they had been before.

"Oh, for heaven's sake, put these wooden toys out, and I'll finish the linens. You really are making an awful mess!" Brenda gently shoved her aside. "It's a good thing your children will have Ethan for a father—they'd get no spatial skills from you!"

Busy rearranging Fiona's disorder, Brenda missed the stricken look on her friend's face. Brenda had mentioned marriage just before Ethan surprised her, and now she had mentioned children. Things were going too quickly. She couldn't marry Ethan, she *was* married. For the millionth time she told herself she'd have to slow things down, even reverse the direction. If only she could think clearly when she was with him.

Who was she kidding? It was much too late to put the brakes on what was happening between she and Ethan. It had happened, they were in love. And now she could no longer hide what she had hoped to never have to reveal.

* * *

Ethan's Jeep squished through the damp earth and gravel of the driveway. The snow was rapidly disappearing. He wanted to get set up to paint as soon as possible.

He wasn't surprised that his car was the only one in the garage. His parents were in Washington again, according to their last report to him. That was one reason he'd wanted to come home now. He wanted things settled between him and Fiona without the loving interference of his family.

He left everything else in the car, pulling out paints, easel, and canvas. He moved quickly, studying the colors of the sea and sky, the white of the snow which was dirtied to gray in places, pierced with bold spears of new grass in others. The sky was beginning to fade, the shades of sunset were subdued, more subtle than they had been just moments before.

He mixed and applied the peach, the rose, the silver, the blue. Here was a sliver of lavender, almost absorbed in the wider band of pink. He looked at the soft beauty and he preserved it with his strokes. The outlines of the few boats were hazy, blurred by the mist around them. Even the cliffs seemed softened by the light. He painted as though what he saw would disappear, never to return, because he knew no other evening would be exactly like this one. Tomorrow there would be less snow, or more sun, or a ship which would be too large and throw off the balance of this perfection.

The finishing touches would have to be done later. The dusk had crept in, wiping away the scene which would never again be duplicated except on this single canvas. He put his things away regretfully, and headed toward the cottage. It was always a little depressing to have the moment of creation end. Without ego, he knew the painting was good, better than good. The light was luminous, the haze seemed made of a million microdots of moisture caught in motion. But he could never quite replicate what effortlessly, miraculously, occurred in nature.

* * *

When Fiona entered the cottage a short while later, several lamps were on, the fragrance of coffee greeted her, and she immediately saw the painting propped against the easel Ethan had set in the corner of the room. Light from a tall lamp softly illuminated the evening scene.

"Ethan, that is the most beautiful thing you have ever painted!" She stood, studying it, as he approached.

"It isn't finished, but the essence is there. I've been working on a different technique. I think it makes the colors more pure, shows the depth of the light."

"It's wonderful." Her voice was almost reverent.

"I'm glad you like it. I wanted it to be special, because it's a gift to you. I want you to look at it and remember I painted it for you, gave it to you, on the day I asked you to marry me." As he said the words, he reached for her hand and turned her to face him.

"Oh, Ethan…" How could she say the words? What were the words? She wouldn't lie and tell him she didn't love him. How could she explain that she couldn't marry him? As many times as she had considered the best way to tell him, she still had no answer and was unprepared for this moment.

He took her chin in his hand and gently lifted it until he could see into her eyes. They were swimming with tears, and he felt fear as he realized they were not tears of happiness. "Fiona?"

"Don't say anything more, please, Ethan." She somehow managed to speak firmly, almost calmly. She pulled slowly away and crossed the room to the fireplace. Backing up until she felt the rough bricks snag her knitted sweater and pull at her hair, she lifted her eyes to his face. He looked wary. Worse than that, he looked afraid.

"I can't marry you, Ethan. I am married."

His head actually jerked back, as though she had slapped him hard across his face.

There was a long moment of silence while she waited for him to speak. She watched his face for any clue that would reveal his thoughts, but it was expressionless. The longer he stood without speaking, the more she feared what he was thinking and what he would say to her. His quiet was unnerving. He suddenly turned and went out the door, leaving it unlatched so the breeze caught it and pulled it fully open. The evening wind was picking up, she thought with an oddly logical part of her mind. The cold felt good, fresh and bracing, as she went to the door and stood looking out at him walking away over the clifftop. She had thought he would ask her questions, hoped they could talk about it until he might even understand and forgive her. Beyond that, she couldn't know what might happen or what they would do, but she had not foreseen his quiet abandonment of her.

She had not had time to really talk to him about Sam's death, his own feelings of mortality, the months of fear as he persevered with the prosecution of the Mafia case, so she did not understand how he had felt today. This was to have been his farewell to all which was grim and dirty, the beginning of his commitment to joy and her. As she stared at the picture, she saw what he had wanted, and knew she had destroyed his hope with a few piercing words.

* * *

She was married. How the hell had she neglected to mention that to anyone during the almost seven months she had lived at Cliff House? He thought of all the times she might have remembered that fact and confessed it to him.

He was angry—furious—and he felt like a fool. She couldn't

have loved him. He must have been something to play with, something she found amusing.

To whom was she married? He hadn't thought to ask. Where was he? Were there children? Surely she wouldn't have abandoned children? But she had abandoned a husband and strung him along for months. She might be capable of anything.

He left instead of asking her these questions because he had to get away, because he couldn't stand to look at her face one more minute, because the depth of his rage had frightened him. Now he had a million things he wanted to say, going over questions and accusations in his mind, but he couldn't bring himself to be near her.

He paced the length of the cliff before heading back toward her cottage. Dusk had become nearly night, and a light was on inside. He turned from her cottage toward the big house, then changed his mind abruptly. He couldn't sit still now and let this fester in his thoughts. He climbed back into his Jeep, leaving his paints and supplies, and began to drive. At first he drove aimlessly, but before long he was purposefully back on the interstate to New York. It seemed to take days to reach the city, but then it also seemed to have been just minutes since she'd delivered what felt to be a fatal blow to his heart. Time was distorted, pain was the only reality.

He didn't bother going to his apartment. Instead he went straight to the office. Work seemed to be his fate, and it was time he accepted that. He couldn't imagine painting now. A painter had to have heart, and his was frozen as cold as the cliffs he had painted—was it only hours ago?

The chair was just stopping its roll toward his desk when his phone rang. "Ethan? Darling, we've just arrived at Cliff House. We grabbed a bite at the café, and we saw Brenda and Adam. Brenda said you'd come home today, but your car wasn't in the garage. And Fiona is just sitting alone in the cottage. She won't tell us what happened."

He waited, too weary to interrupt, as she rattled on. When she finally had to pause for a breath, he said all he intended to say for now. "You'll have to talk to Fiona, I need to finish some work here." Let Fiona explain it, let her tell them what she had done.

Libby sputtered, but he simply said, "Goodbye, Mom," and replaced the receiver in the cradle.

Then he opened the file which he had last reviewed weeks ago.

* * *

The phone was ringing. Fiona had dozed, sitting up in the chair, and she straightened, easing the cramp out of her neck. It was Ethan, finally calling! He had calmed down, and she would, she'd decided in the skewered reasoning of the night which was born of fatigue and sorrow, explain everything to him, and they would think of something. She should have known he would call and give her a chance to explain. He loved her, he wouldn't give up on her now.

She had thought crazily that maybe they would go away, then tell people they had eloped and were married. But now the sun was coming up, and she knew that lie would be exposed within days. Ethan's father was a United States senator. Ethan was well-known himself. Reporters would want to know where they were married and when, and then it would all collapse.

There was no way for them to be together. She had known that months ago, and that was when she should have left.

But still she went toward the phone with hope as it continued to ring. She wanted to hear his voice. He was Ethan, he was strong, maybe he had thought of some way...

"Good morning, my dear wife." Antonio's smooth voice made her gasp. She knew he had heard it when he laughed softly. "Did you really think your little ruse would be successful? No, your brother's loyalty is easily swayed. He told me, without my even having to ask, where you were. Who would think a little scar on your hand would seal your fate? Do not worry, however, I have punished him for you." He paused to chuckle. "I punished your entire pathetically stupid family for thinking they could threaten The Torch."

She tried to make her mind work while he spoke. How close was he? Run! She had to run! She even turned to look around her, seeking a route of escape.

He unnervingly read her mind. "Don't try to run again, Emilia. You would not get far. I am in this very charming little village, only minutes away from you, my darling."

"No…"

"Yes, you are going to leave now, with me. If you do not, I will burn everything on that cliff until there are only ashes for the wind to blow into the sea. I promise you, no one and nothing will be spared. And the very pretty, very talkative waitress in the café has assured me of your deep affection for the Shane family."

The fog of fear in her brain cleared as he said the words threatening the people who might have been her family. Though she was terrified, her voice was steady when she spoke, and she was looking at the piece of paper she had pulled out from under the phone. "They'll see you if you come here. Please leave them alone. I'll meet you on the beach this evening at five, you can drive down there." She calmly gave him directions.

* * *

Ethan's eyes were getting bleary when he unfastened the only photo he had not seen from the Bellini file. It was of two girls who looked remarkably similar, with the exception of their hair. One had auburn hair which was a short, sleek bob, the other was a brunette whose hair hung down her back.

Between them stood a laughing man, but Ethan was barely aware of him, because the woman with the short hair was Fiona.

He glanced at the notes below the photo. The brunette was Emilia Bellini. She had married Antonio Scarpellini and died while visiting her cousin's husband in his office at the World Trade Center on September 11, 2001. The man had also died, but the report said his wife had been reportedly seen at a luxurious boutique hotel in the days following the tragedy.

He was confused. Why was Fiona at the hotel when her cousin was with Fiona's husband? His mind played with the facts as he read more. Fiona's weight and height, her scar on her right knee from a confrontation with a fence when she was nine; Emilia's basic statistics, the scar on her right hand when it was sliced open by her husband's enormous ring.

His heart stopped as he reread the detail about the scar. "I'm married," she'd said. Not, "I was married." He held the photograph close to his face, trying to see any miniscule differences between the two women. Cut Emilia's hair, color it…

"Johnson! What's the latest report from the surveillance team on The Torch?"

"Guy's gone on a vacation apparently. Headed out of the city alone a few hours ago, going north."

"Are they still on him?"

"Naw. He doesn't do any business up that way. They let him go a couple of hours after he left New York. We'll pick him up when he comes back to town. Even the bad guys need a rest, I guess."

He was out of his chair and running before Johnson finished speaking.

* * *

Fiona's head was so clear. She was oddly calm now that she knew what she had to do. Fate had placed Antonio in the palm of her hand, and even the timing was perfect.

She retraced the steps she had taken with Ethan the first day she had watched him paint. When she reached the place where the cliff sank onto the beach, a car's lights were drawing near. She did not look in the direction of the approaching car, but walked steadily to the beach.

The sound of the surf was louder than normal. There had been storms out in the ocean, and the waves were high and wild as a result. True to the chart under her phone, the tide was beginning to come in.

"Emilia!" Antonio's voice was faint, dulled by the water's roar, so she pretended she had not heard him. She knew he would follow her if she ignored him.

When she reached the beach, she turned and waited for him to get nearer. He was alone as she had thought he would be. No man as proud as Antonio would bring anyone with him to retrieve his errant wife. He walked briskly, confidently toward her, a flashlight shining at his feet. Just as he was getting close enough to grasp her arm—she had to time it exactly right, had to force herself not to flee—she turned and walked rapidly into the mouth of the cave. Water followed her.

"Emilia!" His furious voice echoed from wall to wall of the cave as she eluded him.

"Come in here; I want to talk to you, Antonio."

Ahead she saw the slight protuberance of the wall which hid the rough stairs in the rock. She felt safer near it, but she didn't want to direct Antonio's attention that way. She waited for him to find her. A few seconds later she saw him in the dim light, walking cautiously into the cave, still following the beam of his flashlight. The surf was surging, deeper by the second.

"Stop right there, Antonio. We need to talk before I agree to come with you." She must not let him realize she was stalling for time.

"Damn it, Emilia, these are $2000 shoes!" He looked down to see the tidewater suddenly sweep inches over his shoes.

She began to argue with him. A few months ago, she would never have been able to stand up to him this way, but her meekness and fear were gone. Now she wanted to make him angry, and hopefully, he would lose his focus. "Antonio, I don't want to come back with you."

"Shup up, Emilia. Of course you don't want to come back. You stupid fool, do you think I care that you don't want to come back? When I'm done with you, you'll never disobey me again." He was standing only a few feet from her now, not willing to move any further, still futilely trying to keep his pants from getting too wet.

"I wouldn't think you'd want me back. After all, I've changed a lot."

"Emilia, I'm not interested. You're making it worse for yourself. This water is freezing!"

She took a deep breath. "Do you want a wife who hasn't been faithful?"

That caught his attention, and he finally looked away from the seeping water and directly at her. His eyes were narrowed, but he didn't speak.

She continued, pulling out all the stops to make him so angry he would forget everything but his rage. "You were never faithful to me. Why shouldn't I live a little? There are many, *many* interesting men in the world." She gave him a smug smile.

When he took two steps toward her and struck her across the face with the back of his hand, she fell into ice cold water that was now, she judged, over two feet deep. Her head was reeling, her cheekbone was bruised, but everything was going just as she wanted. As she got to her knees and then to her feet, she felt the first strong tug of the water pulling out to sea.

"Really, Antonio, only cowards hit women." She smiled defiantly at him.

He raised his right hand again, but paused. This was undignified.

Instead, he reached for her arm, but she jerked it away and stepped back. "I hate you!" she screamed. "I'll never go back!" She took a few more steps backward, and he obediently followed. She found as she moved that the water was stronger than she was now, and an incoming wave hit at her waist. She was soaked and shaking from the cold.

"Bitch." Antonio said it softly. "I won't argue any more. Come with me now, or I'll kill you here."

She wanted desperately to hit him, but she knew he would win in a struggle. Maybe enough time had passed by now. She looked him in the eye and spit in his face.

For just a moment, he paused in amazement. As he reached to touch his face, she turned and slogged the last few feet through the water and reached the crevasse hiding the steps in the wall of the cave. He was right behind her. She had time to get up a few feet, straining with the effort of pulling herself up with wet clothes and stiff, cold fingers. Then he dropped his flashlight, lunged upward, and grabbed her around the knees. She struggled briefly, unable to kick free. She screamed as Antonio pulled her back with him, and they both fell into the icy water.

There were a few seconds when she was free, both of them scrambling to stand in the deep pull of the tide and catching their breaths. She was still choking when he pulled her back down, dunking her almost to the bottom, so that she felt the sand with her knees and elbows. She was going to drown, she had no doubt, but she was going to fight him. He would not survive either.

She kicked out, but the water was up to her chest, and the force of it carried her leg harmlessly away from its target. His hands moved over her, finally finding her throat. She felt the force of them against her windpipe, then stars burst before her eyes. It was getting black, she was freezing...

The water had carried them to the mouth of the cave as they

struggled, and now a crashing wave battered them, slamming them into the sand so hard that Antonio's hands released her. The pain of rocks and shells tearing at her arms and legs brought her back to consciousness.

Then the riptide pulled them out to sea. She blinked water out of her eyes, tried to breathe, and looked around as she surfaced. Antonio was nowhere in sight. She was being pulled farther and farther from shore. There were lights in the distance, but were they at Cliff House or on a ship? She didn't know where she was, but she was so cold by now it was hard to think anyway.

She would not last long, but she made herself relax and drift with the sea until she could awkwardly battle in a sideways pattern across the riptide instead of against it. Her brain was foggy, and she could barely move at all. She had to be facing the shore, the lights were from Cliff House, and how cozy and peaceful it looked there. As she watched, what appeared to be no more than stick figures began to run around outside, and the lights briefly became brilliant. She blinked against the salt water. The lights were now so blurred, she could see nothing but their hazy glare. Oh Ethan, I'll never get to make things right…

She ducked down into the water so she could remove the heavy sweater. It would pull her to the bottom of the ocean, she thought. She did not want to be found weeks later on the shore. She wanted her body recovered before it was horribly distorted and swollen. She was oddly amused at her own vanity.

As he leaped from his Jeep, Ethan saw the car down by the beach. Then someone near the water clicked on a flashlight and he glimpsed Fiona briefly before she disappeared. Whatever was happening, he knew she was in danger. The tide was coming in. "Dad! Grandad!" Ethan did not take time to go upstairs to rouse the men. He bellowed as loudly as he could as he crashed through the back door. "Get dressed and down here now! Fiona's in trouble!"

He was holding the family's considerable collection of flashlights when the men appeared downstairs in only moments. His mother and grandmother followed, in dressing gowns. Ethan ran outside, yelling over his shoulder, "Call the Coast Guard and the volunteers, she's in the ocean."

By the time his grandfather caught up with them—his father had been only steps behind—Ethan and Keith had the motor going on the sailboat. They worked in silence until Keith asked where Fiona had gone in.

"By the cave. I saw a car and then I saw her down here. She won't last long in this cold."

There was no time to ask why she was there. Keith was thinking of the tide and its effects.

"Does she know not to try to swim against a riptide?" he asked his son.

Did she? It had been too cold for them to swim in the ocean since he'd known Fiona. He searched his memory. Yes, they had talked about how swiftly the tide came into the cave, how his dad had been in danger there. He remembered discussing it later, that he might have survived even had he not found the steps because he knew to swim across the riptide. He was sure she knew. If only she was still alive and calm enough to remember.

But Keith had seen men panic in less dangerous situations than this one. Fiona could have only minutes left in this cold.

"We need to go that way then." But Ethan was already turning the boat. His grandfather held the powerful light so it shone over the water. He moved it steadily across the bay, right to left, left to right, looking for any sign of life.

To their left they saw a body floating. They swerved toward it, and each man felt his heart sink in his chest until they could see the body was male. He was obviously dead.

"We'll worry about him later," Keith said coolly. Ethan once again turned toward the direction a swimmer trying to elude the riptide would have taken.

* * *

For some reason, Fiona thought she was dreaming. She was dreaming again that her father was holding the dollhouse. But this time, she watched, pretending to be asleep, as he stuffed something into the bottom of the base and then turned a key in the tiny brass lock which was hidden there.

Even though she was dying, she felt a sense of victory. She knew where the evidence against Antonio was hidden. Of course, she thought with a distanced clarity, he was going to die too, but there was evidence to be found by someone, someday. If Dominic was still alive, it would destroy him. It would certainly destroy all of Antonio's organization.

The light in her eyes hurt, and she closed them weakly. Was this what she had heard about dying? She could still feel the piercing cold, so she couldn't be dead yet, could she?

"There! She's there!" But the boat was already roaring toward her, where she floated, more dead than alive.

Keith took the controls as Ethan and Tom struggled to haul Fiona aboard. Ethan pulled the sodden clothing away, wrapped each section of her body in blankets as quickly as it was exposed, and sat down with her across his lap.

"Ethan?"

"Yes?" Tears were streaming down his face. The other men were holding back tears too, but it was Ethan's face which was pressed against hers.

"I know where Papa hid the evidence." It seemed important that she tell him. "It's in the dollhouse."

"We'll get it for you." He didn't understand, she realized, but she would explain it later. It was too complicated, and she was too tired right now.

"Yes, Ethan."

"Shh, sweetheart."

"Yes, Ethan…"

"Yes, what?"

"Yes, I want to marry you."

His laugh broke on a stifled sob. He pressed his face, sore nose and all, against hers and softly chuckled. The warmth was slowly creeping back into her body. She snuggled closer and closed her eyes. She was still asleep when they carried her gently from the boat and placed her in the ambulance, and she slept all the way to the hospital.

But she somehow knew he did not leave her side, holding her hand until she awakened to the sunshine of midday. After all, he had done what he most hated, gone out in a boat in rough seas, and brought her safely home.

Printed in the United States
47406LVS00002B/87